SHW

W I ...
P...
BUT...

ALLEN COUNTY PUBLIC LIBRARY
W9-CSX-313
SEP 1 2 2001

"A moody, twisted story of lust, love, revenge, and religion . . . Hill is a truly impressive talent, a master of character and atmosphere. And he weaves a complicated plot, full of flashbacks that layer past and present. . . . *Butterfly Sunday* left me wanting to read more by Hill, and soon."—*Boston Sunday Globe*

"Richly textured . . . elegantly constructed . . . [Hill] deftly employs time shifts and a style at once spare and lurid, to unfold this gothic tale. . . . A gorgeous crazy quilt of a novel, filled with saints and sinners bent on mayhem, southern-style."
—*Kirkus Reviews* (starred review)

"Perceptive, rich writing."—*The Baltimore Sun*

"The strengths are undeniable and impressive. . . . Hill has created some powerful imagery, some memorable characters and an atmospheric setting that will captivate lovers of romantic suspense."—*Publishers Weekly*

"There is no better storyteller than David Hill. There is no better book than *Butterfly Sunday*. In his dazzling illumination of things unseen and things unimagined, David Hill has created an unforgettable cast of characters and an enormously satisfying read. *Butterfly Sunday* is a major miracle."
—Shirlee Taylor Haizlip,
author of *The Sweeter the Juice*

"*Butterfly Sunday* has as many twists and turns as a mountain road and may be the best blend of sex and religion since Elvis."—*St. Petersburg Times*

W

PRAISE FOR
A BUTTERFLY SUNDAY

Also by David Hill

SACRED DUST

Butterfly Sunday

DAVID HILL

A Dell Book

A Dell Book
Published by
Dell Publishing
a division of
Random House, Inc.
1540 Broadway
New York, New York 10036

This a work of fiction. Names, characters, places, and
incidents either are the product of the author's imagination
or are used fictitiously. Any resemblance to actual persons,
living or dead, events, or locales is entirely coincidental.

If you purchased this book without a cover you should be
aware that this book is stolen property. It was reported as
"unsold and destroyed" to the publisher and neither the
author nor the publisher has received any payment
for this "stripped book."

Copyright © 2000 by David Hill
Cover photo copyright by Charles Edwards, TIB/Swanstock
Cover design by Honi Werner

All rights reserved. No part of this book may be
reproduced or transmitted in any form or by any means,
electronic or mechanical, including photocopying,
recording, or by any information storage and retrieval
system, without the written permission of the Publisher,
except where permitted by law.

Dell ® is a registered trademark of Random House, Inc.,
and the colophon is a trademark of Random House, Inc.

ISBN: 0-440-22424-1

Printed in the United States of America

Published simultaneously in Canada

September 2001

10 9 8 7 6 5 4 3 2 1
OPM

In Memoriam
Robert S. Hill Sr.
January 31, 1919–October 30, 1997

ACKNOWLEDGMENTS

Thanks to many, who include:

Lisa Bankoff, Danielle Perez, Wanda Wilson, Michael Cherry, Ann Hughes, Betty Hill, Lea Queener, Martha Holifield, Joey Miller, Bill Wilson, Gary and Rhonda Brown, John Michael Ellis, Brenda Miao, John Pielmeier, Mary Gallagher, Lonnie Hill, Libby Boone, Kate Permenter, Glenn Anderson, and many, many more. . . .

"Henceforth I learn that to obey is best,
And love with fear the only God, to walk
As in his presence, ever to observe
His providence and on him sole depend,
Merciful over all his works, with good
Still overcoming evil, and by small
Accomplishing great things . . ."

John Milton
Paradise Lost, *Book XII*

1

The state would execute her. She knew that. She accepted it the same way she had accepted the fact that there were too many needlepoint pillows in her living room. Someone would stick a needle in her arm and she'd swoon. Her eyes would roll back into her head and she'd transform from a person into a thing. They'd kill her, but not her meaning. They'd get a full confession, but never a word of remorse.

She had so many of her mother's pretty things around the house. It sickened her to think Audena would clean out the place. Her sister-in-law wouldn't know what to keep and what to pitch. Audena would probably keep the rag rugs and use Mama's Aubusson in the doghouse. Well, so what? Without past associations, heirlooms reverted back into things. She slipped two large photographs out of their ornate sterling silver frames: her parents' wedding in '49 with Daddy in his Navy uniform, and her brother Henson's fourteenth birthday at the New York World's Fair in 1964. Those she would keep to the end.

She had to think about her immediate future, what to say, what to hold in silence. What to expect from the police and the legal system. There would be questions, of course, followed by her detailed confession. Then they'd charge her with murder. She'd spend her first night ever in the county jail. A public defender would turn up. There'd be an arraignment. Then she'd have to stand her ground. She'd enter a guilty plea, provided she was allowed to detail not only her crime but also a history of her relationship with her victim.

The world would know and remember everything.

When the deputy knocked, she'd open the door, hand him her overnight bag, and say, "What took you so long?"

Her eyes followed a garland of pastel roses in the carpet to a printed rectangle of lavender paper on the floor at the far end of the sofa. It was this morning's church bulletin. The front was a rough pencil drawing of a myopic Jesus wearing a crown of thorns—Averill's crude handiwork. His insistence on demonstrating his complete lack of artistic talent every week only made sense if you accepted the fact that he had never made a lick of sense. As usual, he'd goaded her into lettering the title of his sermon with her calligraphy pen.

Why did Jesus go to Jerusalem?

It was one of his standby sermons. In her year and a half as his wife, she'd already heard it twice. She had always tuned it out as more of his sanctimonious nonsense. However, now, tracing the carefully drawn letters with her finger—right now, listening in the quiet after-math for the sound of an approaching car—she saw the meaning in the question. Why had the cross-eyed fool ridden that swayback mule into downtown Jerusalem in broad daylight? Why had he placed himself in the eager hands of his executioners? Why hadn't he turned off that doomed highway and slipped into the anonymous sanctity of life under an alias?

Would millions have considered what he had to say for the next twenty centuries if he had? No. He saw the limited value of his existence next to that.

Leona had no desire to start a religion, but she knew that her willingness to die for the opportunity to tell everything would inflate the value of her every word.

She was half-crazy with running to the front porch every time a green persimmon fell on the roof. She could just picture his amorphous specter floating up the road from the church. That was nothing but guilt. Guilt—that pernicious misery. It liked to give her a sick head-ache. Except of course she'd already had one longer than she could even remember. She was a first-class mess. One twit of a sparrow's tail was all it took to convince her that the dead could walk.

Not that she doubted the existence of ghosts. The past—and to her that meant the dead—had ruled her life for several years now. But that was the spirit world; apparitions and images conjured from memory. This all-encompassing terror that she could neither respect nor elude was the impossible idea of dead flesh come back to life.

She kept hearing a nonexistent car on the road.

This wasn't that saccharine, pseudo-remorse that peo-ple used to hide their immoralities. She wasn't "feeling guilty," the way people will when they've done something they wish they hadn't. Certainly, she had regrets around it. Killing him was all bother. She would have much preferred some magic ability to undo the things he'd done. However, that wasn't possible. So, the irksome business had fallen to her. She wasn't a natural killer. The instinct had been raised out of her. She had pondered her way to the brink of it a thousand times, and then turned gutless or moral, depending on your perspective. She figured she must not have had any perspective left—or she would have never pulled it off.

That was giving the situation a wide berth, though. She didn't feel any lack of judgment here. She wasn't suffering any remorse or shame. It seemed very sane and satisfactory to Leona—a good job very well done. So guilt, she was learning this afternoon, had nothing to do with regret. Guilt was contemplation of the inescapable consequences. Guilt was not getting away with it.

The slain might just as well rise up in reanimate flesh armed with immortal powers of retribution.

"The prosecutor will paint me as a woman scorned," she thought. "He'll have me out an avenging, bloodthirsty harlot." He would too. He'd have a Mardi Gras party inventing lurid details. Well, let him. When he was finished, she'd have her say. She'd tell the whole truth in details more lurid and shocking than any lawyer was likely to invent. No, that wouldn't save her life. She was guilty. The lawful truth was, she had planned and carried out this murder. There was no dancing around that part. Yet it seemed to her as she felt the overpowering peace and loveliness of the April woods that his murder was less crime than result of more egregious follies—all of them her own. Well, what murderer facing justice hadn't seen it all that way? Did she think she could convince a jury that the devil made her do it?

Then she laughed out loud. The irony was, she had murdered the devil, as far as she was concerned. She felt a sudden kinship with her fellow killers. Killers blinded themselves to their crimes with the motives. How else would so many otherwise moral people become executioners? To the average killer the victim was always the devil. To the rest of the world he was some mother's darling. She'd do her ultimate cause no good by trying to demonize Averill. Evil didn't require a tail and a pitchfork. Plain human weaknesses, poor judgment and ordinary selfishness were enough to produce evil.

She had to keep a clear head about that. Her motives and Averill's unspeakable actions were beside the point. There were far more important things to put down on permanent court record than mitigating circumstances or criminal evidence.

She'd spent so much time in this house, dreading Averill's footsteps, that she'd developed a warning sense that told her he was approaching even before she heard his truck chug and whine up the hill. She had that feeling just now. She didn't know if the dead could walk, but Averill's car was still sitting there on the driveway, so it was plain he hadn't driven.

"Justice is very little to hold," she heard her own voice speaking silently. "Too damned little when you consider the price you'll pay." All she had to do was wait for sundown, walk up to the church, drag him out back fifty yards into the swamp and let the wet sand swallow him. The notion lit a match. She would pack two suitcases, his and hers. She bent to pull them out from under the bed. Whoever came looking would find the pair of them gone, along with their personal belongings and the car.

She could leave a vague-sounding note for the

mailman—she and Averill called away up north for an indefinite period. Averill's body would sink halfway to hell in that bottomless sand pit before anybody even raised an eyebrow to wonder where they were. Leona could get herself lost in a city.

She saw herself in Seattle, stopping at a quaint little shop to buy fine writing instruments. Leona loved fountain pens. She could amuse herself by the hour drawing and redrawing magnificently looped letters twined with leafy wreaths and ribbons. Now she sat in a shadowy coffee shop redolent of herbs and coffee beans, writing a note on thick velvet notepaper. She would be warm and sincere. She would convey her civil regret like a perfumed countess in one of her mama's worn Anthony Trollope novels.

She would empathize without irony. She would regret destroying poor Helen's hopes. She wouldn't undermine her kindness by suggesting that she had spared Helen the devil's chains. Helen and Averill had been precariously close to riding off into the sunset. What Leona wanted to convey in the most compassionate possible manner was how she regretted Helen's pain. In her ideal world, Helen and Averill would have taken their fantastic flight. As far as Leona was concerned, Helen would always be an innocent bystander.

But Leona was attempting to watercolor a stark black-and-white photograph. This wasn't Seattle. Nor were she and Helen romantic ladies on curling couches in stuffy Victorian novels. Leona's indifference to Helen's adultery with Averill didn't qualify the woman for sainthood. Why did she feel obliged to her? The plain fact was, she didn't feel anything for or against Helen Brisbane. Everything she knew about the woman had come to her secondhand. For that matter, nothing she

had heard about Helen made her seem a very worth-
while person. (A benevolent observation from a murderess.)

No. She had only wanted to draw pretty letters around
the jagged ugliness of her savage action. That was a hollow idea, no more real to her than Helen Brisbane,
whom she had barely met in a shadowy church at a moment when both women were completely absorbed by
other pressing circumstances. Leona had to accept the
thing she had done and its meaning for her. She had to
swallow it whole. She was no longer a welcome resident
of the planet Earth.

Leona had no blood connections left. Averill's only
close relation was his sister. Audena wouldn't raise her
little finger in an effort to find Averill. Her entire concern would be getting her pudgy hands on the contents
of the house. The brackish mule would have a snub-
nosed truck and trailer backed across that miserable excuse for a yard before you could swat a gnat. Well, let
her have it all. All Leona wanted from the mess was
Mama's Lee Ward's sequined Christmas ornaments and
Daddy's christening dress.

Now she heard familiar shuffling feet and scattering gravel. Oh, dear God, she thought, not today. Leona
stepped out to the porch and confirmed her annoyance
and dread. A woman wearing a mismatch of ragged
clothes and a thick red veil crossed the yard. She was
neither apparition nor cause for much immediate alarm.
All the same, it aggravated Leona. Was every freak she
had ever known going to turn up today? The woman's
name was Darthula. She was the local half-wit, the hill
community's first bag lady, a sign of urbanity to come.

According to Averill you had to cross a quarter of a
mile of swamp on foot to get to Darthula's shack. Leona

had seen enough moccasins swimming in that nasty black water. She wasn't liable to run by for tea anytime soon.

"How you, Miss Leona?"

They had a tacit understanding. Darthula would come no closer than the first porch step. Everyone from here to town knew about Darthula. Yet nobody knew very much about her or how to interpret her strange ways. Her long-dead mother had made and sold moonshine and practiced something like voodoo. Darthula had pronounced herself "a guardian angel." Her mission in life was to monitor the devil's movements. She always kept her head covered with bright veils. Red meant the devil was lurking. Blue indicated that he was expected soon, and white meant the coast was clear. Averill laughed in her face. Leona considered it wacky, but she didn't see where Darthula's veils were any crazier than half the things Averill preached.

For the most part Darthula was an annoyance. She had stolen food and picked people's gardens while they were asleep, and nabbed more chickens than a fox. She was lonely and she'd use any excuse to trap you into a conversation.

"What do you want today, Darthula?"

"Seen him in the well house this mornin'."

Darthula's ploy was always her urgent and selfless call to warn and inform Leona of Satan's location. She wanted either food or money. Leona didn't waste time discerning which. She grabbed several cans off the pantry shelf and gave them to Darthula in a shopping bag. Then she handed her a ten-dollar bill.

"He had a raggledy eye, Miss Lee."

"I'll watch my back."

"You bes' warn the Reverend."

"I'll warn him."

"Catch a col' draft on the back of your neck and you'll be stiff and grinning before you hit the ground."

Leona let the inside door close in front of her. In a minute she saw Darthula cross the road and move into the cemetery. She never went near the church. And so what if she did? Someone was bound to find Averill. Why not a half-wit? Why did anyone have to find him at all? What made her so sure of all this? Why not give herself time and space to reconsider? If her conclusion was the same, then she could always turn herself in. Wasn't that better than risking the opposite? Suppose she found herself on death row realizing she had been a fool? It would be too late.

Suddenly she was a frenzy of packing. Averill was easy. All his belongings were neatly arranged in drawers and on shelves and hangers. He was a fanatic about his things. Leona was as clean as a steamer, but neatness wasn't one of her weaknesses. On her best day she had to dig for the other shoe or the matching glove. Today wasn't her best. She was nervous as a cat and by the time she had her suitcase so full she had to sit on it to close it, the bedroom looked like a tornado had blown through it.

It took her half an hour to get it straightened up again.

Then she flooded the truck—which wasn't hard to do. So there she was, under the hood, turning the carburetor screw and spattering her blouse with oil and grease. Now she stood in the shower, scrubbing the petroleum gunk off her hands and arms like an idiot hick version of Lady Macbeth trying to rub off her eternal stains.

Brother, she was cracked now. What difference did

it make about the blouse? Why was she sitting here while it ran through a second wash cycle in heavy bleach and detergent? Anyone could turn up here. God knew how many times anyone had. The more she commanded herself to run away, the heavier she sat in the kitchen chair. Now the blouse was in the dryer. She was sipping a cup of tea. At this moment Averill's body was turning stiff and cold on the floor of his study behind the church sanctuary. Any dog, nut or bum looking for a handout could find him there any second. She had to haul him into the swamp.

She stood on the porch, her knees going weak. There were three vehicles one behind the other on the driveway. She'd move his truck and then his precious Cutlass. She'd take her Blazer. She put the truck on the grass next to the Cutlass. Wait, she thought, I can't take the Blazer. If she wanted it to look as if she and Averill were away, then she'd have to take the Oldsmobile. She still hadn't found that christening gown. But wouldn't people wonder why she'd taken the christening gown if, as she hoped it would appear, she and Averill had left with every intention of returning? Now that was stupid. No one except Averill Sayres had ever seen or heard tell of the christening dress. Now she remembered. She'd wrapped it in tissue and laid it inside of a heavy cardboard dress box that was stored under a pile of wool blankets in the cedar chest.

Or so her deluded mind had convinced her. She had removed the entire contents of the chest by now, and there was no dress box to be seen. Nuts, she was nuts. God alone knew what she'd done with that gown. Some of it, probably most of it, was due to the fact that she hadn't had a real night's sleep or a proper meal in God alone knew how long. Some was a result of having lived so long knowing she was bound by fate to murder him. However, the strain that had worked her mind loose was the daily erosion caused by living with what Averill had done.

Well, sir, he might be dead, but his crime continued encroaching on her sanity. She had to think about that too. Suppose she really did manage to dispose of his body and dissolve into thin air? Suppose she even landed on her feet in some ideal situation? What if she was lucky enough to marry a good man and raise his children?

Wouldn't the past keep eroding her good intentions? Wouldn't the terrible scenes replay in grim detail? You couldn't run away from what you'd seen and knew and experienced any more than you could kill it. No, it would all overcome her in the end. She might even snap like one of those maniacs who heard voices and shot people in churches and shopping centers. Though, if that were to become her fate, Leona was pretty sure it would take place in a church.

She had never driven the Cutlass, never ridden in it, for that matter. It still smelled new. Averill had left the paper coverings on the floor mats. The thin, torn plastic still covered the plush fake velvet seats. It gave her an undesired thrill, a cheesy, slick tingle that recalled the inappropriate and unexpected gestures of needy young men. Now it passed. Now she turned the key and a hot tornado stung her face and legs and a deafening chorus of "Satisfaction" by the Rolling Stones began to play. Everything in the goddamned car was automatic. It was button city. Her trembling fingers found the volume control, then the climate, and the already cooler current diminished into a light breeze. It lifted and crackled the film of plastic, stirring a faint, familiar odor from the back of the passenger seat. It was White Shoulders.

The Rolling Stones became schmaltzy piano. She adjusted the mirrors until she could see the tallest stones in the cemetery across the road behind her.

Then she turned around and looked, as she always did, just before she backed out of the driveway, fixing her eyes on one small stone by a newer grave. She never knew what awful thing her mind would put there. Sometimes it was the outline of the infant herself, wrapped in a blanket. Sometimes it was her own silhouette, bent and digging at the new grass with her hands. This time it was the stone, sitting there like the ignoble, hard fact of the loss it represented. This was different. This might be better. This might mean the vengeance had resulted in some kind of deep, universal ballast. For a moment her mind and heart drifted hopefully toward the meager possibility of some meaning.

No such kindness, no such hovering angel in the surrounding woods. For it came to her in a flash that Averill had buried Tess in the christening gown. What kind of wonder was that? Averill had twisted her newborn neck until it was lifeless, and then dressed her in all that meticulous cotton and lace. Having nothing else handy, he had used the dress box for her casket. Whether or not Averill had bothered to line it with tissue paper was a question that had held her hostage many sleepless nights.

She shook her mind loose from all that. She raised the shining plastic lever to reverse and slowly pressed the gas pedal. Her gaze took in the dry clay road that sloped down through the woods for a quarter of a mile before it cut back sharply to the left and disappeared. A thin haze of yellow dust told her a car was approaching.

She bolted up the driveway on foot and through the back garden into the sheltering undergrowth at the edge of the woods. She stopped to catch her breath, listening to the air rushing in and out of her heaving chest until it died away. Gradually it was replaced by the hollow echo of tires spitting gravel and the whir of the engine as it made the last, steep grade.

Looking up through the trees, it came to her. The thing was done. There was nowhere to run where the swaying limbs of trees overhead wouldn't remind her of an empty cradle. There was no gravel road through any remote forest on this earth where she wouldn't hear her infant girl cry for vengeance like a banshee in the night. There was no reason to draw another breath or take another step or let her tired frame drop down to rest one more night if she didn't stand beside Averill's corpse and tell the world about Tess.

That was that, wasn't it? Then, why did she huddle here, trembling like a hunted doe in the brush? Life was a luxury her soul couldn't afford if she had any character, if she had any good intention left inside of her, if she had ever been a mother. Fear was an indulgence for people who still had lives to lead. She moved across the garden and beside the house. She headed down the front driveway, intending to stand at the very end when the police car turned into the driveway.

She could see it clearly now, making its approach on the road. It wasn't the police. It didn't turn into the driveway. Instead it roared past, disappearing into the dusty cloud in its wake. In another minute, she heard it slow down and veer left into the clay clearing beside the little church. Now a car door slammed, and light, fast feet scrambled over gravel and up three wooden steps. She heard the double doors screech open. She waited, expecting to hear them close. Instead she heard the unmistakable click of high heels on the wood floor of the sanctuary. Now they paused, as if the woman was get-ting her bearings, maybe adjusting her eyesight to the shadowy interior. Then they resumed, fading until she heard the door at the far end of the sanctuary moan. Then she heard a familiar voice call, "Averill?"

She waited and waited for the scream, but the woman didn't cry out. After what felt like three forevers, Leona heard a thud, as if a heavy book had fallen off a shelf back in Averill's study.

2

The voice belonged to her close friend Soames. She was an extremely rich Memphis widow who had come down here to restore her late husband's family home. Soames had put flowers on the altar for the Easter service this morning—a pair of Chinese ceramic vases filled with red buds—apparently she had returned to the church to collect them.

Leona had never seen anything as exquisite in her life as that pair of enameled vases bursting with delicate blossoms. Their perfection had moved her to tears.

Though it wouldn't have taken much, not this morning. Averill was late. The crowd was burning up in that stuffy little sanctuary. The last place on earth she'd wanted to be that morning was sitting in the choir loft, roasting in a heavy burgundy robe. That wasn't the reason, though. She had fed Averill a collectively lethal dose of arsenic in his meals over the last four days. As of an hour earlier, he'd shown no outward symptom that he was fatally poisoned. Nor had he given her the faintest indication he suspected any such thing.

Arsenic was supposed to take its time. It sort of waited and gathered up its potency. Then it worked pretty quickly. Maybe he was doubled over on the bedroom floor. She'd calculated it every way she could. The dose with breakfast should have put him over the line. Her best estimates indicated he ought to feel bad by now. He wouldn't draw another breath after four o'clock this afternoon at the latest. There was absolutely no telling.

The church had been packed. Averill had made himself quite an attraction. Leona would never figure it out. Did people believe what they saw? Or did they only let themselves see what they believed?

The congregation had waited a full ten minutes past the eleven o'clock start-up time. She'd glanced out the window and up the road in the direction of the parsonage. She'd half expected to see him staggering and holding his chest. Though sometimes Averill started late, for the drama. One way or another Averill always had to open his services with arias and elephants.

One time he had leaned off the pulpit and asked a new widow if she wanted to burn in hell with her deceased husband. Another time he hit a little bell with a toy drumstick and announced the end of the world. So, this being Easter Sunday, Leona figured he'd try to pull something bigger than Broadway. Maybe he'd burst in wall-eyed and foaming at the mouth and then drop stone dead in front of the stupefied congregation. That was fine with her. They'd all think he'd had a heart attack.

At thirteen past the hour, old Nina Trace had started a series of treble piano rolls and flourishes, vamping as Averill came down the aisle in loose, billowing sleeves and tight black trousers tucked into pointed black boots. His shirt was open to the third button to display a thick silver cross on a chain against his burnt red chest. He'd fallen asleep while sunbathing on the well house roof yesterday afternoon. He'd let his thick brown hair grow out since Christmas and put some kind of dark rinse on it that looked purple when he stepped under an overhead light.

He approached the pulpit with a strange, muted goose step. He gave each sleeve a prophetic tug. Then he threw his arms out and closed his eyes, tensing his leg muscles while he rocked in silent prayer. He moved his lips, praying fervently, then he moaned and grimaced before he opened his eyes with a beatific smile. Blue Hudson had once commented that whenever Averill prayed you'd swear he was copulating with an invisible angel. Now his whispers were becoming more audible, more fervent. "Yes, Lord, thank you, oh, yes, Lordy . . ."

It was obvious the holy idiot was getting himself more and more aroused, very obvious as Averill had been generously endowed and Leona had admonished him against wearing those tight black pants a dozen times. A decent man would have taken the message to heart the first time. Averill's religion was a noxious blend of Old Testament condemnation, honky-tonk piano and born-again striptease. Leona skimmed the crowd for a pair of offended or incredulous eyes.

None. All looked beatific, easy as sheep.

"Amen."

Next came his Garden of Olives pout. He turned

almost in profile and looked up with a meek and pained expression. That was to divert any lingering impression of lewd overtones. Did they really not see through him? Or did they not want to? Had Leona lost touch with reality? Or was she finally in touch? Averill's gaze shifted from heaven to the congregation. He loved these pauses. He used them to sink his needful gaze into as many pairs of eyes as he could. Finally, he threw both arms into the air and tossed them his big opener. As always, it was a question devised to make everyone sit forward in wonder. Except this morning it came out all wrong.

"Why did Jean Suds goo goo Jerooson?"

He had choked on a self-righteous frog in his throat. In three seconds flat, his pageant was a turkey. It reassured her to notice that the teenagers on the back row were shaking with laughter. However, the rest of the congregation, the adult portion, merely waited in trusting stillness.

Not couldn't. No. They just wouldn't see.

So Averill plodded on with his introduction. He wasn't making a lot of sense. Self-importance made people nervous. Why couldn't the fool know that? His only hope of salvaging his sermon was to abandon it, take five while they sang a hymn, and then start over. Of course, that was asking him to admit a mistake.

Not the sprayed-down, high, holy Reverend Goody Gumptorious. His show always went on. This was only his warm-up. Now he and luscious, lovely Leelinda Spakes stood side by side for their duet of "Just a Closer Walk with Thee." Averill loved to show off his tenor voice. All Leelinda could add to the song was volume. Of course, it wasn't her voice she wanted to display. It was her recent breast enlargement surgery. Soames leaned into Leona's ear and whispered, "Happy Easter. She is risen!"

He was back in the saddle now. His entire being inflated. They finished the song and Averill thanked Leelinda, who responded with a little hug, driving her jiggling torpedoes into Averill's chest. Wasn't he a dragon slayer? A real Johnny Honeymoon.

Finally, Averill swallowed a barrel of air and dove into his sermon.

"Why did Jesus go to Jerusalem?"

Bull's-eye.

His question struck a nerve inside every chest in the room. People leaned forward. They let bulletins and funeral home fans fall into their laps. They laid governing hands on the shoulders of squirming children. Meanwhile Averill's right hand rose and he let it drop forward in a commanding gesture that Nina Trace couldn't mistake. The piano faded.

"Why?" Averill repeated with self-assurance. "Why did Jesus go so willingly to Jerusalem where he knew he would face the gravest danger?" He had them now. And he would roll them around like a Slinky in the palms of his hands. He would knead their guilty consciences and tickle their egos and make Jesus into some holy Romeo and a garden of earthly delights. He had seduced them. Now he would pommel them with their worst fears until they were shouting, "Hallelujah!" Then he'd kiss them good-bye with a promise of more love and bigger thrills next week.

"Why did Jesus go to . . ."

Why did Leona marry the rat and come here to this squalid backwater church with him? What did that matter now? She had done her time on this forsaken hill.

He didn't have a clue, of course, but the sun was setting on his lounge act. Near as she could figure, it would kick in between three and five this afternoon. Brother Joy Boy had ridden into his Jerusalem this time.

Averill had the room halfway up Calvary when the rear doors of the little sanctuary screeched. Leona watched incredulous as his sister, Audena, and her husband, Winky, strolled in like they owned the place. They lived seventy-five miles away. Audena and Averill weren't particularly close. She had only seen Audena once in their four years of marriage. She had never even met Winky.

Well, this was a sign from God, or Noah's Ark and the rainbow and all the rest of it were bedtime stories. An ominous sign at that. If she hadn't been up there in the choir loft where the entire world and the stars could see her, Leona would have brayed from sheer irony. It had to be a sign. It was a warning that she would pay eternally for what she was about to do. All the good in the universe was lining up to tell her not to go through with it.

Fat chance. The wheels were already turning. The train was rolling downhill, gathering speed, and its destination was inevitable now. She could spare herself the torment of any more internal debates over the ethical and the practical aspects. She had set her bargain with eternity. Hell was the fee she had negotiated. Yes, it was all very strange, surreal even. This morning as she put on her lipstick in front of the bathroom mirror she studied her reflection hard, trying to see it.

"You're a criminal, a killer, a cold-blooded murderer," she informed her indifferent features. The only thing her reflection confirmed was the fact that she hadn't slept much all week. Well, what of it? Hell was no more than any mother would give for her child.

She couldn't fathom Audena. She had to stifle a gasp, pretending it was an allergic reaction to an arrangement of ivy and lilies along the railing in front of her. No sense to any of it. Life had its hideous little coincidences, that's all.

When the sermon was over, the congregation rose up to sing "Amazing Grace." He possessed them now. They trusted him. He wooed them back into his clutches every Sunday. They would never believe her. They'd call her a heretic murderess and stand by the holy son of a bitch. He wasn't all that talented, attractive or winning. His secret was simple. He knew they needed to believe he could lead them out of their exhausted, disappointing lives. He was their good ol' honeyman Jesus. He kept the keys to the kingdom on a little brass ring with the ones he used for his car. He had all the answers stowed in the little tin safe in the wall behind his desk in the study. Averill Sayres was their fuzzy country boy, their anointed teddy bear and their baby brother of the Son of God.

Not that she could hold herself above the crowd. She'd played the penitent Magdalene to his bleached cotton Jesus once. She'd knelt down in front of him in a moment of desperation and panic. She had chosen him as her personal light, truth and way. She had come here with him, believing that he had given her the miraculous means to escape her troubled past.

"I once was lost, but now am found, t'was blind, but now I see. . . ."

Oh, if the poor soul who had written those words of faith had only known how they would mutate and reverberate with meaning for Leona here and now. Blindness was exactly what she had suffered. Sorrow had turned into debilitating self-pity. In that useless state, people rarely look, much less see, any danger.

Averill sounded foggy to her. Was that the arsenic already? It was supposed to take several hours. He wasn't supposed to shake or bend with cramps or palpitate or any of that until late this afternoon when the crowd was gone and no one but the wind would hear him beg for a doctor. Audena and Winky sure as hell weren't supposed to be here!

Logic and math were called for. She couldn't let herself slip into paranoid suppositions. There was nothing to worry about. She had read the directions and precautions, hadn't she? Yet try as she would to reason with herself, she couldn't exorcise the image of Averill falling stone dead from his pulpit in front of the congregation. Now, thank you very much, he would go stiff at his sister's feet. Oh, yes, Audena had to waddle down to the front with a half-inch run in her stocking and plop her double-wide behind down on the front pew right under the pulpit. Audena was going to have it known that her brother was the preacher.

No question, Leona would have to feed them dinner—today of all nine hundred ninety-nine million billion days in creation. Though, first and most crucial at this moment, Leona had to sit there and make like a born-again hussy at the well in her crimson choir robe. She had to play like she had three-fourths of her eyes and ears fixed on Averill's message while the remaining quarter of her being telegraphed complete delight at the arrival of her in-laws.

All of which was an act to rival Houdini's. Well, those were life's terms today. She was going to take it minute by minute. No one was going to suspect a thing if she could possibly help it. No one would have the remotest hint of a sign that this was going to be Averill Sayres's last sermon. Nobody would have the legitimate right to claim later that they had seen it coming all along.

Averill was just warming up his sermon, ten thousand feet and climbing. It was already hot in the church and the recently varnished floor and pews had begun to emit fumes. What's more, it was packed, which didn't do anything for the air supply. Averill was talking against all that, trying to wake the crowd from their stupor.

It had thrown him completely off track to see his sister and brother-in-law. Obviously, he too considered it portentous. In fact, he got so addled he lost his place and had to extemporize from his favorite, fail-safe, "Were You There When They Crucified My Lord?" homily. It was several minutes before he regained his next point and went on with "Why Did Jesus Go to Jerusalem?" It was one of those self-righteous topics that made Leona want to stand up and shout, "He went to Jerusalem because the highway to Memphis was closed due to a freak ice storm."

Averill took self-righteous to the fourth dimension.

Everyone in the place kept sneaking glances at Audena and Winky. Leona had only just met Audena briefly several years back. At the time Winky, she had later surmised from gathering scraps of evidence, had been away at Parchman Prison serving a sentence for she still didn't know what. (Averill did, but he claimed not to.)

Audena was one of those people who had nothing to say to your face, but more than you cared to hear in her letters. She was Averill's only sister.

"God bless and keep you, my angel and only blood," she would sign her long, rambling correspondences. Why did people think you gave a damn what they fixed for supper last night?

"Saint Peter came down to earth in a black neighborhood," Averill began his racist joke. "And he walked up to a group of young men drinking liquor on the corner. . . ."

Leona had invited Audena and Winky to visit many times. She had somehow believed it was her duty to nurture Averill's ties with his only sibling. It was one of those arrogant young notions about a wife's duties that she had soon ditched along with any desire to be in the same room with—much less married to—Reverend Averill Sayres. In the beginning, however, she was forever dropping Audena notes, begging them to come for Fourth of July weekend or Christmas.

Audena's letters were also filled with references to this "sterling" spoon Mama meant for me to have and "my bowl and pitcher" you got from Aunt Euline, which at least explained the origins of some of the old dollar-store junk Leona found all over the house.

Was that why she was here now? Was it possible? Audena couldn't know that, if Leona's measuring spoons were accurate, her brother Averill would be a corpse by first dark? How could she? No one knew that except Leona. No one else could have imagined such a thing. She and Averill looked like a happy young preacher and his wife. The rest of the world believed the hundred or more yellow irises that rose out of the ditch separating the parsonage from the road. They believed Leona's kindness and self-deprecating anecdotes, and all the other public effects she incorporated into her role as their dedicated preacher's wife.

Except—and thank God for her one true friend—for Soames. Soames knew just about everything. She was the exception to many local rules, which meant of course that Soames had real common sense. There were about two hundred people in church this morning and, Leona aside, Soames was the only one who saw through Averill.

"'. . . How many of you all want to go to heaven?' Saint Peter asked the motley crew. . . ."

What a pathetic loser, what a cheap little redneck racist weasel he was. How could they listen to him Sunday after Sunday?

Leona had never quite figured it out. Did people believe what they saw? Or did they only let themselves see what they believed? Either way, it seemed to her that the longer you lived the more life clobbered you over the head with the fact that nothing—absolutely nothing—was what it first appeared to be. Sitting there in that stifling church redolent with heavy odors of pine resins and cheap colognes, it struck Leona that she herself was a fourteen-karat example of an illusion. At that very moment she was listening to her husband preach a sermon. Wasn't she? From her beatific profile and the decorous tilt of her head, it certainly seemed so. Who among the congregation would suspect that her charmed chuckles at his worn-out anecdotes concealed a murderer's heart? For she was already a murderer, and the perspiring young man of God who was beginning to work his indefatigable spell on them was already her victim.

People survived by keeping themselves a secret from each other—who they really were, what they really felt, what they had really done or intended to do. Leona had come to think that the things they were created to hide shaped a person's most defining outlines. She would love to know what secrets Audena had stowed behind her virtuous drab brown dress with its ludicrous white collar. And didn't Winky complete the picture in his olive khaki Sunday suit? She could see from the choir loft twenty feet away that his fingernails were black with filth at the tips.

"Honest" country people, the politicians were always deifying people like them. Didn't they seem the benchmark of harmless, faded church supper types? Leona had learned a lot about church supper types over the last few years. Sad to say, ninety-nine percent of it had made her more wary than wise.

She found Audena's weekly letter in her mailbox every Tuesday morning. Audena scribbled pages on pages about hard biscuits and puppy teeth and Winky's bunions. Averill said Audena was just dull but well-meaning. Leona could see into that. Those relentless, bleak letters, pencil on ruled paper, carried messages from sister to brother between the lines. In the year and a half of marriage, Leona hadn't begun to figure them out. Now she was glad to say she would never have the opportunity. A year and a half? It felt like two hundred years in this wilderness.

" '. . . Yeah, boss, I want to go to heaven.' " Averill hung his head to the side and threw out his arms trying to look like a half-wit. " 'But I thought y'all was getting up a busload to go tonight,' " he said, finishing his tasteless little skit. She wondered as she smiled brightly and winked in conspiratorial glee at the choir director, how many of the other chortling Christians really thought he was funny.

At least two hundred, more like two thousand years. The thought had an altogether galvanizing effect on

Leona. Audena, Winky and the rest of creation notwith-
standing, this was going to be the last day of her inter-
minable sojourn in this wilderness of insanity. Unless
she'd misread the large-print directions on the big red
bag of Rat Zap. The print on the back had touted it as
the ultimate weapon in man's endless war against rodents. All the same, it wasn't a thing but arsenic.

By 11:09 A.M., which was what her watch had said
when Audena made the church door cry like a banshee
as she opened it, the poison was deep into his system.
He'd swallowed a collective tablespoon of poison over
the last seventy-two hours. She'd dissolved it into Jell-O
and added it to his iced tea. She'd rubbed it with olive
oil into his round steak and added it with the salt to his
dinner rolls. Three-quarters of a tablespoon was supposed to be adequate. So Averill's big amen was going to
be sooner rather than later.

She'd followed the man's instructions with meticulous care. The man was some kid the manufacturer had
hired to answer questions for those who called the 800
number on the sack.

"How much of this stuff do I use?"

"Depends on what you're killing."

"My husband—"

"You got any idea how many times a day I hear that
dumb joke?"

"This is no joke."

"Then you might better shoot him because this stuff
will take you several days."

"Why?"

"You'd have to administer it in eighths of a teaspoon,
at least four hours apart for three or four days."

"Why not all at once?"

"He'd throw it up."

"Thanks."

"What'd you really need to know, ma'am? I got another call here."

"Don't worry. No one will know you're an accomplice."

What he told her confirmed what she had already figured out. Leona had spent her childhood watching her father weigh and measure and mix chemical compounds at the back of his pharmacy. She had learned a great deal about certain mixtures and doses and how they worked. When Leona was ten, Mrs. Crowe, a widow who lived across the street, was arrested for murder. It turned out she had fed arsenic-laced Jell-O to her mother-in-law, who was in the hospital suffering the effects of a heart attack. Within a few days, four bodies had been exhumed. Mrs. Crowe had murdered her husband, her father-in-law and her own parents with arsenic. She'd gotten away with it all those years because the symptoms were identical to those of a heart attack. Besides, Mrs. Crowe was a good woman, a Christian lady to the core. No one had ever suspected her. No one thought to look for arsenic.

Mrs. Crowe had chosen it for several reasons. The first was its accessibility, since she had purchased it two blocks from her home, from Leona's father. At the time the town was installing new sewer lines. Half the population had been in to buy rat poison from her father. Of course, he kept records of all potentially lethal purchases. He showed the police that he had noted that Mrs. Crowe, like everyone else, had reported an acute problem with displaced rodents nesting under porches and eaves.

Mrs. Crowe had been the high school home econom-
ics teacher. She taught Sunday school as well. Leona
had often spent the night with her daughters. The event
traumatized her. Leona liked Mrs. Crowe. Mrs. Crowe
had read them *The Velveteen Rabbit* and made them cry
with happiness as they fell asleep. Beyond that, Mrs.
Crowe had taken Leona and her girls to see the Ringling
Brothers and Barnum & Bailey Circus in Memphis one
Sunday afternoon in October. The girls had talked about
the event for weeks in advance because Mr. Crowe had
ordered a new Cadillac and the celestial carriage was
promised to arrive just in time to transport them to the
event. However, on the day in question, Mr. Crowe was
in bed with a stomach virus, so his wife, Tilly, drove
them instead.

A week later Mr. Crowe was dead.

It gave Leona nightmares. While they were having
their grand adventure, Mr. Crowe was dying. It was too
horrible. They could have stopped it then. Mrs. Crowe
knew it. She knew it and she drove on up the road,
singing silly songs with them.

For months after they arrested Tilly Crowe, Leona
hounded her mother and father with questions about
every detail. Her mother always deflected her questions
because she feared the grim nature of some of the answers would only add to her child's unhealthy obsession. However, her father took what he considered a
more enlightened approach.

He answered each question in vivid, if nonsensa-
tional, detail. He explained the cumulative effect of
certain poisons like arsenic. He showed her how Mrs.
Crowe had carefully measured and scheduled each
dose, explaining how incremental amounts digested at

intervals would manifest increasingly severe symptoms. Yet each set of symptoms was familiar and attributed to nonthreatening natural causes. Each of her victims had shown a gradual decline that began with an upset stomach. By spacing out the doses, Mrs. Crowe was able to give each victim a false sense of security, as the symptoms would actually diminish for a while.

Almost no one sees a doctor for gas pains and diarrhea. By the time their symptoms had progressed to chest pains, the poor souls evidenced other classic indications of a heart attack. No doctor sees an apparent heart attack in progress as a potential poisoning—unless, of course, the patient suspects as much and informs his physician. All of Mrs. Crowe's victims were well into middle age. None of them suspected poison. Though Mr. Crowe's mother had vehemently asked for an autopsy, which her grief-stricken daughter-in-law overruled so as not to torment his distraught children any further. The old lady acquiesced with apologies and held her suspicions in silence for the next eighteen months.

Tilly boasted that she and her mother-in-law had become like sisters in the months after Mr. Crowe's death. Old Lady Crowe had confirmed this by singing her daughter-in-law's praises all over town. Of course no one, except Tilly, knew that Mrs. Crowe had written a new will, naming her daughter-in-law her sole heir and executrix. Though not even Tilly knew that old Mrs. Crowe had seen a doctor when she developed a sour tummy after she ate a slice of Tilly's lemon pound cake. Nor did Tilly know that the police would impound the container of Jell-O salad laced with arsenic when she rushed to her ailing mother-in-law's hospital bedside.

The saddest part to Leona was that Tilly went screaming and crying her innocence all the way to the penitentiary, and her children believed her. Old Mrs. Crowe took them to raise, but they never forgave her for "framing" their mother. It was too much for the elderly woman, who suffered a series of strokes before they were teenagers. By the time they were sixteen, both girls had dropped out of school and left town, each to pursue her own self-destructive fate.

Meanwhile, Averill's voice betrayed no suspicion of his approaching fate. He was using his sincere tone now, playing bashful, unabashed and self-effacing. It was so empty, so false and conceited, she couldn't begin to imagine what went on inside all those spellbound heads with eyes glued to him.

Odd how a life could come home to roost. Odd and menacing, Audena turning up for Averill's last supper— even though it would be served at midday. It rattled Leona inside out and backwards. What did it mean? Well, there wasn't a damned thing she could do about any of it now. She had laced several casseroles that morning. Then she finished off the arsenic, dumping the last bit into the chocolate pie filling.

Of course, she had carefully prepared two versions of each dish. That was for her and the likely happenstance of an extra mouth or two. People beat anything she had ever seen with their sense of entitlement. She couldn't count the number who had managed to inveigle their way from the church steps to her dining room table for a free Sunday dinner.

Leona wasn't stingy to those in need. In fact, she more than welcomed anyone who earned a plate by making himself good company. These were the threadbare, sanctimonious takers whose frayed cuffs belied savings accounts and whose dinner conversations began and ended with the words "Please pass." Audena would fit nicely into that category. Audena's visit was timed to guarantee her a big meal.

She ought to kill off the whole damned bunch of them. She didn't mean that, not even in thought. Yet the thought amused her to the point that she had to swallow a giggle.

Well, God was merciful after all. Averill's sermon had finally come to an end. Everyone stood up for the hymn.

> "The strife is o'er, the battle done, the victory of life is won.
> The song of triumph has begun. Allelujah."

From the choir loft the congregation looked like a sea of flowered hats. Now, that irritated her. That made her itch between the ears. Choir members never got to wear new hats to church on Easter Sunday.

3

His sermon had made a big impression. They had all fallen in love with him one more time. Averill was glowing with pride at all the compliments he took while shaking hands at the door. Strange how a smile transformed his small, brittle features. His general demeanor was sullen. He held himself in pretty tight. He didn't say much, unless he was mad, then he said way too much, erupting with volcanic rage. So most of the time he wore a downtrodden wince that only made him look all the more like a beady little rodent.

Of what could anyone with half a brain accuse her, other than poisoning a two-legged rat? He kept a rat's habits, slithering around in the dark, carrying God only knew what plagues home at all hours. Not that she even bothered to wonder. Not that Averill ever burdened his seamy mind with anything like guilt or shame. Averill never felt he deceived anyone. Yet there was no one Averill wouldn't deceive. He was oblivious to his own amorality because he was the most ardent believer of all his own lies.

Averill's eyes held on to their decorous spirituality while his torso slipped through the doorway for a second brush with Leelinda Spakes's resurrected breasts that day. He was the Old Testament ram's horn and the windblown enemy of sin. Unless of course he happened to be the sinner; then he wriggled his way around the Ten Commandments by hating not the transgressor but the all-too-human sin within him. Blue Hudson said Averill acted like he had a "Get Out of Hell Free" card in his vest pocket.

No. No, she wasn't going around any bends with thoughts of Blue today. Blue was gone, he was in California with his kids. She wasn't going to get bogged down in all that. She couldn't squeeze anything else into her head. Blue was a fragile little candle in the dark. She snuffed it out. Then for the last time she played the gregarious and smiling preacher's wife, greeting her husband's flock.

"You sounded like a little angel bird this morning, Leelinda."

"Thank ya, Leona."

"Johnnie Nell, how's Miss Leticia?"

"We've put her in God's hands, Miz Sayres."

"Mister Johnson, sir, hand that silly cane to Miz Johnson and give me my hug. . . ."

Meanwhile Chester Spakes, Leelinda's red-faced husband, had watched his wife's breasts brush Averill's shirt and tie. Now he tugged at her sleeve and she moved toward his parked pickup truck. As he opened the passenger door for her, Leelinda turned back around and gave Averill a wistful pout. Her husband, who had seen her, twisted one finger around her hair and tugged hard. He gave her a quick shove up into the cab, slamming the door. As he stepped around the front grille, he flicked a dozen or so strands of blond hair onto the ground. Then he glanced across the churchyard to see how much of his point Averill had taken.

Averill had already turned his back on Leelinda and her husband. He was holding eighty-eight-year-old Ella Stone's hand and listening with an earnest expression while she told him tearfully for the hundredth time that her brother Amos had been killed while fighting in the Philippines on Easter Sunday, 1944.

Meanwhile, Leona had faced down Audena and Winky with all the welcome she had left in her, and introduced them to everyone who walked past. They weren't going to inconvenience themselves trying to make polite conversations.

"Soames, I want you to meet my sister-in-law Audena."

"Winky says he's hungry, Leona."

Soames had heard all about them from Leona. Audena emitted a faint odor of Dial soap and perspiration. Soames, who never missed a cue, asked Audena with a dead-earnest expression if she was wearing Chanel No. 5 and then left Leona to keep a straight face.

She was entering a ludicrous twilight by now. People were crowding around, eager to devour the two new faces like fresh-killed meat. She hoped she wasn't a snob, but she had observed that country people sometimes showed raw edges in situations, while town people regarded such behavior as inappropriate. Averill was lingering over every pair of eyes that walked out of the

church, avoiding his sister and brother-in-law. Audena
embarrassed him. Winky was a walking offense. Leona
was jumpy as a tick trying to preplan how to get the last
dose down Averill without killing her in-laws.

There was nothing to do but escort them a hundred
yards up the road to the house, hand them both big
glasses of tea and listen to them snort at each other.

Later, after Averill showed up and she had run Audena
out of the kitchen, their visit was beginning to feel like
some plan. Audena hated to be alone with Leona. She
was up to something. Then, when she went back into
the living room, Winky fell silent. It seemed rehearsed.
Winky had been pressing some point with Averill, repeatedly drawing him back onto a subject Averill didn't
like. With Audena yakking at her, Leona hadn't been
able to catch Winky's drift. Now she realized that had
been the whole idea. They wanted something from
Averill. They were afraid Leona might object. Winky had
been elected to open the volatile subject with Averill
while Audena distracted Leona.

Now Audena started slicing into Averill's high moral
banter. Leona had to concentrate on the lethal version of Easter Sunday dinner. She did hear Audena say,
". . . our mother's wishes," which even at her young age,
Leona knew to be a certain sign of an attempted lar-
ceny. In a few more minutes, they were too loud to
understand. It was a long-standing argument between
Audena and Averill. Beyond that Leona couldn't make it
out. While they made accusations and denials, Leona
managed to get the food reorganized. She took the
plates off the dining room table so she could fill them
herself in the kitchen.

She had to get them fed and on the road. Averill's
symptoms were overdue by now. Audena was screaming:

they had had streets in hell lined with thieves and hypocrites trying to hide their sins behind a pulpit. Averill
didn't miss the opportunity. He told Audena she was
right indeed, they did have streets down in hell and
they had bloated hags like Audena scrubbing them!
Audena responded with a wail that hung over his rage
like a descant. Winky had seen two lawyers. Audena
was cut through the heart. Averill was innocent. Leona
let them scream and holler for five minutes. Then she
clanged a spoon on a pot lid and shouted, "Dinner!"
When a silence ensued, she stepped into the dining
room and called out as pleasantly as possible, "Take
your seats; I'll serve your plates from the kitchen." She
was going to add that it was because she didn't have any
decent serving dishes, but, surveying her audience, she
decided not to waste the amends.

Within ten seconds the cannon-fire in the living
room resumed. They ignored Leona's second round of
banging. Leona stormed through the kitchen and down
the back steps. The world was a blue-green blur.

Wouldn't it be a delicious irony if Audena pulled out a
gun and shot Averill between the eyes? Wouldn't it be
sheer heaven if the three of them somehow choked each
other to death? What misery and deprivation had nurtured the two of them? What kind of hideous monster
was their mother? It was strange how little she really
knew about Averill's family. The name Sayres was well
known around Fredonia, though it was by and large more
notorious than acclaimed. From what she had known
and forgotten from adult gossip, Averill and Audena had
come back to town as teenagers to live with their grandmother. Rumor had it their mother was a prostitute.

Once, when Leona was still fairly small, Averill had
walked past the house while she was on the porch

swing between her mother and father. After he was out of earshot, her mother asked which one of the Sayres families he belonged to.

"Darcy Lou."

"Sidney's wife?"

"She's no kind of wife."

"Who is that boy's father?"

"A line from here to the courthouse."

"Where is Darcy Lou living?"

"She died of a heroin overdose."

"Hush before the baby hears you."

It was sad. What good could grow out of that? Still, it justified nothing, no matter how much it might explain. There was talk in Fredonia that Darcy Lou had sold Averill to men when he was a boy. If that was true, had it broken his ability to stop himself? Was this all just an eye for an eye? Would it bring Tess back to life? Maybe Leona could still save him. She had to try. She'd feed him raw egg and mustard. He might still vomit the lethal portion. Then she could have his stomach pumped. She could invent some stupid explanation. No one would believe it, but as long as he was all right, they wouldn't bother trying to prove otherwise. Then her mother's voice repeated in her mind, reverberating with wider significance.

"Hush before the baby hears you."

The clouds of doubt and hesitation lifted like veils of illusion and she saw Averill's hands squeeze the throat of an innocent newborn. Compassion was cowardice, morality, an extravagance. Her spirit was bankrupted. She couldn't afford loftier sentiment.

Her eye caught something still and purple and gold just above the tall grass where the yard gave over to woods. It might have been a butterfly, but this was April. Whatever it was, she felt a coolness rushing toward her, an inexplicable calm that overspread the surreal after-noon. A moment ago, she was shaking, hyperventilating and muttering to herself. She had begun to slide away from reality. Now things made sense again.

She wanted to investigate the source of this unex-pected rationality. She hadn't taken ten steps before she understood it all. It was her mother's Siberian iris. She had pulled a handful of stalks the morning she left home. She had thrown them there in the crook of those tree roots the way she could remember her mother and grandmother pitching them around the bases of trees in cemeteries.

Theirs flourished. Hers had withered—all but one. She had forgotten it. Now it seemed impossible and sig-nificant. Why? Because such beauty still existed? Was it a sign that the Creator still had better plans for the world? Or a remnant of Eden? Maybe it was just a flower and it really didn't mean anything or matter. Maybe noth-ing did. She had lost all direction and meaning so long ago that when she leaned down to breathe in the ex-quisite perfume of the floating purple wonder with its brilliant gold throat, she half expected it to disappear like a mirage in the desert. Instead she drew in the es-sence of her childhood.

How could it be the same excessive sweetness? How had that survived when all the rest was gone?

She began to drift back to a world she had inhabited until a few years ago. It was a world where an iris was a small wonder and people meant what they said. She felt a strange hope blending with light green shadows min-gling with overwhelming sorrow for all she had lost. This impossible loveliness reminded her of that striving happiness people back in that believing world took for granted. Somehow there you could get aches and pains balled up with happiness. You could shrug, or smile with irony at all but the very occasional worst things. Now her head began to flow with a great river of people and things she had somehow forgotten or misplaced in this bleak present tense existence where there was neither humor nor hope to sustain you.

It wasn't the memories that stunned her, but the contrast between life then and now. How had she become habituated to this unfeeling hell where she touched no one or nothing real? When had she become this cunning wretch? Worst of all, what was the source of this driving obsession to carry out Averill's death? She had to think. Yet she couldn't. The woods had become a meaningless void, an alien terrain or island where fate had rolled her off its inexplicable tide. What was this murderous impulse that blinded her?

There was a light breeze. It was humid and there was a gathering haze from the woods. It was going to rain. She felt an inexplicable urge to pray—something she hadn't done since she married the preacher. It wasn't the desire to bow her head and attempt to communicate with God. It was a deep longing for the faith to attempt it. Aside from the necessity of seeing this careful, homicidal passion through, Leona didn't believe in anything. Not for herself. Of course, she knew that life still held a great deal of joy and meaning for other people. She didn't see any point debating whether they were more foolish or wiser than her.

Leona had to live by what was in her heart. She didn't know any other way. It didn't matter how much she hated her situation. It didn't matter what the rest of the world had to say about her actions. She couldn't be the rest of the world. She could only be herself, looking into the eyes of intolerable circumstances and doing what she understood to be necessary and moral—even if she was aware no one else shared her view. She didn't like the consequences of those actions. She just didn't see any bearable alternative.

What proof did she have? She had none. All she had was her absolute certainty. What good was that? What evidence was there, for that matter? It said "stillbirth" on the death certificate. Arlen, the county coroner, had obviously decided she was a hysteric when she questioned him on it. He was very polite, sympathetic even, but he'd taken slight umbrage when she asked him if he'd actually examined the baby. He obviously considered her a grieving mother who hadn't accepted the difficult fact of her loss.

The only material evidence lay across the road from the house, six feet under the ground. If her information was right, and she didn't doubt it, Averill had buried it in a cardboard box. Even if Leona could somehow manage it, what would even be left to find after fifteen months in wet ground? There was only one way. Even if time revealed that she had miscalculated everything, if she lived to see that she had done the wrong thing, she would never suffer the bleeding conscience of willful ignorance. She'd never say she regretted her choice. She could only say that there hadn't been one. All the winding roads of her life had converged into one narrow path that seemed to dissolve into nothing behind her as it stretched into a similar bleak horizon.

There was no room on the path for second guesses or regrets—except for one heavy uncertainty she still carried in her heart. And while it slowed her progress and burdened her with its constant torment, it hadn't and wouldn't stop her. It was part of the price. It had to be sacrificed with the rest of her luxuriant notions of happiness. It was a pain to be endured with the rest, a throbbing wound that would never heal, only die with her as the narrowing path descended into a sudden spiral that released her into floating oblivion.

His name was Blue. He was the sum of all her regret for this world, which was already beginning to seem like a fable out of the past. She was still here and alive, yet she had separated from this time and place. Blue was the only thing that prevented her from floating off or dissolving into the perfumed air.

Would he ever understand that she hadn't merely chosen vengeance over him? Would he eventually see that she had spared him a restless existence plagued by the eternal cries of a child's ghost? Would he take any comfort from knowing that she had kept it from him because he would have succeeded in stopping her? She was exhausted with the ever accruing chagrin she endured as life slapped her across the face with one discomfiting truth after another. Yet here was another one. For Leona suddenly felt herself drowning in the realization that their enormous and miraculous love was completely useless, even ludicrous when she considered its power to create unhappiness.

She breathed the exquisite cool scent of her mother's iris. It glistened in the sunlight, stirring an ephemeral shadow of her mother. It almost seemed an exquisite present sent to her out of an impossible, living past. Now it bent and fluttered on a sudden rush of wind like a magnificent butterfly separating its moist wings for the first time and summoning them into flight. In that dissolving moment of jeweled and breathing peace, she heard the scrape of her mother's shoe against the iron shovel as she turned the fragrant earth in her iris beds. It stirred the inimitable comfort of undying nurture. In that moment she understood the power of a mother's love to transcend not only time and place, but also all things real or imagined, including death itself.

Now it was all pure and exquisitely simple. Now the intuitive course she had taken became something inevitable. All that had ever been would always be— including her slain infant and her all-consuming will to nurture its eternal essence with detailed public acknowledgment of her avenging deed.

The argument inside the house was still building. Three outraged voices preached three hissing and popping sermons in a simultaneous din. It was one of those watershed wailing contests people stage when their general fury at life overwhelms them. They were lost in their own little riot. Leona had shifted her position toward the back of the yard, such as it was, in order to turn down their volume a few notches.

She felt better than she had in several days now. She didn't even suffer that gnawing need to have it done. It was already done. Her duties were all but finished. She steadied herself in the knowledge that so little could go wrong now. All those hundreds of frenzied "what ifs" had faded away.

The only part she kept stumbling over was Blue. Why try to fight that? Didn't the sadness pressing down on her deserve its due? Wasn't he a real loss? Didn't this all-consuming ache honor him by its degree? What was the point in pretending it could be any other way? What was the harm now in looking back? It wasn't going to stop anything. It couldn't interfere with things that had already been accomplished.

How could she stop remembering it? She would never stop loving him. She even allowed a guilty gratitude for the fact that he still loved her. She was sorry that it gave him so much pain. Yet she knew it wouldn't kill him. He was strong and young and overflowing with all kinds of passions. He'd love someone else before too long. She had to believe that. She never would have found the strength to reject him if she hadn't known it in her heart. It kept her from hating herself. (Though the truth was, it also broke her heart.)

If she had to sum up Blue Hudson in a word, that word was "kindness." Not that he'd agree or consider that a compliment. He'd much rather be regarded as strong and maybe honest. He was those things too. He took enormous pride in his physical stamina and he worked almost obsessively to maintain it. He walked and talked like a hard-shell redneck—unless you actually listened to him, which most people didn't. And maybe he didn't want them to. He carried himself in an almost menacing manner. There was a tension about him that seemed eternally about to explode.

It was all left over from some kid he had long since determined he didn't want to be. No, the one-word description was "kindness," whether he liked it or not. What made Leona melt into his arms for the first time wasn't his powerful good looks. Experience had long since taught her the folly in that. It was the fact that Blue seemed to know his own strength. He also knew in some essential way that its purpose wasn't self-protection or physical supremacy. Strength was given to some so that they could use it on behalf of those who were weaker than they were.

He'd never said that. He would have made fun of Leona if she had. Yet it was second nature to him. When she was with Blue she was safe. Funny, she had no idea he was any of those things the first time she found herself alone with him. In fact, at first, she smiled to recall, she had actually wished Averill would come home.

4

❦

Saint Patrick's Day always fell in that mystical week of March when a sudden blur of little red and purple leaves floated on the wet black limbs rising out of the mist. Overnight the dry yellow stubble in the yard was neon green and the jagged forsythia bushes beside the driveway atoned for five months of gnarled ugliness with a gossamer burst of sunshine yellow.

She had dragged herself out to sit on the porch swing in the early afternoon sun. It was chilly now. The blanket was too thin to do much good and the mist was slowly turning into a rain that the weatherman said would fall hard and steady through the night. The air was like a cold stew.

It had been nine weeks since the thirteenth of January, the night she had lost the baby. Across the road through a blur of shriveled bramble she could see her gray tombstone near the edge of the cemetery. Earlier she had heard a car and voices from the far end near the church. It was kids, know-it-all teenagers getting themselves stuck up for life.

Several times now Averill had run across their refuse—beer bottles and what the holy hypocrite referred to in a subsequent sermon as "life-preventing apparatus"—designed for adulterers. It might stun his flock to know that Brother Saintly had an old boot in the bottom of his closet where he kept a secret trove of those very same evil implements. Furthermore, their sanctified shepherd had never employed a single one of them in any intimate activity involving his wife. So when Averill pronounced the condom an implement of adulterous facilitation, he had it on good authority.

Not that she felt one way or the other about it—or anything else at the time. Losing her baby had subverted all her feelings under a heavy pall of empty despair inside of her that seemed to reflect the heavy gray winter skies and bare trees outside her window. She had a vague sense that spring might stir her to some plan or forward action. In fact, moving from the living room to the porch swing earlier had been a near monumental triumph over lack of will.

By then Leona was well into her "awareness," as she called it. By then she knew her marriage was an irreparable disaster. She was not only accustomed to Averill's absences, but she preferred them to his company. She knew he had women—or a woman—whichever. That was fine. It spared her any obligation to avail herself to him as a wife.

In the first few weeks of their life as man and wife, Leona had gone to some lengths to arouse and satisfy him. At first Averill's eager facility for pleasing her gave her a fragile hope for their future together. However, it didn't last long. Willingness and effort had ephemeral power at best in the bedroom. He had an intensity she didn't know how to return, and it grew increasingly difficult to substitute gratitude for desire.

Maybe it was because she was almost six months pregnant by then and her swollen shape reminded him that she was carrying another man's child. Whatever the reason, Averill hadn't touched her since their fourth week of marriage. Though she knew she didn't really want him and she doubted that he wanted her. As the weeks passed, they made less and less formal pretense. Averill drifted into his solitary routine, using the house as a place to sleep and change clothes while using her in Sunday public as a prop—his beloved wife and soon-to-be mother of his longed-for child.

She had a head filled with questions about her own future as well as that of her unborn child. If it came as predicted by mid-January, then it would be six months old by midsummer. Sooner than that, it would be too fragile, and soon after that time, it would grow too difficult to carry while she made the two of them a life. Strange, she had never discussed it with Averill, but she knew he wouldn't mind her going. She was so blinded by her desire to leave, she never noticed how little sense the entire situation made.

Even now, Leona still couldn't pretend she understood why Averill had married her. If she had looked more closely from the beginning, if she had examined the incongruous signals from the start, she might have seen what was coming and gotten herself out in time.

Leaving out all the hell of it, giving his philandering some legitimate impulse of certain otherwise well-intended men, she couldn't find the logic anywhere. Why would a man marry an almost penniless eighteen-year-old girl who was not only pregnant but desperately in love with her baby's father?

Love? Did a man love his bride one week and then abandon her the next? Why had he rescued her and lured her here to this lonely place with false assurances and phony admiration? What had he hoped to gain? Was it really as simple as a cloak of respectability behind which he could hide his secret life? Yet if that was true, why had he murdered Tess? Was it the way Soames had said? Was it really possible that Averill truly, deeply, obsessively loved her to the point that her faded passion for Tyler, her baby's father, had fermented in his mind? Were his sudden indifference and silent contempt his means of communicating his misplaced jealousy? Did the sight of her carrying Tyler's child day after day have the cumulative effect that Soames had theorized?

Had Averill been seized by uncontrollable revulsion when he saw the newborn infant for the first time?

How could that be true if Leona had never even suspected such a thing? Even now, looking back from that perspective, she didn't remember much to support the idea. Yet questions only lead to questions. What had compelled Averill to confess these things to Soames? Surely he knew that Soames, a woman whose proclivity for gossip had raised his ire many times, would never keep his terrible secret. Yet he had turned up at her door in the middle of the night and tearfully confessed to his crime as if she were some mother superior sworn and entitled to keep his secret.

Of course, Soames had come to her with everything.

They were best friends. The poor woman was traumatized. He had frightened her. His guilt had driven him
insane. He wanted to be caught. He didn't have the guts
to kill himself, but he wanted to die. Why else would he
provide her with information that could destroy him?
What would he do next? Did Leona feel safe alone in
the house with him? What would Averill do if he found
out Soames had told her everything? Did Leona have a
clue why he had come to Soames? Soames had long had
the feeling Averill neither liked nor trusted her. Was he
setting a trap? Was he simply out of his mind?

More questions leading to more questions. Yet Leona's
whole being was now focused on only one. How would
she do it? How would she avenge her child?

Over and over Soames begged her to let the law
bring him to justice. And how would that be, Leona demanded of her trembling friend. With all those extenu-
ating circumstances that watered down the charges?
With his devoted congregation swearing under oath that
each had seen a one-armed man, or some such, running
through the woods that night? And how much proof
would they furnish? Questions leading to more disturb-
ing questions and then at last Leona had the answer to
all of them: Averill Sayres had to die.

For the next week or so Soames was an almost constant companion, begging her to be careful, to move
slowly, and not to do anything crazy. Yet her good friend's
counsel only seemed to convince Leona a little more
each time that there was no alternative. Finally, even
Soames seemed to reach an uneasy truce with the in-
evitability of it. Right down to the first dose of arsenic,
Soames tried to talk her out if it. By then, however,
both women knew the thing was happening; by then it
seemed to have a life all its own. Nothing was going to

stop it—unless she caved in to her sorrow over its effect on Blue.

It seemed to her that Blue rose out of the mist that gray March afternoon. Looking for Averill, he said, and he kept his distance at first, talking up the porch steps at her from the yard the way Darthula did.

Blue and his wife, Lucy, had been Sunday regulars until about six months earlier. According to Soames, Lucy had dumped Blue for a surgeon out of Memphis. Blue had come in from a three-day duck-hunting trip last October and found their house stripped bare to the woodwork. Lucy and their two little ones had disappeared without a trace. Blue had no idea Lucy was carrying on with the surgeon and no expectation whatsoever of finding himself in an empty house with nothing but the clothes on his back.

According to Soames, Blue had worshipped the ground beneath Lucy's feet. They said the poor man was close to suicide. Leona had taken all that with a grain of salt. She didn't join Soames in condemning Lucy as a double-fanged harlot—not right off like that. Women were always ready to think the worst of other women—especially one who had broken out of local ranks and gone off into the wider world. Besides, Lucy was an exquisitely beautiful woman, one who could throw a moth-eaten cotton sack over her shoulder and make it look like a silk stole.

She had never looked comfortable on an old pine pew in a country church. Leona had also observed that she didn't look right sitting next to a sunburnt kid of a husband. Of course, Leona saw their initial attraction. In his own way Blue was as pretty as his wife. It wasn't hard to imagine them a couple years back, two starry-eyed teens joined at the hip. Yet it struck Leona from her vantage in the choir loft that Lucy had a worldly enervation, a look on her face that told you she had peered up the road ahead. There was none of that anywhere on Blue. He looked like any other kid who was content with the things he could get being cute and always on the lookout for some fun. Thinking back on it, Leona realized that Lucy had already begun to look and act like a surgeon's wife.

Soames knew all the details. Lucy had come from lower, less educated and looser origins than Blue. They had begun their marriage as teenagers with a baby coming. Typical country kids, they'd been high school sweethearts. It was easy to imagine that they had been the prettiest couple in high school. There was nothing effeminate in Blue's manner, and his attraction to the opposite sex was almost comically obvious. All the same, inch for square inch, Leona would have had a devil of a time deciding who was more beautiful. She could just see them at seventeen, stuck on each other like sweat bees on a raspberry jam cake.

About once a month Lucy and Blue brought their little handicapped daughter to church services. She lived at the Home for Incurables in Memphis. No one knew what was wrong with the child, not precisely, only that she had severe birth defects. She was terribly misshapen and virtually paralyzed. She couldn't talk and she had limited mental faculties. Blue always held her on his lap, stroking her baby fine platinum hair and wiping her mouth with a handkerchief. Now and then he'd whisper something in her ear that always drew a little half smile and a sigh from the pitiful thing.

Lucy always sat straight-backed and solemn with the

other two normal kids on her far side. If she moved at
all, it was to warn them into behaving themselves with
an upraised finger or a meaningful glare. She never had
much to say afterward in the churchyard. She was a
tight-lipped woman who rubbed her forehead and looked
over your shoulder when she was talking to you. Leona
never made much of that. Not with Lucy's wretched
freak of nature looking up at the world from her canvas
stroller. People had no call to judge the poor woman
harshly.

Yet they took it upon themselves to disapprove of the
fact that she had placed her daughter in an institution.
So when Lucy left Blue, her Christian neighbors demo-
nized her immediately. They had a tremendous love for
plucking out eyes and rotten apples, a passion for a sacrificial woman at the well. Of course, she was gone and
doubtless impervious to the fact that she was being crucified on the cross of respectable opinion.

Leona wasn't devoted to Lucy. She was hardly ready
to take up the woman's cause. She had barely known
her. All the same, she had to admire any woman from
this backwater who could unshackle herself from a husband and a badly misformed child and land herself in
five bedrooms overlooking a beautiful East Memphis
golf course. No, there was nothing noble in it. It probably indicated some moral weakness. Yet, all that aside,
she had an empathetic regard for her accomplishment.
Though she wasn't sure how she regarded Lucy's ex-
husband when he showed up late that Saint Patrick's
Day afternoon.

"Is that Blue?"

"Yessum."

Blue lived on the far side of the hill on a three-
hundred-acre cotton farm he had inherited from his

father. He was on his way to becoming one of those grinning young men of many enterprises. He'd acquired half interest in a video store and a drive-in grocery. She had also heard that for some unknown reason he'd recently hired on as a part-time deputy sheriff. He later admitted he went into law enforcement to avoid staying home alone at night.

Averill had been gone since early that morning, called away to Senatobia to preach a funeral. A little boy had drowned. That had set her own mind drifting over her recent loss. Strange to say, at the time she still believed her daughter had been delivered as a stillbirth. Aside from grief, she was half-crazy from loneliness. She was trying to stir herself a little, pressing herself to make some plans. As deep as her sorrow lay inside of her, she was beginning to understand that she would get up and go on from here—even if that only meant carrying the pain wherever she went.

Blue came on foot. She had spotted him as he emerged from a vine-covered ravine behind the cemetery. Above him, the path he had walked rose sharply to a wide, grassy plateau that rolled back for about an acre before it slanted higher into a hardwood forest.

"Scare a nervous ol' ninny to death."

"Don't wanna do that, now."

He slipped into the ravine and out of sight for a moment. During the few seconds it took him to reappear, she felt an inexplicable delight of panic, a half-forgotten rush of blood she had experienced as an adolescent whenever a boy she liked walked past her father's house while she was on the front porch. It was an exquisite angst of hope that he would stop and speak with her combined with an absolute dread that he might really do it.

Blue was crossing the road now.

"Reverend Sayres home?"

"Naw, I'm sorry to say, he's not," she said. "Gone to Senatobia to preach a little boy's funeral."

"A little boy, I'll say . . ."

"Terrible thing. It was his uncle that came for Averill."

If Blue thought it was peculiar that a family from a big town of several thousand people had sent for a country preacher twenty-five miles away, he gave no indication whatsoever. She studied his long oval face and pale blue-green eyes. He was as blond as they come, but with a dark complexion. Leona figured him to be twenty-five or twenty-six. He moved up the driveway, absentmindedly kicking up clods of dust with the points of his yellowish leather boots.

"Didn't mean to scare you."

"I never know what might come out of those woods."

"Tell the Reverend I came by, please, ma'am."

He tipped the front of his dirty white hat slightly, like in the movies. Its wide brim made a halo around his longish white-blond hair. His constant scowl and careful monotone gave him a comic edge, like that of a small boy trying to act like a man.

"Please don't rush off."

She was embarrassed by her unintentional plaintive tone. He didn't respond. He just stood there looking at her a minute. Something flashed in his eyes, something meant for Averill, she guessed. Apparently, he wasn't going to share it with her. For some idiot reason she blushed with jealousy. She pointed lightly toward a chair.

"I reckon you noticed there's a storm coming."

"All day long . . ."

She continued with a silly harangue, saying the storm,

if it was really going to make it there, would apt as not be a shower or several showers at most, certainly not torrential or menacing to any degree. He just looked at her. She wanted to chastise him for leaving without any consideration for her loneliness or extending his sympathies for her recent loss. She wanted him to stay, but she was afraid he might. She wanted no part of men, especially the good-looking kind like Blue Hudson.

Men loved to talk about the treacheries of women. Ha! Wasn't this the dark side of that moon? Was she supposed to believe he didn't have a clue as to his effect on a lonely young woman like her? She had to say something before she started acting weird and desperate or he got wise to her odd sense of longing.

"Was it a religious matter or a personal matter that brought you?"

He didn't want to answer. His scowl deepened into consternation. He was country, but he was a country gentleman. He couldn't ignore the question. Yet there was an undercurrent of something like resentment in his silence. Her query threatened his secret.

"A little of both and neither, really," he said boldly, then he turned on his heels.

"If it's religious, then I never interfere," she said to his back. "Even though I know more Old Testament than Averill does," she added, and instantly regretted her braggadocian editorial. Blue kept walking down the driveway toward the road. "However," she added in a tone that revealed a little more desperation or tension than she had intended, "if it's a matter of a personal nature, a question of morality or the heart—well, sir, it has been said I'm the one to ask."

He stopped and turned around. She couldn't tell

from this distance, but she would have almost sworn tears were welling in his eyes. He cleared his throat and spoke in a barely audible voice.

"It's just man to man, I reckon."

Man to man, he reckoned. Didn't that usually mean there was a woman involved? Well, he'd been in turmoil over Lucy for weeks. That was no secret. He just stood there, his face getting longer. Any second he'd turn away again, and she'd be alone with the sun going down. She wouldn't let that happen.

"I won't have it said you came and went without me offering you a cold drink."

He nodded. He almost seemed to half smile, as if he was glad for the invitation. She tapped the faded flowered cushion of a metal chair. Then she disappeared inside of the house.

"You need another one," Leona said after Blue inhaled an entire can of Dr Pepper and crushed it in one smooth motion.

"I'm fine," he said, stifling a burp.

"Well, it's sure enough turning spring. . . ."

"Yessum." He grinned, but he was already shifting his feet toward the driveway.

Already the despair was gathering around her, like it was a demon hiding in the woods, watching for the chance to overpower her again the minute Blue was gone.

"Much obliged," he muttered. Then he was down all three porch steps in one leap.

He'd read her despair and he didn't want to be saddled with it. She watched him move toward the road. There was something almost fluid about him, something unreal, as if he'd dissolve into the atmosphere if he turned sideways. She couldn't begin to explain it, but every step he took seemed to pull her down another foot into her dark mood. She couldn't, she wouldn't let him pass through in a wink. She didn't know what he wanted, but she was pretty sure it had to do with his broken marriage.

"Blue!" she cried out, frayed edges showing in her voice.

"Ma'am?"

"It doesn't hurt forever. It won't kill you either."

She had mortally wounded him. He just stood there, his back to her, his shoulders bunched, shaking head to toe.

"Blue, you got a hole in your heart the size of Texas. . . ."

He turned toward her, his face beet red and creased. He was trying to talk, but his lips were quivering and he was afraid if he opened his mouth, he'd start crying.

"Go on, let it out; it's just feeling."

"Aw, hell," he said. Then the tears flowed and he was a blubbering mess. He cried for a long time.

She had wanted company. She'd manipulated him into this for the sake of some company. Now she had no idea what to do or say to help him. What did she know?

"Come up on the porch and sit down."

She brought him lemonade and a towel. It was grief. One minute they talked about any- and everything. The next they sat without words and watched the thunderheads blanket the evening sky. Then he'd cry again, heaving and raining tears down the front of his white cotton shirt.

"I'm sorry," he sniffed.

"For feelings?"

After an hour he seemed to be all right again. He went into the house and washed his face. When he came

back outside it was almost as if his earlier sorrow had
been a dream.

"Better run."

"Why?"

"Things to do."

His distant, polite self-possession insulted her. She
felt like some stupid girl who'd lured a sailor home and
regretted it later. Why shouldn't Blue leave? What did
she have to say about it? This sudden rush of resentment caught her off guard.

"I'm glad you came by."

"We'll see y'all."

It felt like, "I'll call ya, babe." Was she losing it? He
had come up on the porch at her insistence, sated his
tears on a kitchen towel and voraciously helped himself
to the intimacy of two glasses of lemonade.

Blue walked across the front yard toward the road.
The sky wouldn't fall. Nothing would jump out of the
woods and gobble her up. She'd been through an eternity of lonely nights in this house since the baby. She'd
endure this one and more. Eventually she'd pick up and
go on living. This would all be some blurry memory of a
strange sojourn in the wilderness one day.

When he reached the road, Blue stopped and leaned
against a tree, thinking about something a minute. He
was too deep in his miasma to peer over the edge of it
and see hers. Well, no one could take on another person's happiness. She had to find her own and he had
to find his. Maybe growing up was understanding that
love wasn't the answer. At least not just one kind of
love. She had things to do and be that would somehow
absorb her immediate sorrows and make her life good
again.

Blue turned around and walked slowly across the muddy stubble and peered up at Leona.

"Please forgive my rudeness for not telling you right away how very sorry I am to know about your terrible loss. . . ."

His unexpected kindness elevated her. The ominous black forest turned silver under the rising moon.

"That really helps."

"Nothing helps. Nothing people say."

The unembellished truth violated her a little. It was as if he knew a secret she had never told anyone. Now he seemed a little dangerous. She didn't want company if that required her to open feelings she had stored because they were too intense to control.

"Well, as you say, you have things to do. . . ."

A shadow crossed his face, no more than a half blink, but Leona saw that she had insulted him.

"Where are my manners?" she cried with alarm. "Where is my common decency?" She rattled on for a minute, explaining that solitude made people a little quirky and egocentric.

Blue hadn't reached the steps before a deafening peal of thunder shook the house. Every towel she owned was on the back clothesline. She shot through the living room and kitchen and out the door and reached the clothesline just as the first drops began. She gathered one whole line in her arms, letting the clothespins fall where they may. Then she turned and saw that Blue had been working behind her, clearing the other one.

They were standing opposite each other, folding linens at the kitchen table when the first hard rain hammered the roof.

"You're pretty good at that, Blue."

"I'm getting better, I reckon."

"How long have you been divorced now?"

"Divorced, three days. Separated, nearly half a year. It's the worst."

"No, there's worse," she let slip without meaning to.

They were folding a sheet. He held it while she turned one half into the other. The rain had brought a cool breeze with it. The air was alive with wild, moist scents. As she handed him the corners, her finger grazed his palm and they felt a jolt of static electricity so powerful it lifted the damp strands of hair plastered to his forehead.

The silence that dropped between them made the rain seem surreal and loud. Now that the initial cloudburst had turned into a steady downpour, the air seemed warmer. It was suddenly very close in the little house. The lull in their conversation was by mutual agreement. It should have felt awkward; or if not, indecent; or then strange. Yet it wasn't at all strange or indecent. It was lovely. Something hidden away, something tightly rolled and stowed and almost forgotten—though living—some breathing blade of grass bent through its captive gate and eternity was new.

Now they were back on the front porch, watching the silver veil of falling water. Now and then the sky would ignite with yellow and then it would hiss and crackle before the sonorous thunder rolled out of the woods.

"What did you want to see Averill about, Blue?"

He now got out of the wicker rocker and sat down beside her on the glider swing. Then he lifted her hand, sliding his long fingers in between hers. There were no wild hearts beating, no lunging passions, and no furious needful flesh. He released her hand and slid almost out of reach, defining that necessary country between speaker and hearer.

"I'm trying to find some meaning in my life."

The rain, which had been a steady drizzle for half an hour, became a torrent. They followed their instinct to move ever so slightly closer.

"Leona, do you think God punishes people?"

That stopped her cold. Not because she had any definite opinion on the subject; rather, because he had obviously meant to take it up with Averill.

"Say it."

"Is that what you wanted to ask Averill?"

"Kinda."

"Now you say."

"Well, now, I'm embarrassed to."

"In that case, the answer is no, I do not."

Slowly, he spit it out. He just didn't think he could take much more of his heartache over Lucy. People kept telling him to let go and he wanted to, he really did. Only, no matter how many ways he tried to get away from the terrible emptiness, it sneaked up on him and pulled him into a pit of despair.

"How do you quit wanting something that's taken complete hold of you?"

"You don't."

She said that she believed some hurts never went away. People talked about getting over things and "letting go," but the truth was you couldn't and you were a fool to try. You had to embrace what you couldn't overcome. You had to go on. Eventually time taught you how to pick up your hurts and carry them with you as you went forward.

"Life has to make more sense than that." He said that he had talked to Averill about Nancy, his little handicapped girl. Was she a happenstance or did Averill believe God had created her that way for a reason?

Leona shuddered. She already knew Averill's answer.

"He said she was the price of our sin."

Lucy had been pregnant with Nancy when she married Blue.

"Which sin was that?"

"Fornication."

"That's what he called it?"

"Yeah."

Averill was a snake. He used his church members' greatest vulnerabilities as a way to shake them like money trees.

"So, anyway, Leona, I've combed my Bible for weeks, now, and I can't find what he's talking about."

"It's not there."

She might have slapped him, from the look on his face.

"There's not a solitary word in the Bible against unmarried people having sexual intercourse."

"What about 'Thou shall not commit adultery'?"

"That's married people—cheaters."

He didn't like that. He wanted her to turn water into wine. He wanted some magical penance or charm that would bring his family back. His was the sort of vulnerability and despair on which Averill thrived. Averill would get hold of someone like Blue and convince him he had God's answer. All a sinner had to do was write him a check or paint the church or bring Averill a cord of wood. Presto! Wrong was right, down was up, and Blue was going to drive his reunited family to heaven in a sky blue pink Cadillac convertible. She had bruised him. He got up to leave.

"I don't reckon this rain will kill me. . . ."

"Didn't mean to sting you, Blue."

"Nah . . ."

But she had stung him. People weren't much interested in what was real if it got in between them and what they wanted. Everybody had his or her own shield of lies to hold up against life. That was how they protected themselves from it and each other.

"Sorry I was so little help."

"Don't be silly."

Blue was the silly one. He felt sorry himself, so he felt he deserved her empathy. He was condescending to her views. He'd failed to extort her pity with his watery good looks and sighs. Now he was miffed, now he was going to leave her to the warm, suffocating solitude.

"Don't try to make the Book of Isaiah out of it, Blue."

"I best be going."

"It's not such a spiritual matter, really."

"I reckon not. Well then . . ."

"She just doesn't want you."

That silenced his fancy farewells.

"You don't have what she wants, Blue."

The volcano inside of her was going to blow. It was already sending up blasts of boiling air. It was unstoppable now and it was going to consume them both. She was no longer merely in this situation, she was observing it from a distance. Blue didn't even suspect the gathering liquid fury.

"Maybe Lucy didn't think you were enough reason to throw her life away."

"Throw her life away? On me!?"

"Yeah."

"No. It was always going to be Lucy and me, from way back in high school."

"Well, Blue, I guess she graduated."

The only thing that kept his anger in check was the shock that came with it.

"I could have had a hundred girls, but I chose her."

"You knocked her up."

"She had a choice."

"With you pressuring her?"

The look on his face told her that she was right. She just knew she had to be right. Maybe it hadn't taken much. Maybe Lucy just wasn't a girl who would go and have an abortion without suffering for it.

"What do you know about it?"

"I know how you knights in shining armor think."

"Do tell."

"Making a baby makes you a manly man."

"Horse shit."

"Horses' asses! You trapped her. She stood it as long as she could and then she went and found a man who treated her like she had two legs instead of four."

He was one more suit of armor that had turned out to be hollow on the inside. He reminded her a lot of Tyler Crockett. He didn't understand himself at all. He was scared to death, terrified because Lucy had shattered his idea of who he was. When it came to women, he was still a kid.

"Say, Blue, on what basis was Lucy obligated to stay with you?"

"On the basis of loving and needing me."

Leona eyed him, stunned by his sincerity. He didn't have a clue.

"Like she did when you were both seventeen?"

"What do you know?"

"I know about seventeen. I know about giving in to him in order to keep him."

"Do you know about her telling me she felt God inside of her our first time?" Blue turned beet red with embarrassment. Leona was suddenly very uncomfortable. Blue looked at her a long time, sizing her up.

She was lovely. That was obvious a mile away. Put a hundred women in a room and the one you'd see was Leona. She was a willowy beauty with thick chestnut hair, a long, oval face and almond-shaped eyes that shifted from emerald to jade green in the sunlight. She had high, round, raspberry cheeks sprinkled with brown sugar freckles. The rest of her made him think of some breathing alabaster sculpture. Beyond all that, Leona had an aura, a grace that came from within.

Blue had noticed it even before he had met Leona, back in the days when he and Lucy had attended Averill's church. Many times he had stood in the churchyard after the service and watched Leona move through the crowd, talking and shaking hands with people. There was no one in the world but you when Leona tapped your shoulder to say hello. There was no sound but your voice when she gave you her ear in a noisy throng. It was as if she pulled an invisible cord and left a light on in every living soul she met.

Though now he saw something in Leona he had never noticed. She was lonely. There was a long, sad story in her eyes. He almost wanted to tell her everything would be all right. Yet she hadn't exactly comforted him just now. Where did she get her license to act so damned sanctimonious? And what made her think she knew what had happened between him and Lucy seven years ago?

"Forgive me, Blue. I talked out of turn."

"Fuck you."

"I meant no harm, I apologize."

"I worked two jobs so she could go to nursing school."

"I misjudged you and I apologize."

He had more to say, though, a lot more, and it made her feel even worse. She hadn't guessed it all wrong. Blue had talked Lucy out of an abortion. They were seniors in high school. They kept her condition a secret until after graduation. She was four months by then. By the time their parents knew and calmed down a little, she was almost five months. That was when her mother finally took her to the Memphis doctor who told them there was something wrong with the baby.

"She never forgave me for talking her into having that baby."

"That doesn't matter, Blue. You have to forgive yourself."

"She tried to love her at first."

"Then why is she in an institution?"

"Lucy got afraid she'd kill her."

Everybody lived with something. Everybody had some kind of blood on their hands. How many killed themselves and each other trying to hold the lid down on their secrets?

"Lucy was brave to tell it."

"I know."

"Blue, I didn't think anything could be worse than delivering a stillborn child."

"Who's to say, Leona?"

"Lucy is."

"Why?"

"My loss is terrible and immense, but hers lives and grows."

"All she had to do was love her."

"Do you?"

"I have to."

"From guilt?"

"It's what fathers do. Mothers too."

"But Lucy . . ."

"Refused to love her. That's what's twisted her."

He was no Tyler Crockett. He didn't need a suit of armor. She had been a thousand percent wrong about him. She was ashamed, but more than anything she was happy, happy to know he was so much more than he seemed. More than that, it gave her all kinds of hope to look into a man's heart and admire what she saw there.

It was very dark outside. The moon was a strange yellowish blur through the thinning clouds. She didn't know what it meant beyond the moment, but she had never felt as close to another person, or as safe. She had no idea if he had the same tender inclinations. She didn't tell him any of that then. She was afraid to breathe out loud, terrified it would scare him away. They sat in close stillness some unmeasured time, then a clap of thunder broke the spell.

"Enjoyed my visit."

"Stop by any time."

"Thank you."

"I'll give you a ride."

"I know the path like the back of my hand."

Then the darkness swallowed him. She listened to his footsteps fade. She had no idea when she might ever see him alone like this again. She had no other situations against which to compare this particular lightness inside, so she couldn't give it a name. One thing she realized with a start, one little star switching on somewhere. She was stunned to know it, but know it she did. She could love somebody again.

Meanwhile, Blue had run about a quarter of a mile up the dark hill and his breath was giving out. He felt silly now that he hadn't accepted Leona's offer of a ride. He couldn't see more than three feet. A cold wind had kicked up and he could smell the rain in it. He stopped to rest. What was the sense of getting soaked? She'd offered him a ride. Why didn't he go back to Leona's? The thought made his cheeks burn. But why? She had taken him a little aback, brought him up a bit short, Daddy would say. He couldn't fit in his head all the things they had said to each other, all the things he had said out loud for the first time. Did she know how right she was about a lot of it? Did he?

He felt better. Yet some things she said practically sliced him in half. A woman who had so much bad to say about him couldn't hold him in very high esteem. Still, he couldn't fool himself here alone in the dark, she'd nailed him. And she'd done more good than harm. How much umbrage could he take when he felt like laughing out loud? The cold air smelled clean. The wet bark of the trees glistened silver blue. The warm earth breathed back the chilly mist.

He thought of her there alone, closing her window and slipping on something to keep her warm while she slept. Was it true? Had she married Averill to give his name to another man's child? What a desperate thing in this day and time. It made him feel very sad for her. Did she know where Averill went at night? Did she know it had been going on before she came to these parts? Was it betrayal or an understanding? Why did she stay there with him, dying of loneliness?

Now an idea took over his mind, an idea so big it smothered all other thoughts. He should rescue her. He should save her from her dark existence. How he'd go about it, he wouldn't dare dream he knew. It was just a powerful inclination at the moment. She was finer than people around here seemed to know. Did other people already know the depth of her honesty? Did they appreciate her candor as sincere and second nature? Or did they think she was rude? Did they also see how beautiful she was? Did they realize she played it down because she had the gift of self-possession?

Not these people, not his cousins and his neighbors and lifelong friends. They were good people. They meant well. They just didn't always look close enough to see all the details that drew your careful attention. What was he thinking? Not these people? No. Not him. That was what he meant. He referred to his own blindness. The woods were so lovely just then that he almost had to retch at their exquisite isolation. Earlier he thought they had never been like this.

Now he felt his heart release a heavy burden. The woods had always been this lovely. He'd covered every square foot of them in much worse weather than this. It wasn't the rain. He'd easily be at the house in another fifteen minutes if he kept up his pace. It was Leona. He wanted to see her again. As he turned around on the path, the toe of his right boot jammed in a gnarled tree root. He lurched forward, trying to avoid twisting his ankle. He barely had time to see the limb before his forehead smashed into it. Pain burst, searing yellow and splintering into cascading stars that extinguished in the blackness as he fell forward.

5

❦

Alone in the darkness, Leona was grateful for the rain. It muffled the usual creaking and moaning of the trees and wild dogs barking and owls and such. The showering quiet overspread her thoughts like a luxuriant blanket of peace. She didn't sleep much since the baby. Though part of that was Averill lumbering in at all hours, startling her. She had never quite settled her mind on what he might or might not do. Tonight, though, there were no thoughts of loneliness and dying to keep her burning eyes peering into the boding blackness until sunrise. Tonight as she had climbed into bed, she had felt a swirling rightness about things, as if a band of gentle spirits hovered close.

Blue's boot on the porch woke her. She knew it before he knocked. She hadn't expected Blue to come back, and not after one A.M., yet she couldn't say that when she switched on the yellow porch light she was surprised to see him standing there. They had already entered that tender country where inchoate lovers dwell in the same hopeful mystery.

"What's that welt on your forehead?"

"I hit a tree limb. It knocked me out."

"Oh, boy . . . Come on in. I'll get an ice pack." She might just as well have said, "I'm so glad you hit your head."

"I'm fine. I just came back . . ." He took her hand to prevent her from leaving him there alone. He held on to it. "I just came back."

"I know. . . . Let me give you an ice rag."

He stepped into the living room and waited while she pulled a tray of ice cubes from the ancient Frigidaire. He heard the back door slam, then the hammer. It was a good-sized room, probably the only one of any consequence in the house. The furniture and rugs looked old and expensive. There was a shining black baby grand piano in one corner. It was as if he had stumbled against a door in the night and opened it into an unexpected elegant lair.

Like the woman, the furnishings didn't go with the house. He read her in the solid, old things in the room, lace-curtain Methodist, merchant types. Solid.

"Sit down, Blue."

It was too late to call someone for a ride. Though he couldn't ask her to take him at this hour. Several inches of rain had already fallen. The county hadn't laid fresh gravel on this section of the road in years. There would be twenty-foot-long mud puddles by now.

She gave him Averill's best robe and he took a hot bath while she ran his clothes through the washer and threw them into the dryer. Then she sat in the living room sipping hot tea while she waited for him.

"I feel like one of the wise men in this thing." His enormous hand dwarfed her mother's delicate china cup when he took it. "Trying to make a gentleman of me?"

"I don't know what to make of you."

If Averill walked in right now, would it look like they had just slept together? It didn't feel anything like that. There was too much trust and budding affection. Love, she thought, before she had time to consider the implications, isn't lurid or sensational. From her fragmented experiences of it, she had always imbued the real thing with lurid sensation.

"If it wasn't so late, I'd light a fire."

"It's never too late," Blue observed, setting down his cup. In less than two minutes Blue had a log on a bed of small flames. The kindling was damp. It hissed and crackled as the fire slowly filled the hearth box. Something rattled near the top of the chimney and a delicate shower of leaves drifted into the blaze. In a minute they heard a squirrel scratch lightly across the tin roof.

"We've never laid a fire," Leona explained. She had battled an odor of mildew in the house since her arrival six months ago. Obviously it had come from the unused fireplace. Blue reached over and switched off the lamp. Now the room was bathed in pink and gray shadows. She had entertained hopes for this room in the first week or two. It needed new windows, the plaster had been repaired too many times, the floor sagged at one end. Still, by design it was an airy room. Painted beams crossed the high ceiling. There were long, narrow alcoves for bookcases on either side of the fireplace. A row of French doors, their glass panes long painted over, separated the dining room.

"It's a good house," Blue observed.

"Nothing wrong here but neglect," Leona amended.

"It'd be fun to put it right."

"I've considered taking a match to it."

They sat on the sofa and watched the fire and talked and talked and talked. Leona was like an enchanted flower that kept opening and revealing more and more layers.

"Try as I might, I can't put you and Averill Sayres together."

"It's not a marriage, Blue."

"You don't love him?"

"Never pretended to."

It was a well-made black cotton robe with buttons on the pockets. The fabric was smooth. The collar was made almost like a suit. It was made for smaller shoulders than his, and longer legs. She had never seen a robe like it, except in movies with English lords and Russian princes. The hem lay on the floor under his bare feet. His long, slender toes and narrow heels fascinated her. The masculine refinement of the robe highlighted his animal grace.

Clean bare feet, she kept thinking. Long, lovely fingers and clean cotton and the honest aroma of a hickory fire. Why did people make it so neon bright?

"Why did you marry Averill?" His voice reminded her that she had drifted away into her thoughts.

"I was pregnant."

"A lot of girls today don't see that as a reason."

"Life and death hit me over the head all at once. I couldn't think."

Everyone knew Leona's story in more detail than she

probably even remembered at this point. Though Blue sensed that she was unaware of that. The last thing he wanted to do was upset or humiliate or embarrass her. They were sitting very close. Somehow they had crept comfortably onto tender ground. Yet neither felt the slightest fear of the other. Both understood that whatever happened would be all right. They had reached that velvet plateau of mutual accommodation. Each felt his needs and desires would be best served by facilitating the other's.

Then he kissed her and the kindness of his lips sent her soaring. Tenderness swallowed every ache and sorrow in her crowded young life. She took him by the hand and led him into the bedroom. Before they lay down on the bed, she opened the closet door and showed him which boot to reach down into.

His guileless need and intuitive understanding of hers disarmed her. She had never before experienced this friendly passion. It was impossible to discern conversation from lovemaking. There was as much laughter as there were sighs. It was charming and innocent and pleasant for a long time. Then they were jolted by a climbing need that took them both a little by surprise. There was nothing sordid or secret in it, none of the painful pleasure she had experienced with Tyler and Averill. Blue's eyes never left hers. His body never imposed a separate agenda on hers. When they burst together, it was thrilling. Yet the hours of soft conversation and comforting flesh that followed were wonderful too.

It all seemed connected, all part of the same thing: love and touch, sleep and talking, moonlight and shadow and dawn. She drifted to sleep with her head on his shoulder and, dreamless, she breathed the opiate balm of his affectionate flesh. Then it was morning and yellow sun flooded the room.

She opened her eyes and sat forward. Blue was sitting on a small wooden chair next to the bureau with his feet propped up on the footboard. He was so deep into his thoughts that at first he didn't seem to notice that she was awake. His manner gave her the impression that he had been there for some time.

"Are you painting me?" She smiled.

"I don't need a painting. I have the real thing."

She smiled. Tears poured down her face. He smiled at her. Neither of them spoke. Tears came hard for Leona and almost always without warning. They were the private language of her inarticulate depths. She never meant them for the rest of the world's sympathy. She rarely wanted to discuss the things they addressed with whoever happened to see them. Yet people meant well and she didn't want to be rude. She waited for Blue to notice them and comment or presume to offer unsolicited comfort. Yet his smile didn't seem to take them into account. It was extraordinary. It was exquisite to draw in his already beloved outline, to embrace her deliverance from that now ancient wretchedness that yesterday was her waking and sleeping fate.

It was impossible to believe when he kissed her that this wasn't all some yellow image of an ideal love painted in thick oils on canvas. Or a film or a moving dream. Life was a layered series of illusions. Innocence, passion, sorrow, despair, and now this sunny new awakening of bliss. Would it ever take a discernible shape? Could she believe in this wondrous solid ground? Yet these arms around her were more than canvas. She wasn't a painter. This moment—which she already knew in her heart was what people meant by glory—was not to be observed or sketched or even doubted. It was for embracing. This was happiness, heaving and tumbling through her. This was singing flesh and trust and warm giggling in her ear. This was new, impossible good. She had stepped on too many of life's rusty nails, she had cradled too much everlasting sorrow to take the clear blue sky above the new green hills for granted. If love wasn't eternal, then neither was sorrow, but here and now Blue's relentless affection was enough meaning for her.

Later, when the sun had dried the shining leaves and the warm wind had chased last evening's chill, she and Blue walked up the hill into the woods, leaving the path where it veered and skirted a steep incline of boulders in front of them. Climbing another ten minutes, they stood at the edge of the flat, grassy plain that stretched a quarter of a mile across the top of the hill. On the far side they found a broad, flat, mossy stone, which jutted several feet over a bowl of farmland below. Three miles away, at the top of the next wooded hill, they could make out the west face of the courthouse clock in town. Blue had discovered the place when he was a boy. He said half his memories were here.

"Why did you marry Averill?"

"I told you last night. I was pregnant."

"You haven't told me anything."

"I might have done differently if . . ." She didn't want to tell him. She had been blissfully free of all those ghosts since last night. She was afraid it would bring them back. She changed the subject, but he wouldn't let it go that quickly.

"They'll kill you, Leona."

"Who?"

"Your secrets."

If she closed him off, she'd lose him. Yet it frightened her. The idea that she might overcome the dark influences of the last few years was very new. Hope was a precious commodity. She wanted time. He was waiting for her to tell him about it. How much did he already know? He read her mind.

"The more you hide, the more people see, Leona."

"Why do you want to know?"

"Because it's eating you alive."

They drifted into an almost wordless quiet, napping while a vast hoard of gray-and-white sheep swam slowly westward on the pale blue sea above them. By two o'clock the clouds were scattered threads and the day was white. It was warm, almost hot, the sort of mid-March afternoon that had brought a steady trickle of old ladies into her father's drugstore to declare they just didn't know when they had ever been so warm a solid week before, sure enough, spring arrived.

Why not tell Blue? Why not share that world? Did she think it would bore him? Did she fear his judgment? Why not? Didn't it ennoble her when he shared so much with her? What did he mean? What was eating her alive? She was crying, not that exquisite pain that had engulfed her with tears this morning. This was more terrible and overwhelming and heavier than that. This was the fear of telling him everything; this embodied eating her alive. This was the unmitigated mortification that overwhelmed her every time she looked back.

Now his arms were holding her. Yet their kindness was unbearable. She didn't deserve kindness.

"What is it, Leona?"

"They gave me everything, Blue. . . ."

"I know. . . ."

"And look what I came to. . . ."

"Leona, I told you, I know."

"I'm . . ."

He gently loosened his arms and let his hands slide up to her shoulders. Then he lifted her chin and looked into her eyes.

"You're ashamed, Leona. . . ."

"Yes."

"That's good."

"Then why do I feel so bad?"

"Evidently you did a lot to feel bad about."

"That's easy for you to say."

"About as easy as you telling me to forgive myself."

They sat down in an ocean of tall grass and watched the fleecy sky ravel and drift away like a white iceberg dissolving into a silver blue ocean. When they kissed and lay down, the grass waved, and when he was inside her she felt the earth sigh. There on the glistening, heaving flesh of his shoulder she saw a white butterfly drying its perfect wings. When it rose, it seemed to draw them into the sky with it as peace burst within her. Then, as they lay in the still grass, she watched it climb higher and higher until it was tiny and shining and indistinguishable from the first spray of evening stars.

That was when she knew she could tell him.

Facing down the years, it was strange how her memory had kept details she had missed altogether when she was there in the flesh. As she told Blue about her girl-hood in Fredonia, Mississippi, Leona saw for the first time that hers had been a very privileged childhood. Her father was a prosperous druggist and her mother taught elementary school music. Both of her parents had used their comfortable income to smooth a lot of rough edges for Leona.

They were pillars of the First Presbyterian Church, but they had a more tolerant approach to other people and certainly to child rearing than most of their friends. People said they couldn't help spoiling her. Leona was their only daughter, but not their only child. Lloyd William and Viola Clay raised two children, each a generation apart. Her brother Henson had been born while her daddy was still in pharmacy school. Henson was drafted into the army in 1970, the summer after he graduated from the University of the South at Sewanee, Tennessee. He was killed in Vietnam two years later.

Leona was born in 1980, a complete surprise, and to their dying days her parents never failed to seize the opportunity to tell her she had come like a miracle. They coddled and protected and adored Leona, raising her in a home where everything revolved around her happiness. Lloyd William Clay made a very solid living as a pharmacist. Leona's world was comfortable and pretty and soft and sunlit. She had everything she wanted all through her childhood, and she had never doubted that she always would.

Maybe that was her parents' one big mistake. She had too little awareness of life's darker potential. It created a false sense of security and left her vulnerable to people and situations. She was blinded by her self-importance. She had little practice with looking at other people's needs and motives. She had come to the opinion that selfish people were the easiest to manipulate. Or maybe her mother and father meant to postpone some of life's lessons until they felt she was old enough to accept them. In any event, Leona's childhood came to an abrupt and permanent end two weeks after her fifteenth birthday. After winning second place in the Fourth of July Five Mile Run, Lloyd William bent over to tie his shoelace and fell dead at age sixty-nine.

It was as if fate had decided that Leona had experienced too much light and laughter. The skies would never be as blue again. In the wake of her father's death, Leona helped Viola struggle to keep the drugstore open. However, without a pharmacist it quickly deteriorated into a high-priced sundries store. It limped along for a little over a year. Then Wal-Mart appeared at the center of a parking lot on the north edge of town and Clay's Drug Store succumbed with half of the other businesses on Court Square.

Viola was in her sixties, well liked and certified as a schoolteacher, but she had lost more than her husband had when her son died. The ancient wound left by that loss had never really healed. Viola and Lloyd William had been conservative Christian people who believed in the tenet "my country right or wrong," when Henson was killed. However, the intervening years revealed a great many facts, slowly convincing Viola that Henson had died for the profit of a military-industrial complex that had staged the war like a multibillion-dollar flea market for its military goods.

By the time her husband died, Viola was already suffering dark periods lasting several weeks. The futility of her son's death had overpowered her former faith in life. She had once been a strong woman. However, these difficult losses seemed more affronts than bad luck. Her despair had become a formidable opponent before she lost her husband. Her grief afterward, coupled with her inability to save the business, seemed to draw the life out of her as well.

More and more she sat at home all day while judges and lawyers and bankers cut up her late husband's assets. When Leona came home from high school, she would often find her mother seated in the same chair that she had been in when Leona left for class in the morning. Gradually Viola became a semi-invalid, managing only to get herself to church in good weather. By the time Leona was sixteen, all her mother's duties had fallen on her shoulders. Viola had caved in to despair. She not only ceased taking care of Leona's needs, but she neglected herself completely. Her nourishment, her hygiene, the small business dealings and income left her—everything became Leona's responsibility.

One by one Leona had to give up her outside activities. She had worked for the school newspaper and played a series of comic parts in the school drama club productions, which won her a reputation as a cut-up. The special fund her father had created to fulfill his dream of sending her up north to a good girls' college went to pay estate taxes.

She wasn't going to college. She wasn't going anywhere except maybe to type and answer the telephone for some lawyer.

Then one June night Tyler Crockett stood looking at her through the front door, his eyes red, his hands shaking and his trembling lips begging her for help. After that everything changed.

She was miserable and afraid that her mother would keep her from having a life. From her shadowy vantage, Ty Crockett seemed like a sudden angel of mercy. She and Ty had always been buddies. He was her first boy pal when they were children. Even then they just saw things the same way. Later, in high school, they continued their easygoing friendship. Leona had never thought about Ty as a boyfriend. It just never occurred to her. Everyone knew that he was going to marry Gloria London one day.

Even when Ty came to her devastated by his breakup with Gloria, Leona hadn't attached any romantic significance to it. She was merely returning the same shoulder to cry on that he had lent to her when her father died. She was just helping out a good friend. Even when they began to do things together in public—the picture show, church, summer parties—they were always surprised when people considered them a couple.

They had always liked each other. They had always understood things in a similar manner. They shared a delicious, sardonic sense of humor and an indomitable passion for dreaming up all kinds of future adventures, like backpacking through Europe. Neither could say when the friendship turned into something more. It just evolved. It seemed the most natural thing in the world when they started loving each other. When they slept together, it seemed right that Ty was her first lover. Hadn't she always loved him in one way or another? He was dear and familiar and it all made perfect sense. It was as neat as any movie. Life had come through with her happy ending just when it had seemed impossible.

Looking back, the memory of her naiveté turned Leona beet red. She laughed nervously as she recalled it for Blue. He didn't comment or wince or smile. He just waited with inscrutable interest for her to continue.

6

They'd had everything planned. Ty would go to the university one hundred miles away in Oxford. She'd stay in Fredonia to work and live at home and attend secretarial courses at the local junior college. When Ty graduated, they would be married. They would live in Oxford while he went to law school and she worked in an office.

Six weeks before Ty was scheduled to enter the university as a freshman, Leona began to suspect that she was pregnant. In the first week of August, with her second period overdue, she and Ty took a train to Grenada, where a doctor confirmed that she was expecting a baby. A terrible irony of fate had been working that summer in the weeks between her first suspicions and the proven fact. Viola's doctor had finally revealed that she had been suffering terminal cancer for several months and now she was running out of time. On the train ride back to Fredonia Leona and Ty amended their earlier plans. They would marry right away, as soon as their parents were informed of Leona's condition. Ty would go to the university and Leona would stay in Fredonia to see Viola through to the end.

Ty went home to tell his parents the news. He'd come over to the Clays' house after supper to be with Leona when she shared the news with Viola. The lovers embraced and parted, certain their devotion would see them through. Leona couldn't help her happiness at the prospect of the new life to come. The being that was growing inside of her was a promise of all the life ahead, a tonic and a balm that gave her the perspective she needed to face her mother's illness and the past that was now lost forever.

Leona waited until eleven o'clock before she switched out the porch light and gave up on seeing Ty that evening. She went to bed worried that his mother and daddy were giving him a hard time. Ty's parents had the highest expectations for him. She was confident that nothing could stand in the way of their deep bonds. Leona believed that she and Ty had been linked in their spirits back when they were still just friends.

When she hadn't heard from him by the following afternoon at four o'clock, she made several attempts to reach him by telephone, but there was no answer. Fighting panic all that night, Leona went to Ty's house around nine o'clock the next morning.

There was no one at home. In fact, the drapes were drawn across the downstairs windows and the shades on the second floor were pulled down. Still, whatever it meant, she didn't doubt Ty for a second. She knew this inexplicable absence was unavoidable. Destiny had brought them together. His love was the inextinguishable torch illumining her darkness. Ty would never fail her.

"Something's happened, child."

It had been ten days since the doctor told Leona and Ty they were expecting a baby. She had gone by his house every afternoon, hoping against dwindling hope she would find him there. She was almost to the third month. The puffiness at her middle wouldn't wait for Ty or anyone else. So far it wasn't showing as long as she wore a loose dress. But her ideas about any kind of wedding with guests and a reception were useless. It was probably her imagination, but people in general were taking an odd, inquisitive step backward when she walked into a store. Was it her, or was it odd no one ever said, "Leona, where's Ty?" Now Viola was about to ask her that very question.

Viola's condition had deteriorated. She was bedridden. She'd lost her color, and her dry, gray flesh hung off her chin and arms. Her eyes were two tragic ovals sunken in wrinkled holes. They were yellow. They had given up all their hopes for this world.

"Nothing's wrong, Mama."

"I'm not dead yet, child."

"Rest. Get better."

Viola began to cry. It was terrible to think her mother knew about her predicament. Her cruel disease already tormented the poor woman. Worse than that was her knowledge of its approaching, inevitable outcome. It seemed awful enough to Leona that people lived with general knowledge of their own mortality. In her mother's case, she had been compelled to lie in pain and watch her death make its slow, steady progress like a ship with black sails moving into harbor.

She couldn't bear the idea that her stupidity had created another source of pain for her mother. So she denied all reason for it, though her denial was as much to protect herself as well. The future, though immediate and inescapable, was imponderable and impossible to face. Leona didn't know, looking back, what might have transpired if she had shared her dilemma with her mother. However, she was certain that other, more sensible arrangements would have been made.

After two desperate weeks of calling and knocking and mailing notes to Ty's house, she saw his father's Oldsmobile in its familiar place in the driveway on Sunday morning.

"Hey, Leona."

"Morning, Mr. Crockett."

"What can we do for you this morning?"

"I just came by to see Ty, sir."

"He'll be sorry he missed you."

"When do you expect him?"

"I couldn't say, sweetheart. He's touring the Continent with his mother."

"But he has to start classes at the university in two weeks, right?"

"His mother and I felt he should travel for six months or a year while he decides where to attend college."

Mr. Crockett excused himself, explaining that he had to teach the Presbyterian Men's Sunday School Class in half an hour.

It rained that afternoon, a torrential harbinger of an eternal season descending. Viola slipped into a final lethargy and Leona sat holding her hand while her mother drifted in and out of the withered shell of the life she had completed in this world.

"I worry about you."

"I'm fine, Mama."

The dying woman summoned her last strength and placed her hand against Leona's stomach. Her eyes flooded with joy and sadness.

"I love it so," she whispered. Leona bristled with shock. She didn't mean—she couldn't know. Then Viola's withered hand rose slowly and she brushed Leona's tummy with the tip of her index finger in a gesture that could only mean one thing.

"Tell it I loved it."

"I will, Mama."

"You were my delivering angel," she said in a barely audible tone.

"And I'll have mine," Leona heard herself say, experiencing the notion as she imparted it. Viola's lips drew back into a heavy smile. Leona saw her mother abandon her eyes, and she felt her drift away.

She was dead. Love was dead. Days and nights became indistinguishable.

For the next several days the house was filled with women who kept cleaning the house and wrapping food in aluminum foil and keening every time another hideous red-and-orange flower arrangement arrived. They told Leona what to wear and instructed the minister which hymns to sing. It relieved her to know that her mother was no longer in pain. Yet the loss was astounding, and the sadness sat on her shoulders like a mountain of stone. It made Ty seem trivial, and the baby, who was still not in evidence, feel distant and remote. Everything and every moment was saturated with the terrible emptiness, the unbearable longing for her mother.

There was an edge of autumn coming in the breeze as she stood listening to the minister recite the dreadful rhetoric of dust and eternity over Viola's casket. There was an echo of life dying in the shuddering bursts of falling leaves on the faded grass. All around her the worn granite tombstones stood like a mournful tribe of headless phantoms, their shoulders stooped and useless against the crushing weight of time.

That night a small circle of women who had known Viola from early childhood lingered after the condolence crowd was gone. Bit by bit Leona found herself penned in by a group who already knew about her predicament. In fact, they knew several things she hadn't discovered. The first of them was that Ty hadn't left the country at all. Ty was in South Carolina playing football for the university at Columbia. He'd been awarded a scholarship during his senior year. Leona had known all about that, but Ty had insisted he didn't want to go that far away from her. He'd wanted to attend the University of Mississippi like his father and grandfather.

The women shook their heads and clucked and, using as much grace as possible, they explained that Gloria London, the steady girlfriend who'd jilted him last year, was already enrolled in summer school there. Several weeks back Ty and his parents had gone to Columbia, where he and Gloria, who was expecting a baby next month, had been married. His mother had stayed on for a few weeks to help them settle and prepare a nursery.

"You've proven yourself with Charmaine!" one woman pressed on. "You're a genius at wedding decorations."

After the drugstore failed, Leona had worked part-time with a local florist, helping the inept fool plan and design weddings. "You get yourself straightened around and avail yourself of a good floral concern!" another chimed in. "This is all just a bad year, baby," mused a third.

Later Leona would look back at those women and see that she had been their sacrificial lamb. Almost all of them had or would shortly drive their own unmarried, pregnant daughters to the anonymous sanctity of distant cities for abortions. Therein lay the dangerous differences between individuals and groups.

Of course, she wasn't listening to them anyway. She didn't hear a word. She was struck deaf and dumb by the cold, hard fact that Mr. Crockett had lied to her. Leona felt the fire die out of her passion and grief. Nothing grand had been lost, nothing mystical or destined or poetic was gone. She was one more stupid, sorry bad girl in a jam.

Yet his abandonment and the insensitive indifference of the sanctimonious world around her were merely burdens beside her mother's death. That was incomprehensible and cruel, as if life had waited for this difficult summer to bare its teeth with a haughty smirk.

As she lay in bed that night, watching a moving armada of clouds sail past the moon, it seemed as if the army of death were surrounding her, seizing her future and tossing her along with it into prison. It seemed that her mother's dying had permeated every cloud shape, every leaf on every tree. And when she slept, it was only to chase her mother, who outpaced her as she fled through the meaningless void.

7

FRIDAY, AUGUST 28, 1998
12:00 NOON

Mr. Crockett's office was at the back of the Bank of
Fredonia, a gray marble temple of finance built in 1899
with NeoClassical faith in the impending twentieth century. The receptionist was at lunch. Mr. Crockett, who
was the first vice president, didn't go to lunch. He liked
to work straight through from seven A.M. to three P.M.,
when he headed for the country club golf course. She
slipped down the polished granite corridor, leaning one
hand on a carved Corinthian pilaster beside his open
door. He looked up before she could speak. He pasted
on an affable smile and jumped to his feet, moving
toward the door to prevent her from taking a seat. He
was an unpleasant, fastidious man who always seemed
about to fly into a rage. She had a childhood memory of
her father leaning over her head in church to comment

to her mother that Mr. Crockett was a man tormented by secrets.

"Hey." His smile shifted into a sympathetic look. "We're all so devastated about poor Viola."

"Poor Viola's troubles in this miserable world are over," she replied with distant cool, raising her palms slightly to prevent him hugging her. He became as neutral and matter-of-fact as he could. "However, my troubles are growing by the minute," she continued, choosing the tasteless expression in an effort to express her disdain by arousing his. He crossed his arms, tucking his hands into the crooks of his elbows, and waited for her to continue speaking. When she didn't, he dropped his hands into his pockets and walked around behind his desk and leaned against the back of his chair.

"What can we do for you, sugar?"

He said it loud enough for anyone in the surrounding offices to hear him, and he used a tone of voice that might expect her to say she wanted a car loan.

"Sir, I'm here to make an honest appeal."

He flashed a broad, mechanical grimace and leapt around her to shut the door.

"Have a seat, precious."

She sat down on a leather sofa. He leaned back, half sitting on the front edge of his desktop. It probably gave him some confidence because it positioned him above her.

"All right, honey. Is this about Daddy's time deposit account?"

That disingenuous rhetoric delivered with a punch, he made several louder than necessary steps toward the door, which he opened a crack, and seeing that the corridor was empty, he closed it again.

She was wrapped in a veil of unreality that protected

her from condemning her effort with an angry overreaction. How could any of this be real? She was eighteen years old. This time yesterday she had stifled terrible nausea, hiding it from the whole town, while she watched her mother's casket descend into the ground. She wouldn't disgrace herself or insult her mother's memory by allowing the swirling inferno in her stomach to erupt. When she wept she didn't know if she was mourning her mother or Ty or expressing the terror she felt at surviving as a woman alone with a fatherless child.

And this son of a bitch knew it. This empty bastard was well aware that she was carrying his grandchild. Was this really about his position at the bank? Was Mr. Crockett devoid of all human decency? Would he deny his son's child and tear him away from a girl he loved—all for some job? Then, in the name of the brass plaque on the door, would he further force that son to marry a woman he despised and accept another man's child as his own?

No. No one was that cold. Were they? Had she missed the point? Were people in general far more devious and dangerous than she was willing to see? No. She wouldn't believe that. The strain of the last weeks was catching up with her. She had stood by her dying mother to the end. She had planned and overseen the arrangements. She had carried her terrifying sadness with determined grace, greeting the onslaught of people, behaving as if she had one and not two losses to bear, as if she had any idea what to do or expect.

Meanwhile this contemptible jackass had manipulated Ty—of that she was certain—into a miserable marriage. "My father used to say that a man's secrets are his doom," she began. She had gotten the idea if she confronted him with some truths about the situation, she might win him over.

"Ty and our darling Gloria have been inseparable for years." He took a little step into it. "They had a silly lover's spat last year, but they can't argue with destiny. They need each other. They might as well be Pyramus and Thisbe." Mr. Crockett thought he came across upper-class when he made obscure references. It just so happened that her mama had reared her on mythology. She knew all about Pyramus and Thisbe.

"Pyramus and Thisbe were eaten by a lion," she replied.

He reddened at the affront.

Leona knew the score. In the first place, everyone who went to high school with Ty and Gloria knew that they had bickered and argued for months before they broke up. Ty had told Leona that his and Gloria's parents had exerted a lot of pressure on them to date each other, and talked as if they were engaged. Everyone in school knew Ty's father was the reason he hadn't already dumped Gloria. He'd made it clear to all his friends he planned to dump her when he got to college, where he wouldn't have to listen to his parents' badgering.

For that, Gloria told the whole world she thought Ty was dopey. She was just dating him because he was the best-looking boy in school and he'd look good next to her in the yearbook. Sometimes, if she'd had a few pops of gin at a party, she'd "borrow" another girl's boyfriend for a frenzied romp in the backyard. She defended her practice, saying that Ty's loving amounted to an appetizer and she was starved for a T-bone steak.

"There's lots more fish in the—" Leona's shriek cut

him off. He was going to make her tell him she was
pregnant. He wanted to feign shock, dismay and sympathy and then tuck a few hundred dollars into her pocket
as he shoved her out the door. She could also count on
the fact that he was going to dangle the money over her
head until she made some concession to his theory that
there was some real reason to doubt the actual parent-
age. That would give him the kernel of a half-truth on
which to base the lies he would tell about her. He'd fic-
tionalize it into her full confession that this was all a
ploy to extort money. Why, his own son had asked him
how best to rebuff her lascivious advances. He said
she'd been with so many boys, he was afraid he might
catch something.

"Mr. Crockett, let me repeat this for you, sir. I don't
want your money. I'm not here to threaten you either,
sir. Everywhere I look in this town there's a hard memory
staring back at me. That would be enough to make me
leave town for good. But on top of all that, I have no intentions of giving birth to an illegitimate child here
where it would have to grow up the bastard of a father
who wouldn't claim it."

He had an expression of terrified hope. He couldn't
tell whether she was telling him something too good to
be true, or whether this was leading to some impossible
condition.

"So you want to know why we encouraged him to
marry Gloria and not you?"

She detected a slight tinge of sarcasm in the question. The man not only misread, he underestimated her.

"No, sir. Gloria's father is worth a fortune. Among
other things, he even owns the controlling interest in
this bank."

Ty had explained all that to her. His dad was fighting

for his life at the bank. He had enemies on the board. As chairman, Mr. London carried enough influence to protect Mr. Crockett and support his ambitions for moving up to the position of president.

"I'm glad we understand one another," Mr. Crockett said in a tone that indicated the conversation was over.

"Mister, we've got a situation here and I have something to say to you."

He went red with fury again. All the same, he pretended he was happy to listen to anything she had to say. She laid it out for him with great care. On the first Saturday night in April, a large group of senior class girls including Leona and Gloria had the traditional ladies' night party—which meant that they all spent the night at one girl's house. It was a custom observed by the local senior girls, who kept the boys away in order to indulge in their last of many slumber parties since junior high school. Gloria was suffering heavy cramps, as she had the curse.

She was going to leave with her parents the next day at noon. They were going to spend the two-week spring vacation at their family home in Palm Beach. Gloria worked her way down a bottle of gin and confessed that she had a secret lover waiting for her in Florida. The man was twenty-three years old, married, and worked at a tennis club where her father was a member. She said he had taken her virginity when she was fifteen and they always met on the golf course late at night. She finished off the gin and fell asleep crying because she said she loved him.

Mr. Crockett was turning pale and almost seemed to shrink before her eyes as Leona continued. He saw where she was headed. It was obvious he considered it a dangerous destination.

Now she explained what she had learned from Ty. After spring vacation Ty had run track, as Mr. Crockett knew. The track coach was a Spartan about maintaining his regimen, and that included no dates or spending time with girlfriends during the four-week season. However, Ty did see Gloria every day during school hours. There was one big scene between them during lunch hour, which everyone within half a mile overheard. Gloria was hysterical, shouting at him, hitting him in the chest, calling him names. Her period was over a week late. Ty was, in all innocence, trying to reassure her by reminding her that they hadn't even held hands in six weeks.

The loud breakup in early June was all for effect, according to Ty. Gloria had come home from Florida carrying her married paramour's child. She was trying to characterize Ty as a liar who was trying to shirk his responsibilities. Gloria had admitted the truth to half the girls in the senior class. One of them had been with her when she made the call to Florida to tell her grand passion he had to marry her right away. The man denied any acquaintance with her and ignored her hysteria. He stonewalled her threats to call his wife by suggesting in a polite tone that she consult her local clergyman.

Always the loyal son, Ty had dated Gloria in order to please his parents. However, as Mr. Crockett well knew, he wasn't about to hand his future over to a girl who was cold enough to use him to hide her promiscuity.

"I fear you've gotten your facts twisted there, Miss Clay."

"Sir, Ty loves me. Why have you forced him to abandon his own child in order to marry a woman he hates and play father to another man's child?"

Mr. Crockett didn't have an answer. There wasn't

one that wouldn't incriminate him. She and Ty knew his parents wouldn't take their marriage well. They'd accuse Leona of trapping him. They'd try to find a way around it. They'd bribe or threaten or do whatever they thought might work regardless of who it might hurt. Ty and Leona had been braced for all that. Something had happened. Something monstrous enough to persuade Ty to take on a life of unhappiness while abandoning her and a child they both wanted. Someone behind a door or under a woodpile or lurking in a hallway, someone was in more trouble than Leona was at the moment. Over and over she heard her father that day in church, "tormented by secrets . . ."

"Mr. Crockett, this has to do with your secrets, doesn't it?" She was bluffing of course, stalling, grabbing at straws. Then to her amazement Mr. Crockett's sudden pallor told her that he believed she knew all about it.

"I understand you," he said after a long silence. Then he stood up.

"Excuse me a minute, Miss Clay."

For the next twenty minutes she heard his officious feet scurrying up and down the marble floor of the corridor, slipping in and out of half a dozen offices where soft, obedient voices replied in the affirmative. High heels scampered, metal file drawers clicked open then whooshed shut and clicked open again. It was like listening to an eerie radio drama without words. Strange how unnecessary words became as indiscriminate voices high and low blended with scrapes and bumps and hard leather on stone, the tempo increasing, the pitch rising as throats tightened in fear.

It had an element of familiar dread, like waiting in church while the deacons removed the starched cloths from the communion cups and plates, knowing the symbolic cannibalism of drinking blood and devouring flesh was coming. It echoed coercion as each employee initialed his involuntary complicity, dreading the inevitable day when his own ink would document his felonious cowardice for a jury of his peers.

Strange, too, how the thief caught red-handed and accused (". . . you have some deep problems . . .") denies what is incontrovertible and then, like a windup toy dog lifting its hind leg at the turn of the key, he duplicates his crime in a mad attempt to escape prosecution for his original sin.

Leona had seen nothing to which she could testify in court. Yet her heart knew she had seen Mr. Crockett in action. His light frenzied steps sped up to the door. Now he paused. She could hear his heavy breath. Now with enforced reserve, a slow hand twisted the knob and his shadow fell on her like a pall. He took a business envelope from his inside coat pocket and withdrew a stack of new one-hundred-dollar bills. It was two thousand dollars.

"No!"

He was certain he had her. He smiled with omnipotent disdain as he slipped the money back into the envelope and pressed it hard into her palm. Then he removed a revolver from his desk drawer and cocked the trigger. He pointed it at her.

"If you ever come near me or my son again, I'll kill you."

Her mind reeled with the possibilities. If she lunged or laughed or made any sudden move, she knew he would kill her. There were strong odds he was going to kill her regardless of what she did. She couldn't understand why she wasn't afraid.

Maybe she was too tired and beaten to care. Maybe her prospects had dimmed to the point that living didn't look that much better than dying. A person's life wasn't the one you read about in the newspaper. Life wasn't all about the wars and disasters and revolutions that made the headlines. Life was a matter of the secrets that ruled people, themselves and others. Each life was a scraping and trudging caravan over a meaningless desert until you either died of loneliness or went berserk from it and got yourself killed for harming others.

It seemed to her that every few seconds a spinning tunnel swallowed the room. It was her first experience of death as an outside force, an entity that approaches. It had been summoned by the preparation of the bullet and chamber. Her perception of all this was instantaneous. She rose very slowly, keeping her eyes on the shining pewter gun barrel. She understood at once and completely the living power of acquiescence. A voice in her head taught her the plain truth of the matter. The gun was God. God was the gun. She hated communion, but she had always loved God. She dropped her head to show Him respect. Then she stood. When she had removed all trace of defiance from her eyes, she let them show Mr. Crockett that she regarded him as all-powerful. She turned and opened the door and walked into the corridor. She heard him drop the gun into his desk drawer.

The chief of police had been a lifelong friend of her father's. She told him everything. Then she handed him the two thousand dollars, which Mr. Crockett had stolen.

Later that afternoon the chief brought Mr. and Mrs.

London to see her. Things started very badly. Leona had assumed they would be as despicable as Mr. Crockett. After all, they had accepted his son as restitution for all the money he had stolen from their bank. Or had they? She had expected them to treat her with canny wariness. She was sure they would wear the same haughty air of superiority Mr. Crockett had shown her. Yet they seemed taken aback by her resentful manner. She kept making oblique remarks to get them to address the situation, but neither indicated any awareness of where she was leading them. In fact, after an uncomfortable twenty minutes, Mr. London finally admitted he had no idea why the chief had brought them to see her. The chief asked Leona to start from the beginning and tell the Londons everything she had told him.

It was a shock to realize how little they knew about Gloria. Like a lot of parents, the Londons turned out to be much nicer than their daughter. They were typical of rich people with only children. They were too afraid of losing their daughter's affection to teach her anything. It became painfully obvious that the Londons had believed their daughter's lies. They didn't seem to know that blind faith in a child's veracity teaches him to lie without guilt. Mrs. London turned gray when Leona told them about Gloria's married lover in Florida. She kept her calm, though. When Mrs. London grilled Leona in the obvious hope of spotting a crack in her story, it was from concern for Gloria, and much more sad than malevolent.

The Londons left Leona's house in a state of deep despair. Yet they had both demonstrated the largesse to hug Leona, and offer to help her in any way they could. Of course they could, but she didn't feel she should say it. They could unchain Ty from their daughter and send him back to her. Leona sat vigil in the heavy quiet of the house that was still redolent with illness and death, keeping watch, as it were, for some sign of hope that her actions would bring Ty home.

She had taken some encouragement from the Londons. Their character would lead them to insist on the right thing. Did they want their daughter to live all those lies with a husband who not only despised her, but wasn't even her baby's father?

The situation with Mr. Crockett was more clouded.

It had begun to appear as if he had been the driving force behind Ty's marriage to Gloria. If that was true, then Mr. London hadn't blackmailed him. When the chief came by one afternoon to tell her the Londons were making inquiries on several fronts, she asked his opinion and he said that Mr. London had confided that he and his wife had reservations about Ty. They suspected Mr. Crockett had pushed his boy into dating Gloria. In matters relating to the bank Mr. London had the utmost faith in Mr. Crockett to verify that Mr. London was conducting his own secret audit. He didn't expect to uncover any impropriety.

All the same, he did, though. In fact, everything turned out exactly as Leona had told herself that it would. Mr. London's private investigation had turned up with nothing. He couldn't find a missing penny or an unaccounted-for nickel. That was the tip-off. He knew there was at least two thousand dollars missing. He had Leona's envelope in his pocket. He brought in a team of auditors, to whom Mr. Crockett served high tea every afternoon. Mr. Crockett thanked them and Mr. London for what he called this opportunity to demonstrate competence

and honesty. The auditors uncovered his trail. It was
their conclusion that Mr. Crockett had stolen almost
fifty thousand dollars over a five-year period.

Before he informed the police, Mr. London called
Mr. Crockett into his office to tell him he'd been found
out. Then he told Mr. Crockett to go home and tell his
wife and call his attorney. He was going to allow him
the dignity of turning himself in to the police. Mr.
Crockett well knew there was no point in further denial. He also accepted the fact that any attempted flight
would lead to a certain and disgraceful death. Mr.
Crockett went back into his office to retrieve his car
keys. While he was in there, he shot himself in the forehead.

That evening around eight o'clock, Leona found Ty
at the door. Her joy was immeasurable. She threw her
arms around him, but he didn't react. He let her hang
off of him as if he were a fence post. Of course, she told
herself, he was heartbroken over his father. His grief
had swallowed any happiness he might have otherwise
felt at seeing her. He was numb with shock and sorrow.
Her joy was completely selfish and inappropriate.

"Forgive my insensitivity, Ty. I'm so sorry about your
father."

"As far as I'm concerned, you pulled the trigger."

She began to pray as she had never before prayed
that she didn't understand what his words meant. Yet
it seemed the inevitable outcome, as she remembered
him pointing his pistol at her in his office. Mr. Crockett
had wanted to shoot her then and there because he
understood that she would never suffer in silence. He
couldn't do that and get away with it. He wasn't quite
ready to kill himself, not yet. He was only a step closer
than he had ever been.

"Ty, I'm so sorry," she said. "I couldn't let him sacrifice you and me and our child."

"So you sacrificed my mother and my younger brother and sister instead."

"I didn't intend to."

"Tell me another one, slut. And then tell me who really knocked you up, you vengeful whore!"

His accusations and epithets hit her like a steady stream of molten rocks. His searing hatred was so intense that she drew back into the deepest corners of herself until his voice was distant and his unbearable words were unintelligible. Then he was hitting her with his fists and she experienced falling down, but like in a slow-motion dream. She felt the room grow dim. Then from the other side of the room she watched him hitting and raping her. Later she saw him crying and laying his head on her breasts, and his remorse didn't make sense. She remembered him picking her up.

Then it was early morning. The rising sun burned into her good eye. The other was swollen shut. She was trying to stand up. There was vomit on her dress. Her knees were bloody. She made it to her feet and looked in the mirror over the fireplace. She looked as if she had been badly burned. Coming closer, she saw bruises and dried blood wherever her flesh was uncovered. She passed the day in bed. The telephone rang fifty times. There was insistent knocking at the front door every hour or so. Did he think she didn't know that he was sorry? Did he think that made any difference? She was sorry too; sorry he hadn't killed her.

Or was he coming back to finish the job? She had her father's pistol on the bedside table. She almost hoped that he would come back. She envisioned telling the police when they took his body away that her only regret was that he had suffered such a short time. She would have enjoyed his terror.

After two days the bruises began to fade yellow and her swollen face regained its regular outlines. Without the constant pain to stimulate her, Leona's bitter resolve turned to despair.

She let him in on the morning of the third day. She hated him for looking so weak when he begged her forgiveness. She hated herself for loving him. That made it next to impossible to rebuke his reasons for abandoning her. It wasn't ambition for himself. It wasn't even ambition on his father's part. It was desperation. His father had been a drowning man. He knew his game was almost up. If Ty was married to Gloria, he might use the connection to negotiate some solution. Public scandal would disgrace their daughter as well as hurt her husband's future.

This was his abject apology?

He was trying to make it all work. Gloria needed a husband for the moment. She didn't want him for the rest of her life. They'd make it work for each other. Then he was going to square it with Leona. She could even live nearby so they could be together. Of course, she didn't believe him. He didn't even believe himself.

He'd left her to bury her mother alone, knowing she was carrying his child, knowing she had to be devastated by his cruelty. No. He hadn't married Gloria as a sacrifice for his father. He married that unlovable witch for her father's money. Now Leona had uncovered the truth and his guaranteed annual income was in jeopardy. Tyler Crockett didn't have any tears in him for his father or his unborn baby. The only grief or joy he experienced was for himself.

He had called her names and raped and beaten her

unconscious. No, she wouldn't waste umbrage on his empty proposal that she live like his backstreet tramp with his bastard. That was his pathetic attempt to convince her he felt trapped with Gloria. He had no plans to see Leona or his child. He didn't want them within a thousand miles of his love nest. He had it all now. He had a rich wife who didn't give a damn whom he slept with or how often. It was perfect. He and Gloria could live their debauched and separate lives in perfect harmony, coming together to perform their duet as a happy young couple from the right side of the tracks whenever it served them.

What was he doing here then? What did he want?

"Tyler, I want you to leave now."

"I need you."

"You need my silence."

"You, I want you."

"You want to control me." That was it. He'd beaten her badly. Had anyone seen it? Had she gone for help? Did the police know about it? Or worse, the Londons?

"I love you."

"Leave now!"

That was it. She had it figured out. Gloria was in love with danger. She'd play one crazy game after another with Tyler until she got bored with it all. Then the endgame would start. If Tyler had beaten Leona, then he'd treated Gloria the same way. Maybe that's why she went down to Florida and got herself in trouble. Maybe she had already experienced his brutality and she was trying to force him to let go.

"You beat her, don't you?"

"Never. What happened here was grief."

As if she'd pressed some button, he pulled her close to him on the living room sofa. He started nibbling at her neck the way he usually got amorous. He'd made a disaster of her life. His poor widowed mother was at home receiving condolence callers. He had a wife he didn't want who was knocked up by some other man. Leona still hurt from his beating, and he was pressing his hardness into her thigh and digging his fingers into her pants.

Yet she couldn't let him know that he was hurting her. He'd go crazy with the thrill. She kissed him. He was all over her.

"Oh, Ty, I need you so badly. . . ."

"Beg me."

"Baby," she whispered, letting her fingers play with him lightly, "hold up a second." She stood up. "Wait there," she said. "I've got a surprise for you." Then she kissed him and squeezed him, letting him nibble her breasts through her dress. "It's a big surprise," she promised as she backed away from him and left the room.

He had taken his pants off by the time she came back.

"Sit down on top of me," he commanded.

He was a hairless ape. She straddled him and he pushed himself all the way up inside of her. She watched him bucking and rolling his head from side to side with his eyes closed.

"You might better slow down or you'll finish before we get started," she whispered.

He ignored her, pumping harder now, moaning and sweating, his eyes glued shut.

"Baby, stop a second," she said with more force, but he wasn't listening. He was slamming and puffing and using her to make full-throttle love to himself.

"Stop!" she shouted.

"Can't, can't, can't," he panted.

But he suddenly discovered that he could. And he did—when the cold steel of her father's revolver touched his forehead.

"Get your clothes on. And get out," she said.

Later in the darkness it gave her a measure of comfort to think that this time at least she had sent him away.

8

❖

FRIDAY, SEPTEMBER 19, 1997
6:15 P.M.

Averill sat on the hard sofa in Mrs. Churchill's overly air-conditioned parlor waiting for her like a cold potato in a refrigerator drawer awaits the inevitable hand and paring knife. It was reputed to be over a hundred degrees outside. Yet here, separated from that sweltering realm by lace-covered Italian windows, it felt like it could snow any minute. If this was the difference between rich and poor, then Averill didn't see much point in endeavor.

"I'll be right down, honey."

Mrs. Churchill's voice drifted down the magnificent curving staircase like clouds from a better world. She and Mr. Churchill had seen an old pump organ on sale in an antiques store down at Oxford. She wanted Averill

to look at it. If it met with Averill's approval, she wanted
to buy and donate it to his church.

Like he wouldn't approve? Like she valued his ignorant ideas over her educated ones? "His" church was
"hers." He was her puppy dog, her hobby this month,
and that was all right with him. The Churchills were
regular patron saints of Averill's fledgling church. In
fact, since they owned it, they were totally responsible
for its existence. It had been built by Henri Churchill's
ancestors on their enormous cotton plantation in the
1840s. Succeeding generations of Churchills had married and buried and baptized one another beneath its
lavender-and-ivory stained glass windows.

It was a beautiful little church that revealed an unexpected richness of architectural detail—"mini-
magnificence," Mrs. Churchill described it in her
self-deprecating banter. It had historic significance as
well. In the early days of the Civil War, the Confederate
army had used it as a secret arsenal. Two years later
General Ulysses S. Grant, who evicted the Churchills
from their home in order to ensconce his wife Julia
there, stabled his horses in the little sanctuary. There
was a small, elevated gallery at the back with a double
row of pews. A line of iron loops set into the floor in
front of them had once secured the ankle chains of
Churchill slaves.

The family hadn't used it since the early fifties. Or
so the current Churchills had told him on his first interview under the swirling plaster filigree of their cav-
ernous parlor ceiling. That was four months ago. He
had come in response to their advertisement on the
bulletin board outside of the dean's office. Averill had
just finished a general course of studies at Gulf Coast

Theological School. GCTS was really just a run-down
two-year college that offered a few extra Bible courses.
Graduates who wanted to become ministers of more established Protestant denominations moved on to four-
year colleges, followed by graduate seminary studies.

Averill had neither means nor inclination to endure
that. He had already outperformed any known member
of his family by finishing high school. His two years
at GCTS were all the icing he intended to spread on
that cake. The mainstream Protestant churches held
no temptation for him. They were quirky and out of
touch with people. The Methodists were too damned
sanctimonious. You could feel it in their handshake,
their self-righteous squeeze. The Presbyterians were as
dry as fire, as if they could bore people onto the right
path. The Baptists had it all, no question. Their sheer
numbers and holdings were impressive. A facile young
Baptist preacher could make quite a life for himself.
But you needed backing to enter those arenas.

Averill's backing consisted of the sweat of his brow.
As for the Catholics, well, their idol the Pope was driving all of them to hell in Italian sports cars. Which
really only left the Episcopalians. As far as Averill was
concerned, the Episcopal Church was the Pope's bastard child, a place for divorced, egg-headed and/or sexu-
ally deviant Catholics.

A true man of God had no need for all their fancy
theologies. All he required was a well-worn King James
Bible and a handful of faith. The Apostle Peter had said
it all when he declared, "Upon this rock I shall build
my church." Averill had determined to find his rock and
start building when the Lord led him to Mr. and Mrs.
Henri Churchill. The multimillionaires were restoring
the old plantation that had been in Henri's family

"since the birth of Christ," Churchill explained with a dry sneer.

"We're restoring the entire plantation," his wife confided while Henri was out of the room on the telephone. Henri's enterprises had taken them all over the world. Now it was time to reattach to old family ground, to put all the old things right, to polish up traditions and values the rest of the world had forgotten, and pass them on down to their children.

"What children?" Henri asked from the doorway with a smirk. The Churchills were childless, as it turned out. Of course, they had only been married four years. She didn't look to be much before or after thirty. Churchill was gray and there was a settled look about his face and shoulders. Averill put him around fifty. This was at least a second go-round for him.

In any case, Henri Churchill wore a very sour expression for a guy with so much to smile about. Averill included Mrs. Churchill high on that list. She was a striking red-haired beauty with a warm smile and a natural ability to put people at their ease. Churchill seemed to regard his wife's charm as personal property. He sat there like a stone while she explained all the details. The position came with funds to restore the dilapidating church and parsonage into habitable condition. Beyond that, there would be an annual stipend of sixteen thousand dollars. Of course, Henri knew a man couldn't do much more than subsist on that. Averill was welcome to devise any additional means of income he required.

"So this is a part-time pastorate?"

"If need be . . ." she answered.

Averill read the deeper meaning of that between the lines. Churchill wanted Averill to attract and build up a congregation large enough to support himself and his operation from the collection plate.

"Since you're Presbyterian, Mr. Churchill, will I follow the Presbyterian doctrines?"

"You can practice Dionysian rites as far as I'm concerned," Henri sneered out of the blue. Then he shook his head, chuckled with private relish and excused himself. Mrs. Churchill turned pale and took several moments to suppress whatever she was feeling.

"He carries too much on those poor shoulders of his, Reverend Sayres."

That didn't faze Averill one way or the other. The enormous opportunity overruled that. If he couldn't make what he wanted of all this, then he was an idiot and a fool. He had answered their ad fully expecting some fatal catch to turn him away from their offer. Instead, Henri Churchill had made it even more tantalizing by virtually assuring him he wouldn't be breathing down his neck.

Could a man ask God to make His Will more clear?

He took a room in town and got to work cleaning up the old church. Henri was always away on business, but Mrs. Churchill—"Soames," as she insisted he call her—was there almost every day. At first he thought she was keeping tabs on his progress, but he soon realized that she had a great deal of expertise about restoring the old place. After all, she had just restored a twenty-four-room mansion designed and built by the same New Orleans architect. She seemed as excited by the prospect of turning it back into a real church as Averill was.

In fact, when Soames realized that Henri had given

Averill a woefully inadequate budget, she provided additional funds to get the job done. She also proved herself an able, willing worker, climbing a ladder to help paint the ceiling, operating an enormous power sander to help strip a century of finish off the cypress floors.

They had chosen the first Sunday in August to rededicate the sanctuary. Knowing Averill wanted a good crowd there when he preached his first sermon, Soames had made the day a special event. She had mailed out hundreds of engraved invitations announcing that she had arranged that the restored church building would be placed on the National Historic Register during the service. Those in attendance were invited to remain afterward for a barbecue luncheon inside an enormous pink-and-white tent that a Memphis firm had set up on the church lawn.

The county's main newspaper, *The Orpheus Gazette*, ran a full page of pictures and stories about the history of the church and the great event itself. Averill had preached his heart out that morning. It was a well-heeled crowd for the most part, coolheaded, educated types who looked at his raw, old-time religion as nostalgic entertainment. Still, he had taken a handful of twenty regulars from that first Sunday, and a month later he was proud to say that it had grown to forty.

Averill was deeply indebted to the Churchills, especially Soames. He was just crazy about her. She was gorgeous and vibrant and she believed in him and what he was doing. Of course, Averill wasn't blind. Henri's absences left her bored and lonely most of the time. Henri was always calling her at the last minute to say he'd be gone another two days. Averill didn't see how a man could be married to such a wonderful creature and stay away from her so long. Of course, Soames never

complained about it. She had never said a word—
except when Henri failed to keep his promise to give a
small speech at the dedication service.

His name was in the program when he had reneged
the Saturday night before. Soames, whose nerves were
already stretched thin from trying to get things ready
for Sunday morning, was bitterly disappointed about
that. Averill had sat with her in the tent after everyone
else had gone, and listened while she unloaded a little.
Though her disappointment never descended into criti-
cisms or complaints and she had been all smiles for the
crowd on Sunday.

"Henri's stuck in Atlanta all weekend . . . as usual. . . ."
Her voice trailed off. It was one of her rituals, holding
him hostage in the parlor while she called down the
stairs every few minutes. Averill didn't want to bite
the hand that had fed him so well, but it seemed like
she was everywhere he turned night and day. The poor
lonely lady needed some companionship. More and
more she tied him up on one pretext or another. This
trip to Oxford to look at a pump organ was a perfect example. He knew nothing about pump organs and he
didn't care whether or not she bought the stupid thing
for the church. No one would ever play it—not while he
was in the pulpit.

In fact, the whole idea for the excursion had come
up at the last minute. He knew in his heart Henri
Churchill wouldn't materialize. He didn't want to spend
the next several hours in a car with Soames. She was
bound to insist they stop someplace to eat. She always
did. He liked her. He thought the world of her, in fact.
He owed her more than he could say, but just didn't

want to play house with her while Henri Churchill was away. That's where this was all heading—if he didn't slam on the brakes in a hurry.

All by itself, the idea of helping her cure her loneliness had undeniable appeal. Soames was the most voluptuous and glamorous woman he had ever known this well. His duties and obligations as a clergyman aside, it was tempting in a lot of ways. The problem was discretion. Soames didn't know what the word meant. Nor did she seem to understand the idea of moderation. They would start a waltz that would never end. Or get him shot between the eyes.

Averill knew himself a little. He knew that women could be almost like madness with him. He had longed for many with a desire so intense it scorched him. He had gone too far with the wrong girl too often and skated out of all kinds of scrapes. He had promised God the night he accepted the ministry here that he would turn away from his obsession with the ladies and serve His Will.

Averill crossed to the tea table and lifted a cold bottle of French chardonnay out of a silver ice bucket and filled a glass. This was a pleasant little vice he'd picked up from Soames. He was getting hooked on those English cigarettes of hers as well. It was all part of what Soames called "urbanity," a quality she said any ambitious young clergyman would do well to cultivate.

"Or don't you want to be Bishop of Barchester," she'd say in a tone so imperious and pouty he could never summon the nerve to ask her what she was talking about.

"Henri asks me to convey his apologies."

She was dressed in white. The top of the garment barely managed to conceal her breasts. It almost looked to him like she had wrapped herself in an enormous towel. The wine always made him a little drunk right away. Averill's conscience worked overtime and the wine relaxed it. He refilled his glass and then sat back sipping as he enjoyed the scenery.

"I'm beginning to wonder if there isn't another woman." She laughed.

Judging by Henri's actions, it was more a question of how many. Of course, that was between a man and his wife. Averill had his strict view of the general topic, but he was also a man. He would be loath to violate his obligation to his gender by discussing any man's infidelities with his wife.

"Forgive the pathetic hors d'oeuvres," she begged, pouring herself a glass of wine. She smelled like a field of lilies.

Soames sat on the edge of a small sofa trying to collect her thoughts. Henri had just walked her through his usual bullcrap litany of reasons why he wouldn't be home this weekend. The miserable weasel wasn't even in Atlanta. He was in Miami, waiting for Honey Bun's plane to land. Of course, Soames had a detective on him. She knew the weekly drill. Babycakes came in from Atlanta, first class no less, at 6:35 on Delta. At 8:00 they boarded a chartered seaplane for the ninety-minute flight to his private island of joy near St. Lucia.

Three generations of Churchill good ol' boys had splashed down in that adulterous surf with a chorus line of Honey Buns. Soames had never known Henri's father or grandfather. Henri had told her about it himself when he first took her down there twelve years ago. He was of course married at the time. Soames was twenty-three and working as a secretary in Atlanta. Every extra dime over the rent went to Jeanine, an old

French whore who quoted Voltaire and sold her match-making services to a certain caliber of ambitious young Southern women. Beauty and brains were essential. You had to be well educated or pass for it. You also had to be self-possessed and eternally graceful. That meant some harridan magnolia had molded you from childhood for the role of an American geisha. Though no one ever said "geisha"—they said "Southern lady" instead.

You also had to know what you wanted. Henri met every one of Soames's specifications. Henri was a Southern prince. Naturally, his wife was a lady. According to the ancient code, that meant he shared her bed enough to make a few babies while he bought his serious fun on the side. Henri was one of the breed when it came to that. What set him apart was a certain rigidity, a temper that flared when he sensed a woman had the upper hand. Then, in bed, there was an unmistakable air of cold necessity that told her Henri never had a good time in bed with a woman. Not that he was homosexual. His desire was real. It was his execution, somehow more determined than passionate, that told her she had found The Man she understood.

He was a mama's boy. A matriarch who inflated his ego with constant references to his innate superiority had ruled him. He was a demigod, a paragon, and women should prostrate themselves before him and glory in the fulfillment of his every whim. The South was loaded with those iron battleaxes who stroked their sons' egos while they squeezed them down below if they made a move to break away. At that point his elevated nature turned base and idiotic. He was cruel, conspiratorial, unconscionable and disgraceful.

Soames knew that a man like Henri expected perpetual adulation from all women, and certainly from a paid escort. She knew that his world was filled with self-effacing females who tried to attract him by demonstrating their natural civility and delicate, deferential style. Would the genuine heir to a textile empire grown out of his ancestor's cotton interests settle for any less?

Her considered opinion was yes, he would. A soft-spoken angel might win his praises in public, but her acquiescence in private would bore him witless. She was right. She mocked his mannered lovemaking and insulted everything about him—when they were alone together. In public her emasculation took the subtle form of ordering for him in restaurants, sending his wine bottle back to chill ten more minutes, taking up his cause with waiters and bellmen and concierges and drivers.

She practiced her manipulations by trial and error until she had almost complete control over him. Of course, his friends complained. Certain business associates stepped back when Soames began to offer opinions. Most of the people Henri Churchill knew were too deeply involved, too financially dependent on his approval to do anything but listen and nod and figure a way around her later.

Not that she ever had any real power. He was using her like a shield. Meanwhile, his wife held down the family fort in Memphis, playing the indomitable angel who suffers her husband's outrage in relentlessly cheerful, obsequious public oblivion to his disgrace. When Henri finally began making insincere overtures to Soames about "some day," she promptly changed the subject every time. Of course, her dismissal was more than he could resist and he brought it up time and again. Like a great actress carefully calibrating the most important role of her career, Soames very gradually changed her tone from dismissive to baffled. It took her months to extract his first indignant demand to know why she discarded any attempt to seriously discuss marriage.

There were a hundred wrong answers, a thousand glib responses that would have tipped him off. Soames had become an expert on manipulating Henri by then. She knew the one that he would find irresistible.

"Because Henri, darling, I adore you, but we both know you don't have the balls to divorce her and then ruin yourself by marrying me."

Though he did both. He divorced his first wife, charging her with frigidity and accusing her of having attempted to remedy her condition by virtue of the favors of several young men, two of whom he paid handsomely to support the lie on the witness stand. Rich men had done worse things to rid themselves of unwanted wives in Memphis divorce courts. He aroused some disapproval in and near the country club. But he was too rich, too facile, and too Delta to be ruined by any such epithet.

Until the broken woman took a pistol and shot herself in front of his young sons.

Soames had counted on Henri to become bored with her in time. She had assumed she had several years to wrangle and maneuver a large enough slice of his pie to live in luxury for the rest of her life. But the suicide turned his world against him. (It also made Soames front-page news and a household word in certain Greek Revival bastions of New South Republicanism for decades to come.) The party was over. Her cleverly constructed house of illusions began to crumble in the heat of this all too lurid spotlight.

They'd used up all their honeymoon fun and games during their courtship. It hadn't taken him long to realize he'd been manipulated, hoodwinked, maybe hypnotized a little. Soames had expected that. She had figured rightly, though. He had behaved very badly toward his first wife and his children. He'd gone soft in the head over a trollop. He wouldn't turn around and beg that world he had defied to forgive him. He wasn't about to admit his mistake. Then he had his first wife's blood on his hands. In his mind, Soames graduated from unrespectable to evil.

Now he saw everything. He would have to take this slowly. He couldn't divorce her now. She'd have the whole savage drama on cable with daily installments nightly from Little Rock to Atlanta. Worse, she'd beat him. She'd walk away with millions as a reward for her scheme. He had to move slowly. So he settled her into the farm in Mississippi where she had less to spend and less on which to spend it. He let her sit there, knowing she was bored to death and frustrated while he auditioned willing candidates for her replacement in the foaming Caribbean.

What could she do? He could buy as many lawyers and witnesses as it would take to expose her scam. Meanwhile he'd pay lip service to her, admit and betray nothing. She was bound to go crazy from loneliness. She'd crack. His lawyers would find a way to get rid of her cheaply. It was a waiting game. Meanwhile he was having his fun. What did he care how long it would take? Time was always a better friend to the rich.

Averill Sayres had no idea of the situation as he sat in the parlor drinking too much wine and imagining his head on Soames's breasts. It wouldn't be accurate to say that by that time he hadn't picked up on the fact that there was trouble between them. The cold fact was that Averill didn't particularly care, as long as it stayed between them. Maybe he understood on some level that Soames's seductive manner was connected to it. He was pretty sure he'd be sorry if he followed her swaying torso up the stairs.

"I'd best be going."

"Why?"

How he would have loved to tell her the truth. He had a place to go that night and someone waiting he very much wanted to see. Unfortunately, for the foreseeable future that had to be no one's business.

"Things to do."

"On a Friday night?"

She smelled like orchids. She wasn't wearing a bra. She was practically sitting on top of him by now. He had to get up then and there. He had to go. There was no time to worry how insulted she'd get or how he'd explain it later. Women woke madness in him, a foolhardy ache that measured considerably higher on the scale than ordinary desire. It troubled him. It kept him in a near constant state of excitation. That in itself was a terrible distraction. How often had he begged God to cast that demon out of him?

"You're a very sensual man, Reverend."

Now her hand brushed his lap and found the zipper. When she softly wrapped her fingers around him, it was finished. Heaven lost a zealous guardian and somewhere down in hell he thought he heard a tango as he followed her up the stairs.

She told him everything as they ate breakfast in the kitchen the next morning. Henri had a lover. Soames would soon have nothing. Though Averill was quick to discern that "nothing" didn't mean nothing, it meant Henri. Then she cried with shame at her seduction. She had dragged him down to her sewer. It wasn't his fault. He mustn't blame himself. She was without shame or character, she said. Her desire had been building over weeks of neglect and loneliness. He was a very sexy man. Never had she been so completely satisfied.

In the end, of course, he was no match for her. This time he took her in the shower, the same shower where an hour earlier he had knelt under the cleansing stream of warm water and repented of his sin. Now in his state of arousal and depravity he understood that it wouldn't be much of a thrill unless it felt like sin.

"You're getting me addicted to you."

Averill woke like a drunken man, which he might have been a little earlier, a still-drunk man who finds himself naked and compromised and afraid of the consequences of the desultory flesh sleeping beside him. Friday night had become Saturday and now it was Sunday. In one panicked action he was dressed and down the stairs. The front hall clock read 5:15 A.M. The sky was silver. It was muggy. He followed Henri Churchill's wax-green cotton crop down the curve of a bowl of land into the pink-and-orange sun. When he came to the creek bed he dropped to his knees and, trembling from head to toe, he wept with shame and remorse.

"God, Lord God, forgive my debauched and wicked acts."

He had been sullied and defiled as a boy, rendered filthy and depraved by strange men. From the last time he was used until this day, he had kept his solemn vow never to pollute another human being with intimate contact. He was low and worthless and condemned. This vow of abstinence was his private, holy covenant with God, his means of remaining acceptable to heaven.

Now, in the space of a few hours, he had allowed himself to lie down with the whore of Babylon. He took out the small portable Bible he always carried inside his jacket and he opened it to a familiar quotation from the Book of Proverbs, one on which he had based his first sermon at Whitsunday Pentecost Church:

> *". . . A harlot may be hired for a loaf of bread,*
> *but an adulteress stalks a man's very life . . ."*

Soames's perfume mingled with the salty odors of lovemaking all over his body. He removed his clothes and waded into the clear, cold stream, letting the waters wash him, praying and baptizing himself new again, repeating God's promise of redemption for repentance. He floated near the middle of the stream for a long time, giving his curved limbs to the healing water of life and offering himself in service to heaven, rededicating his life to salvation.

The sun was warm on his back, the velvet moss was dry and soft beneath him where he slept on the rocky bank of the creek. When he woke, it was hot and the sky was white. He stretched and then he carefully dressed himself. He was renewed. The answers had come. He was restored. Soames was a fallen woman, a priestess in the temple of evil, a witch sent from Satan to tempt and beguile God's innocent servants into their eternal damnation by way of her lavender and silk seduction.

He dropped to his knees, closed his eyes and offered heaven gratitude for his deliverance. When he opened them a shadow had fallen over him, blocking the cruel sun. He breathed an alluring scent of feminine tenderness and beauty.

"Why'd you run away, lover?" Soames whispered, and the hair on the back of his neck bristled with sudden need. Then she kissed his neck. When he turned to her, she had already set a large woven basket on the ground. She shook a large quilt open and he helped her spread it.

"I saw you skinny-dipping," she said with a giggle.

"We better hurry," he said, "I'm preaching in one hour."

Then for the second time that morning, Averill began removing his clothes. Forgiveness and redemption would have to wait until he had thoroughly scratched this wonderful itch.

"It's a drug with people like us, Averill."

"It's done now."

"Until the next craving."

Later in his guilt and mortification, he was in such a hurry to leave the place and its fateful implications that he flooded the truck engine. It wasn't just what he had done. People committed these spiritual misdemeanors every day. Sin was always forgiven. No, he wasn't proud of himself. He knew she'd come back around again some afternoon when his resistance was low and there they'd drop like a pair of weasels on crack.

Sometimes he wondered why God made him if all he could do was fall down in evil. Had he come upon this earth with the curse on him? Had he been sprinkled and immersed and baptized in depravity so powerful no force of heaven could overcome it?

He turned the key again and throbbing bedlam erupted under the hood.

Though someone else, someone not much more than a mile above him through the trees, a ragged woman of no discernible consequence, had been moving in a roundabout way in his direction for several hours that morning.

Darthula always rose with the sun and went to pray at Honey Sweet's grave. Mama, whom this world had known as "Honey Sweet," had walked this hill more than one hundred years when she was taken in nineteen hundred and eighty-eight. Nine solitary years had passed since Darthula had gently lifted her from the iron bed, wrapped her in the shroud they had embroidered by the fire and laid her away in the abandoned cemetery, the dry remnants, the useless shell out of which Honey Sweet had risen on magnificent white wings and flown away in the moonlight.

There was no one else left. Nothing much to say, neither. Just Darthula shoveling clay into the hole until she strained her back. After that she sat on the mound till half past dark trying to pull a tune from Honey Sweet's mandolin. Nine, almost ten years ago.

Darthula had lived alone there in the woods on Whitsunday Hill ever since. The mound was long gone. Twice it sunk and she refilled it. Twice. The second time she used a good bit of gravel. The second time did the trick. Now Johnson grass hid the unmarked grave down on the low end of the run-down cemetery. Honey Sweet had demanded it just that way.

". . . *where the devil can't find it; you hear me, child?*"

"*Yessum.*"

The ritual behind her, she had left the cemetery this

morning, passed the church and the abandoned ram-
shackle house beyond it. She followed the all-but-over-
grown tire tracks down Whitsunday Hill, leaving its
ghosts behind her. She came to the path at the hardest
crook where a sudden bank rose on the right and September Woods looked down. From here she could see
a fair stretch—more specifically, the driver of an approaching vehicle could see her.

Her mind couldn't make a person so low that he
wouldn't stop and offer her a ride to town.

Her mama, Honey Sweet, had been a sanctified
woman, blessed with second sight. She had raised
Darthula in the knowledge that she would one day in-
herit Honey's gifts. It would be Darthula's mission to
advance Honey's duties in this miserable world. But
time had taken most of that. Darthula hadn't displayed
any of Honey's fabulous abilities. She received no pre-
monitions, angels or visions. She heard no voices from
beyond except Honey Sweet's, and that was to be expected. Worst of all, she had never encountered Satan
in the woods, as Honey Sweet had promised she would.

*"Girl, you keep out the churchyard this morning; I
done laid a spell."*

"Why?"

"Why!?!"

Honey Sweet looked like an old lizard squinting over
Darthula's head toward the sun. Then she slapped the
child so hard across the mouth that Darthula fell back
on the ground.

"Seen him in the woods this morning."

"Ol' Scratch?"

"Beelzebub, yes."

"How he look?"

"Fine."

Darthula didn't get that. But she didn't ask any more questions. Honey's slap still stung her cheeks. There'd be two or three more behind it if Darthula provoked her. Sweet generally took a sick headache after she'd laid a spell. Sometimes the pain ran down into her tooth. Ol' Sweet would beat her own mama blind when she got that way.

"*What you think he say to me?*"

"*Devil?*"

"*No, Ugly Bitch, Eranaham Lincoln!*"

The best part of Honey Sweet's conversation ran between mocking and trifling.

"*He ax me did you like chocolate candy.*"

"*Do I?*"

"*Do a baby pig like shit?*"

"*Then what did the devil say?*"

" '*Hag, lemme kiss you and turn you young as Little Ugly.*' "

Sweet played it out for Darthula.

"*Back away from me, Satan!*"

" '*I can make you pretty as Eve when I laid down with her.*' "

"*Step down, Evil!*"

" '*All right, Hag. You see me leaving.*' "

"*I do.*"

" '*I'll get Little Ugly when you're gone.*' "

"*I know it well.*"

Now Sweet aimed her story at Darthula like a pistol.

"*He gonna get me?*" Darthula cried.

"*With a bar of chocolate.*"

"*I'll refuse it.*"

"*You'd swallow a sack of Milky Ways.*" Sweet was already battering her face like a drum.

"*I'm sorry.*"

"*Then he unzip and stick you, cut into you like a damned sawmill!*"

"*No, Mother!*"

"*And you all hunchin' and beggin' the devil for more evil seed!*"

"*No!*"

"*A thousand hellions, an army of hell will drop out of you on the ground.*"

"*Don't slap me no more, Mother.*"

"*And then he'll drop you to boil forever in the lake of fire.*"

"*Stop it!*"

"*You will be the mother of all evil!*"

Darthula took to holding her breath when Sweet got this bad. In a minute she blacked out into peace. After Honey Sweet had dosed her tooth with corn liquor, she lifted Darthula into her arms and called her "Precious."

"*Unless . . .*"

"*I know, Mother.*"

"*Unless you keep watch night and day.*"

"*I will, darling Mother.*"

"*He'll hide. He'll wait you out. He'll disguise himself.*"

"*I'll keep vigil.*"

Years came and went. Darthula kept watch, but she never saw a sign of his presence. It must have been Honey Sweet he'd wanted. Honey Sweet was resting safe this fine September morning—as she had for nine years now—sleeping dreamless in the arms of Abraham.

Just the same, Darthula got around. Sometimes she listened from the darkness under the open window behind the crossroads store. Sometimes she hid in the crook of a tree above a house down on the blacktop and watched somebody's television. Certain cellar doors and kitchen windows became well acquainted with Darthula.

She came to know more than must be told observing people and things, but she never saw the devil.

Though Honey's voice came back to her on hot nights.

"Lisssten at me. . . ."

Her heavy whispers crossed the black dampness of the house and woke Darthula. She didn't even open her eyes, much less pretend to sit forward. She knew it all by heart.

"I know about the devil."

It was hot. Darthula wanted sleep.

"Shade of night, be gone!"

"Devil can't cross water, Darthula."

"You done tole me that."

"Devil on your roof right now!"

"Hush! You dead!"

"Nobody never dead. Scratch come cravin' you."

Darthula threw off her sheet and shouted at the dark, "I'm gittin' tired of that!"

"He know how to look good to you. Know what to say!"

"I ain't been with no mens and I ain't goin' with none; so you lay your nasty head back down on that pillow and die in peace!"

Darthula had garnered enough stares here and there to know that Honey Sweet had made her a freak. She had no way to deal with people except to keep her head low and avoid them as much as she could.

"Nobody want me, Old Bag, not from this world or the next."

"You think the devil gonna tell you his name?"

Honey Sweet was dead. Darthula was wrestling her in the lonely dark.

"Go away!"

"What his name, child?"

"Satan."

"What?"

"Beelzebub."

"What's his name?"

"Scratch."

"How Scratch get over on you, child?"

"He say, 'Girl, you look fine.' "

"And what?"

"Bring me a big Hershey and he touch me soft."

"And then?"

"Climb up on me in the bed."

"That all?"

"Ol' Bitch, you long dead, now why don't you get away!"

Time had slowly faded the voice in the dark. With the years Darthula took a measure of worldliness. Darthula had run up on the world as it were, cleaning houses and churches in town. She had not inherited Honey Sweet's calling. She was as mortal as a dog. She was no angel. No, Darthula didn't believe it all straight out the barn door no more.

Yet she could not shake her exasperating belief that Satan was destined to cross her mortal path. Darthula knew that was true. She knew it because Honey Sweet spared her no mercy when she beat her for stealing quarters. She knew it because Honey Sweet threw her half-naked and barefoot into the ice storm when she peed the bed. Darthula knew it with that perfected faith that has been cut and burned and beaten into a child's soft bones and baked by time.

That was done and gone and behind Darthula this fine September morning. She had her cleaning money and she was intent on yeast and a banana and one or two other things from town. She waited, and directly the sun was melting her and she was torn between a half-mile walk home, or two and a half more miles into town. Then she heard the truck engine in the distance.

Averill clutched the steering wheel but he hardly saw the road or noticed the sudden incline. He was seized by a boding terror of his weakness and Soames's apparent power over him. Hadn't he prayed that it wouldn't happen this time? If he prayed and it happened, then heaven had failed him to some extent. God had said no. That made Averill think of the old country song that said God's greatest blessings came when He said no to a prayer. Still, he just didn't want this to happen again. The thrill came and went, but there could be longer-lasting effects. Suppose the Churchills divorced and old Henri got wise? He'd haul Averill into court, make him a public disgrace and take his church away from him.

"Lord, I'm counting on you," he prayed.

Then he drifted into a reverie as he remembered her scent and her red hair tickling his chest and how she bore down on him and goaded him into a bucking frenzy as she nibbled his ears and whispered hot, sweet, dirty come-ons. And here he caught himself. Here he realized he was sliding his backside around on the worn leather seat, enjoying the rising sensations there and, worse, he was precariously close to letting the truck sink into the soft silt shoulder.

"Lord, my God, cast this demon out!" he shouted.

At the same time, Darthula saw a curl of dust a good ways up the road, and it was moving this way. Now she could make out a truck, an old truck, but none she could call to mind. She knew all the hill people, Spakes,

McFayes, McAlexanders and on. Try as she would, Darthula couldn't match a single one of them up with that truck. Now it got into the straight slope that ran into the crook, and that's what the fool was fixing to do if he didn't slow down.

Then she saw the man and felt herself turn to stone. Oh, terrible that beauty and thrilling the dread that shot through her. And she prayed.

"Lord, undo his evil!"

Averill saw her too, or thought he saw a strange figure standing on top of a high ridge of eroded red clay from which tree roots hung in a bearded fuzz beside the truck. Whether it was man or woman, he couldn't say. It seemed to be a person covered head to toe in layers of ragged clothes of every description with a white veil on its head. The figure startled and distracted him from the road, which took a sharp downward curve just ahead. By the time Averill looked back to his path, he realized he was going much too fast to avoid crashing into the clay bank on the outside of the curve.

He slammed on his brakes and the truck spun three times in the road, raising so much sand and dust that it obliterated his vision in a pale orange fog that choked him as he slid to a stop, though gently, against the crumbling clay. Through the dissolving fog he heard a voice from the ridge fifteen feet above him. Whether it was man or woman, song or chant, curse or prayer, Averill had no idea. The best he could make of it was some kind of muttering growl.

"Memphi . . . Memphi . . . Memphi . . ."

Now the dust had settled enough that he could see the ragged figure standing just above, stomping its brown bare feet and rocking as it chanted. A red one had replaced the white veil.

"Memphistopheles, be gone!"

Now a gloved hand raised and pointed something down at him. He took it to be a gun. He floored the engine, jerking the wheel left and, careening almost on its side, the truck rumbled and sputtered onto the road and roared downward into the woods.

The ragged figure kept the instrument pointed in the direction of the truck until the woods had swallowed it sight and sound.

"Satan, go back to hell," she said by way of completing her first crude exorcism. Now she waited for the last dust of her boiling spell to settle back onto the road.

Satisfied at last that the devil had been momentarily driven out, she let the hand holding the weapon of glory drop to one side and laid it on the ground. Then she removed the red veil that she wore to signal all living things and heaven above that Satan was afoot in these woods. Well pleased that the environs were safe once more, Darthula covered her head in the white veil of sanctity she had worn earlier. She lifted the weapon, which was no more or less potent than a worn copper-and-silver-plate crucifix, and tucked it into one of a dozen pockets. Then, holding her head erect so the breathing world could read its propitious message, she descended into the dry amber shadows of September Woods.

9

❦

For a moment, as Leona drifted out of her crowded reverie and let her tired mind readjust to the present situation, everything in her immediate vision was yellow-throated irises and new green shadows and sunshine. It seemed a fragmented vestige of long-lost Eden, but it was only the back corner of the unkempt yard, seen at a momentary angle of the sun in the temporary glory of later April. In a matter of weeks these tender, opaque vines that laced the grass would erupt and swell and smother the ground. They would circle and climb the trunks of these hardwood trees, choking the leaves, spreading across the upper limbs, sucking the strength out of the forest and blocking out the sky.

Summer, fall, winter or spring—in the end it was all just one long season of the witch.

Inside the house the yelling had died away. The quiet unnerved her, but for a moment she lost track of why. Then she remembered the deadly feast on the kitchen counter.

From the kitchen she could see the three of them sitting at the dining room table waiting in a kind of stupor or trance. It was that wary silence of people forced by unwieldy circumstances into a truce neither side wanted. They were hungry.

"Looks good," Winky observed after Leona had served each of them a full plate and returned with one of her own. Audena picked up her fork.

"Let us bow our heads!" Averill snarled at her. She let the hand holding the fork drop into her lap. Then she bowed her head. Leona gave Winky one hand and laid the other one on Audena's shoulder.

"He is risen!" Averill began.

"I could still save his life," Leona said to herself.

He prayed for a long time. He never did that when it was just the two of them. This was showing off—and not his religion, but her own deceased mother's sterling flatware and Irish linens and Wedgwood plates.

It wasn't two more minutes before their argument resumed. From the large amount of food Averill had consumed, Leona was convinced that her mission had been accomplished. She had to get rid of Audena and Winky.

"A fine Christian family, you all are!" Leona exploded with genuine contempt.

Averill looked thrilled. He wanted the pair of them out of his face. Audena and Winky exchanged mortified stares. Then Audena glared at Leona as if she were about to bite off her head at the neck. Seeing their departure in sight, Winky lifted his plate and started shoveling.

"I won't have it," Leona hissed.

"He's a thief!" Audena spat.

"Don't insult my husband at his own table on Easter Sunday!"

"You're living almighty damn high on what he stole from me!"

"Get out before I have the law throw you out!"

"You took the Sayres name down lower than mud."

"That's not possible!"

Winky burst out laughing and spit a mouthful of mashed potatoes over Averill's head and onto the flowered wall behind him. It had no discernible effect on Audena; he probably did it all the time at home.

"Oh, yes, it's possible," Audena hollered, standing up to leave, "considering how you ruined a good family in Fredonia and drove a poor man to suicide with your accusations. Then you turned around and tricked this fool into giving our name to your bastard."

Now Averill was laughing as hard as Winky. That cured Leona of any misgiving she had about poisoning him. Because even Averill knew that Leona had swum rivers of pure burning sulfur in an effort to find her way out of hell after she lost the baby. And Audena well knew that Leona had crossed hell on bare hands and knees accepting what she had believed at the time was a stillbirth. Leona took no pride in winning a verbal scrimmage with a swayback mule. Nor was she later pleased to recall that she had dismissed Audena by comparing her to a bloodhound and calling her husband a grabby little Chihuahua.

It got rid of Audena and Winky, though. And it put Averill in grand humor. He could barely quiet himself before he'd start giggling all over again. After that, all she had to do was wait Averill out while he drank coffee and ate two slices of triple chocolate cake, enriched of course with a pinch of her secret ingredient. Averill snickered and choked and belched his way through two slices of that special mix. It was his favorite cake recipe. However, that wasn't why Leona had chosen it. Leona had gone to no short lengths with that particular cake because of its name, "Devil's Last Wish." That tickled her cornball funny bone. Now, as Averill walked out the front door snickering, she just had to smile, thinking that the fool was going to literally die laughing.

10

EASTER SUNDAY, APRIL 23, 2000
1:46 P.M.

Watching Averill's narrow torso dissolve into the undergrowth on the opposite side of the road, Leona sensed a circle completing its strange returning path. Seeing him move off into the shadows now, she was overwhelmed with the desire to follow him, to hide and watch the sickness come over him, and then see him die. It wasn't the vengeance. She wanted to see it for herself, so that she could creep up to him while he was still warm and shake and slap and otherwise assure herself that he was really dead.

Audena had no idea how right she was to say that Leona had taken her family's name down low. Or how much further it would sink when the world knew what he had done. Audena's resentments toward Averill were within her family. In a wider context, Leona knew that Audena not only coveted his comparatively elevated lifestyle, but bragged about it to the rest of her squalid world. So these pitiful souls who had listened until their ears burned with Audena's bragging would take no little pleasure in media accounts of her brother's hideous acts. She had no less doubt that Audena would waste no tears on her when they killed Leona. However, it would be a cause of deep mourning to endure a second wave of notoriety as one with the family name was punished for capital murder.

Though she was dead wrong to say Leona had tricked Averill into marrying her. Averill knew better than that. He should have said something and Leona would have forced some acknowledgment of the truth out of him, except of course he was full of poison and she had to get rid of her sister-in-law and husband before it became obvious. Now, this was an irony, resenting a man you had just finished murdering because he wouldn't defend your honor. Still, it flew all over Leona every time she thought about it. She hoped and prayed Audena would turn up for the trial. She wanted her to hear in person just exactly how it had been the opposite. Averill had tricked her. And when indeed he made a contract with her to give her baby his name, he omitted one clause. He left out the one stating his right to choke it to death.

Low? There was no question. Leona was lower than she had ever imagined when she made her bargain with the devil. Obviously, Averill had heard that timing is everything in life. At that point she was willing to follow anyone's lead. She was blinded by pain. She would have done anything to relieve it. If he'd suggested shooting herself, she would have gone along with it. She couldn't help thinking that it would be a better world now if she had.

Leona married Averill a month after her mother's funeral, when she was at the bottom of her grief. The immediate rituals of flowers and kindnesses were over. Her mother's death hadn't begun to turn brown and dissolve with the mound of flowers on her grave. Instead, it had taken on a life of its own, its impact had grown to an unexpected and frightening degree. Then of course the unhappy finale with Ty and his father's suicide had added their unbearable weight. And she was by then almost four months pregnant.

He had come back to Fredonia late the previous spring. The local Church of Christ minister was going away for the summer and Averill was going to take over his duties until September. Averill had always floated on the periphery of Leona's world. He was one of the Sayres who lived near the bottom of a squalid downhill street where poor people lived. In spite of the fact that Fredonia was a small town and the inevitable paths always crossed, Leona had grown up believing that there was an impenetrable border between herself and people like the Sayreses. It wasn't her creation or an affect of snobbism, but something that she accepted as the natural order of things. And something she assumed the extended Sayres tribe accepted as well.

She had gone through school with plenty of Sayres children, at least through junior high, when it almost seemed unwritten law that Sayres girls got pregnant, got married and took cashiers' jobs at the Big Star while the boys went to prison or the army. Not every single one of them, though. They were a huge family. A few had drifted upward over the course of several generations. If they wanted to do or be anything in the world, they always left town. It would have been easier to dance barefoot on top of a flagpole than it would be for a Sayres to overcome the name in Fredonia, Mississippi.

If there was ever going to be one Sayres who had what it would take to cross over into the realm of ordinary, decent people, it was Averill. Leona had heard her father remark to that effect as well. She was more than ten years younger than Averill Sayres and wouldn't have known him from any of his four brothers or umpteen cousins. Or so she had always believed. In that regard she had been very mistaken. For Averill Sayres had passed by her house a thousand times and exchanged polite greetings with her all her life. Leona had mistaken him for one of the Baptist minister's adopted nephews.

Why wouldn't she? He didn't look anything like a Sayres. No freckles, frizzy red hair or anemic eyes. He evidenced none of their benchmark enervation. He wasn't loud. He didn't have a nervous bray. You never saw him at the wheel of some throbbing old jalopy that was destined to rust among half a dozen others on concrete blocks beside little shacks that had planks where the front steps should be.

Like so many evils, Averill had entered her world as a seemingly inconsequential shape, a familiar smile among the steady parade of visitors hovering over her mother's sickbed that summer. Viola's friends came and went almost like round-the-clock nurses. There were others as well, some curious, some distant relatives carrying out familial duty, and there were clergymen. Apart from the Methodist, Episcopalian and Baptist ministers, there were at least a dozen from other denominations who called on a regular basis. Leona didn't know them. She let them into the house because their visits seemed to touch her mother.

Averill was the youngest of these. He was courteous, attractive and especially attentive to Viola, who soon took a shine to him. Leona didn't always stay with her mother's callers throughout their visits.

By the time Leona finally realized that he was one of the "untouchable" Sayres, he had already earned her esteem with his kindness to her mother. So his unfortunate background added rather than detracted from her regard for him. The young man had overcome a great deal of adversity. If you looked at Averill one way, he was a very attractive man. He was tall and long-boned, with a strong jaw and emaciated cheeks. He wore his thick curly hair parted at the side in a Princeton cut. He took pains with his clothes. His one obvious Sayres attribute had been a pronounced overbite corrected by braces, which he had somehow managed to pay for himself. Now he had a wide, straight, toothy grin.

That was one way. The other way to see Averill required a certain worldliness or intuitive discernment. It meant looking through his unremarkable, decent looks and seeing the broken, resentful, self-entitled criminal lurking there. Strange, looking back on it now. Ty had somehow seen through him. Once when Ty came to pick up Leona he commented on the way Averill looked at her.

"It's not right, him being a man of God."

"What's not right?"

"The way that snaky Bible wiggler undresses you with his eyes."

How she had laughed at that. She had never felt Averill look at her any way at all. He was a regular and much appreciated visitor at Viola's sickbed during her last weeks—one of the few who seemed to do her heart good. He brought her communion and read to her from the Bible and listened to her as she inventoried her life. To this day Leona couldn't deny her gratitude for his kindness to her dying mother.

At that time she had allowed herself to believe Ty was so chained to her, so desperately afraid of life without her, that he had invented it. She was far too naïve to understand that jealousy is never touching, never cute and never an expression of genuine affection.

She had no memory of Averill during the wake and the funeral. The longtime friends of her parents, whom she had called aunt and uncle from the days when they towered over her, crowded in and decided everything, dwarfing her once again.

It had comforted her that there were still so many older and wiser people left in the world who knew just what to do. She was young then and unaccustomed to death. It seemed freakish and cruel and it made all of life seem meaningless. Yet these bustling gray-haired people who had loved her mother could smile and talk about her as a blessing. None of them retched or cried out in protest. They gave her a sustaining particle of hope that she might one day understand and accept it.

It wasn't until she walked out of the bank with the image of Mr. Crockett and his pistol burned into her mind's eye that the shock of things began to recede and she became aware of her sorrow and her solitude.

People were puffed-up images of what they thought the world expected them to be. They wouldn't accept you as anything less. Wasn't that what Mr. Crockett meant by killing himself? He wasn't a man. His weakness and failure and fear weren't acceptable. So he tried to please, to measure up by playing a role that cost too much money. In the end he had succeeded by turning himself into something he couldn't bear to be. There was no way out.

She might have succumbed to a similar despair except for her unwillingness to hurt the child she carried. It was a gathering light in the midst of utter chaos. She wanted it with ferocious longing. She dreamed about it, talked to it and saw its life open like a great glowing flower on a dark blue landscape. She watched it stumble and grow and helped it up, and when it was grown and flying off, its brightness flooded the world.

What odious scripture had poisoned those decent ladies into believing she would actually birth this miracle inside of her and then hand it new and helpless into the unknown dominion of strangers? Where was the meaning in her life if she wasn't the mother of this child, unless she nourished and protected it and helped it find its way in the world? Why didn't they understand that she could manage to do that much good without a husband or much financial means? She could endow it with the courage to place its heart in the palm of another human being, unafraid to bear the consequences.

Yet all that was half-focused, half-experienced within the gathering cloud of sorrow as the terrible emptiness created by her mother's death intensified. If Ty had left her an everlasting heartache, it was at least possible to imagine some distant future realm of existence in which life in its exacerbating, slow processes would lead her to its deeper meaning. Not so with Viola's death.

It angered her beyond expression to be alone. It flooded her with rage to think of how life had cheated both her and Viola out of her father. Worse than that was her mother's long-suffering widowhood, her agonizing descent into the grave. These weren't conditions to change like hearts and minds with the seasons. These were life's raw, inexplicable and cruel terms. In light of them, hope itself seemed fatuous. As she contemplated the new being inside of her, she began to question her role in its existence. What kind of monster would bring an innocent creature into such a world?

As the first few days became a week after her mother's death, Leona began to consider the peaceful alternative of taking her own life and sparing the child-to-be all the agony of human existence. Then one night she found herself at the front door, staring into the determined eyes of three women, the most efficacious of the larger deputation who had lingered the evening after her mother's funeral.

They rushed in with an air of officious intent. It was past time to get on with practical matters. A space had been reserved for her at a home for unfortunate young ladies in Pascagoula. She had to vacate the premises anyway. Her mother had signed something; there was a bank lien on the house. The thing to do was sell the contents, pay the interest, stave off the bank and sell the house. It was one of those miraculous plans of financial salvation that would rescue the bank's interests, reinforce a few lawyers, give the state and federal governments their due and leave her a virtually impoverished unwed mother without a roof over her child's head.

As young as she was, and as pretty, why, it wouldn't be any time before Leona had her prince—somewhere else, of course—someplace where no one would ever be the wiser. They were almost giddy, a conspiring cabal, nothing to it, really.

It was pointless to argue with them. They were in love with their combined ability to right so much wrong, to keep their Protestant sun in their Methodist sky, to whitewash her woes with Presbyterian platitudes like some old picket fence. By the next afternoon they were back with three cleaning women, sorting and pitching and packing up things she would want and need in her next life in a new town with her attorney prince.

The rest of her mother's belongings they polished and straightened and otherwise got ready to sell the following weekend. Their Christian zeal was strengthened by their awareness that Leona's condition was now obvious even in her loosest dress. That meant, of course, she had to be gotten out of town before the sight of her swollen midsection desecrated her beloved mama's memory.

Leona chose the path of least resistance, keeping herself back and watching them sort, fold and dispose of life as she had always known it with astounding facility. She hated them, of course. She thought they were cold and uncaring hypocrites. She had been too morose and deep into her decision to take her own life to argue with them. Now, of course, she was glad for that. She couldn't say that time had convinced her the women had done the right thing. However, she knew they had gone to great lengths to salvage her situation the best way they knew how to do it. They had done it as loyal friends of her mother.

There was nothing more multifaceted or bizarre than the truth. She realized now that, as they dismantled everything she had desperately longed to hold on to, those women were stowing and organizing their own hard emotions at the loss of a beloved friend. They took comfort in honoring her memory by arranging things for her daughter.

By the following Saturday evening three-fourths of

the contents of the house had been sold. After the interest on the bank note was paid, she had several hundred dollars. The silver and china and linens and several antiques that Viola's family had brought from Virginia to Mississippi in the early 1800s went into storage. Reverend Sayres had volunteered his own storage shed for safekeeping several less valuable items Leona had refused to sell.

Leona didn't own a car. Her father's had deteriorated in the years since his death to the point that it was no longer safe to operate. Tomorrow she would take the five A.M. Sunday New Orleans bus. There she could transfer out to Pascagoula on a commuter train. She would leave the next morning and arrive in her new home "pro tempore" in time to wash her face before joining the other ladies for luncheon.

Averill backed a small truck to the front porch that Saturday night. He and a helper loaded Leona's things.

Leona's sorrow was laced with an odd tenderness for this kind young man. Ministers were supposed to be somewhat Christ-like, at least in her mind. Maybe it wasn't fair, but she had always felt let down when one clergyman after another eventually turned out to be an ordinary mortal. Yet Averill had given a great deal of himself to her mother, and now to Leona, without any hint that he expected anything in return. It was an effort she felt obligated to acknowledge.

No question her vision was clouded. Life had broken her that summer. She had no intentions of leaving town on the bus in the morning. She had gathered a bottle of painkillers from her mother's room and she had her father's pistol loaded and ready inside of her purse. The future was a black box of oblivion. She watched them lift the tailgate and rattle the steel chains and hooks.

He made easy work of a considerable task and she couldn't help but admire how he took pains not to over-burden his helper. When his eyes had met hers to ask if a carton contained glass or if the drawers of a desk had been emptied, she couldn't help smiling at his shyness.

Leona stood inside the screen door. "Can I offer you some ice water or a Coke?"

He was all appreciation as he nodded. When she opened the screen door to admit him, he waited to be asked. It was impossible for her to express how much it comforted her to leave this world knowing there was still some measure of humanity left in someone. She didn't say that, of course.

"Your sadness honors a real and irretrievable loss," he told her in a soothing, almost hoarse voice. "Your mother was a great lady and I include myself among her many admirers." It wasn't the words. It was the kindness in his voice as he imparted them. "You gave her such im-mense comfort in her suffering," he went on. "Let that comfort you now."

It did. His were the first sentiments that didn't at-tempt to persuade her she should feel better.

"Your sorrow is going to bend you for a long time to come."

His empathy flowed through her like a balm. It was as if she had suddenly been granted the right to exist. He put his arms around her and held her while she cried. There in that sad, empty house from which all life had fled, his comfort was like a benediction.

Later, because there was no furniture left in the house, they sat on the front porch and she told him everything she felt, including the fact that she had been planning to kill herself. As the blue darkness fell and the streetlights came on, gathering intensity while the night settled in, she almost felt as if the normal world had returned. It was like visiting late on the porch with a high school friend while her mother and father slept upstairs behind the screened windows.

Telling Averill was the first good she had succeeded at in a very long time. Telling him told her how lonely she had been since Ty had deserted her. It made her aware that she hadn't seen or heard from half a dozen friends who she would have expected to call after her mother died. Of course, everyone knew about her predicament. They had all backed away, not to shun her in shame; rather because, as Averill explained it that night, their families had financial entanglements with a certain banker who didn't want Leona's side to gain credibility.

"You're a preacher man, don't you regard my situation a sin?"

"Well, my Bible says to let the one without sin cast the first stone."

His answer touched her that night. In fact, the generous way he listened without judging had lifted her spirits more than she would have believed possible. She told him as much. He looked embarrassed for a minute. Then he said something that, when added to what he'd said about the first stone, told Leona that Averill Sayres was a man the world never saw.

"Nowhere in the Old or New Testament does it say that a man and a woman must be husband and wife before they become intimate." It was a statement the likes of which he would never risk in front of his congregation. Nor was he very likely to reveal that much worldly good sense to her after that. Later she would almost wish he hadn't said it that night because it made his mask of ignorance harder to endure.

To this day, even with the slow-acting poison she

had fed him doing its secret work inside of him, Leona couldn't deny the very high probability that Averill Sayres had saved her life that night. For, even while they were sitting there talking, Leona had decided on another course. She wouldn't serve out her pregnancy like a sentence in a home for unwed mothers. Nor would she give her baby away—ever. She'd leave town on that bus, but she wouldn't change for Pascagoula in New Orleans. She'd get a room and figure out the rest of her life from there.

"People are cruel," Averill observed after a long silence had drifted by. More than his sentiment, Leona was struck by the fact that she hadn't felt the least bit awkward or compelled to clutter the quiet space between them with forced conversation. It indicated an underlying trust. He was a very decent, sensitive young man with an intuitive skill for reassuring her. It mortified her to think of the thousand past opportunities that she might have taken to get to know him. It was genuine mortification because she could see as clear as day that the reason she had missed out on him was snobbery. She had taken complete license to prejudge and avoid all but the most distant contact with Averill because his last name was Sayres.

Now it was too late, too late to know him, and too late to help him gain a much-deserved foothold with all the other self-anointed ignoramuses in town. It gave her another reason to regret leaving town.

Suddenly she hated to leave, though not because she felt any great affection for it just then. In fact, she felt betrayed by her own community. She had learned a terrible fact about people's beliefs and friendships. Until recently she had assumed that an idea had a value of its own. You stood behind a principle in direct accordance with the good you saw in it. It was the same with people. Their intrinsic decency was the important thing.

Now she saw that it wasn't so. People attached themselves to whatever advanced their financial status and spurned whatever might have a negative impact on their pocketbooks. It bothered her to admit it, but she could recall any number of times when her mother and father had paid lip service to opinions they didn't hold. There were hundreds of little injustices they accepted and perpetuated out of fear of alienating customers at her father's pharmacy. In fact, Leona had been carefully instructed by her mother in the fine art of keeping your opinions to yourself. She hated to give in to the oppressive hypocrisy. She would have loved nothing better than to stay right there in Fredonia and raise her child on her own.

The problem with that wasn't people's reactions. She was savvy enough to pressure their consciences into accepting her on those terms. She no longer questioned the morality of bringing a new life into the world, but she had an obligation to protect it from people's ignorance and cruelty. If she stayed in Fredonia, her baby would grow up Ty Crockett's unwanted bastard, the mistake of a summer night. She wanted it very much. It would come into this world an adored innocent. She would raise it where no one had ever heard of Ty Crockett or Leona Clay. It would be itself, free from all that, unharmed by the sharp tongues of fear-driven people.

"It's late," he said. He had to drive a hundred miles that night. He had to teach Sunday school and preach in the morning. He was also going to stop at his sister's on the way to stow Leona's things.

"It's my fault you're getting such a late start," she said.

"It was a privilege to spend the time with you, Leona."

"You've been a grace to me and I'll never forget it."

"You'll make it, I know," he said, and his bottom lip quivered. He steadied himself with a breath and touched her shoulder. His eyes held hers for a few seconds, bathing her in a benediction of kindness. Then he turned and moved down the porch steps.

She wanted to cry out and beg him not to go. He was only a few feet away and already the loneliness was weighing back in like before. She didn't have the courage to face life on her own in a strange city with a baby. She had lost the will to take her own life. As his outline began to soften while he moved farther into the gray darkness, she felt the despair overtake her. She was going to give in to that coven of fear that had arranged her sensible and cruel future. She was going to surrender to the daily rituals of that house of shame where she would suffer her penance and, by letting them give her child to more deserving hands, she would redeem herself and regain the hope of heaven.

"Averill, don't go!"

He turned around and looked at her, his eyes brimming with sadness. He didn't say anything. She didn't know what she meant by asking him not to leave her alone in the dark. It didn't matter just as long as he stayed. She had no one and no idea what to do. She only understood that he cared very much what happened to her and he was willing to help any way that he could.

It was a long, strange night. Hope and doubt and confusion dominated everything. She couldn't stay there. He had no idea where to take her. They were drawn together like magnets, yet they were for the most part strangers.

Something assured them both that their pairing-off was inevitable. Yet neither could begin to broach such a preposterous intuition. Hours passed and Averill had no choice, he had to leave. She didn't know how she could let him do that alone.

Somehow they reached a tenuous compromise. She would get into the truck with him. They would discuss the next step on the road. It was crazy. It was terrifying and exhilarating all at once. The journey might conclude with her waiting in his truck in the church parking lot for his service to be over so that he could drive her to the nearest train station. This still didn't mean that Pascagoula wasn't her final destination.

He tossed her suitcases into the back of his truck and they took off. She would never forget her last look at the Fredonia Court Square and commercial district. They stopped at a red light. The pale sky glowed blue gray with muddled clouds behind the charcoal silhouette of the stucco courthouse. All her life she had believed it was an inviolable fortress of justice. Now its row of twelve long, bleak upper-floor windows became six pairs of eyes witnessing her departure. They seemed immutable and guilty.

She thought, when at last they crossed the city limits and moved into the open country under a moonless canopy of night, she might just as well have ridden in an open cart along some seascape of hell, letting her bare feet drag across the smoldering sand. She pressed her shoulders into the back of the seat and closed her eyes, drifting in and out of consciousness until she floated into warm, moist oblivion.

She opened her eyes once for a few seconds when rain slapped the metal and glass surfaces of the truck. From her vantage his hands seemed enormous as they held on to the steering wheel, and the meager tufts of hair below his knuckles bristled when there was a flash of lightning. When it was dim in the cab again, she noticed a gathering pink in the rearview mirror and glanced back at a shining web of silver trailing into the rising sun. Then she saw him look at her and smile. She couldn't decide whether or not he was handsome.

"Know what I was just thinking?"

"No, sir."

"I should come clean here and now."

"Please do."

"I've been in love with you for a long time," he blurted, and his voice cracked as tears burst down his cheeks like a flash flood. (She had no idea how often she would see him weep on a dime to disarm a woman.)

He seemed so earnest, so harmless and well meaning, and she couldn't overcome her need to believe him. He'd had an eye on her. Leona's failure to pay more than polite attention to him when he called on her dying mother had cut him to the quick. He didn't ask her to love him or stay with him forever. However, for the next year or so, she was going to need a great deal he would consider it an honor to provide.

He seemed honest. He fascinated her. He was an unusual combination of long masculine angles and unexpected feminine touches like his thick, dark eyelashes and porcelain skin. He was at once bold and shy, innocent and seductive. She couldn't help her inexplicable suspicion that he was, or at least had once been, a little dangerous or wild. She couldn't pin it down, but she read something rakish or bad his seminary training hadn't quite erased.

It made her the slightest bit uneasy. She didn't find the bad boy type at all appealing. She knew that girls who did always wound up in a lot of pain. Of course, Averill hadn't done or said anything she could interpret as suggestive.

Later the sky was powder blue. The ground was dry here. They were on a narrow blacktop that twisted and climbed and dove into eroding banks of red clay from which the gnarled roots of trees hung in tornadolike swirls.

"This is hill country," he said.

She had been turning his confessional words over and over, examining their implications for her. He wanted to take her in. What would his church members say? What would their relationship to each other be? Was he expecting her to bed down with him? Though he didn't seem to realize it, Averill was a young man whose body language communicated an almost constant need for a woman. It was too intense for Leona. It made her nervous. Although she trusted him completely.

"You're far too decent for me to take advantage of you."

"I'm not asking you to love me."

"You deserve to be loved."

In future moments of anger, Averill would say that Leona had deceived him. She didn't have the guts to tell Averill she was using him for a port in a storm. She wouldn't propose the nonsexual, public façade she wanted. Rather than embrace the fact that she was desperately terrified of facing the world alone in her predicament, she played a high-handed game of moral and emotional chess. It added up to a pretense of affection and concern she had manufactured to disguise her terror of physical intimacy with him.

Leona had never made anything like a formidable objection to his charges because the truth in them always made her burn with shame. In the end, and not without deep gratitude and, at first, great affection, Leona married Averill (for the benefit of his congregation) and tried to give a believable performance as a young country preacher's expectant bride.

They passed through Orpheus, a small county seat town like Fredonia, but obviously built by a far more prosperous class of plantation owners. It was hard to imagine so many hulking, antebellum dinosaurs, several occupying large estates surrounded by tall, elaborate iron fences. As they left the edge of town behind them, the paved street gave way to a gravel road as the town ended abruptly. They descended through soy fields interspersed with stands of hardwoods and cedars. After a mile, they crossed a wide creek dotted with sandbars. Now the road inclined sharply upward and a dark forest loomed.

Now the gravel road forked right, skirting a small mountain while the left branch, which Averill took, was little more than two clay ruts that climbed it. Cotton fields became rocky woods and the shoulder disappeared as clay banks rose on either side—ten, sometimes twenty, feet above them where soaring oaks leaned off the forest floor. It was the steepest road she had ever traveled. The truck engine protested its battle with gravity. Banked by the dark silhouettes of the towering trees, the view straight ahead was endless pewter sky.

"Wouldn't want to be on this road in a rainstorm," she said, talking to dispel her inexplicable boding. How stupid that must have sounded to him, knowing as he did that her fate was sealed, that she would indeed travel this road in rain and snow and hail and blinding lightning with tree limbs crashing. They were moving up a steep incline now. The engine was grinding and clattering now, straining against the steep road.

"When we get to the church. I'll introduce you as my wife," he said. The way he said it made her feel a little conspiratorial, like kids late for supper and deciding what excuse to give. She didn't delve into it. It was something he had to do to protect himself. She saw no harm in following his lead.

Besides, the long ride, the intensity of the situation and her condition had conspired to make her a little nauseous. She was just glad he didn't expect her to wait in a hot truck while he taught his Sunday school class and preached a sermon afterward. She'd figured out enough life for one day. It was no small relief to be with someone she could trust who, for the moment anyway, seemed to know what she should do.

Just when it seemed to Leona that something under the hood of the truck would have to explode or crack in two, they crested the hill and the road flattened and curved through dense forest. Daylight darted between the trunks of hardwoods on the horizon in front of them. Above the trees, a pale scrap of moon hung behind the pallid morning sky. It seemed used up and as dead as a dry leaf.

She wanted to ask him if it had been his plan to bring her here. She wanted to know his expectations. There was a great deal of room for the answers to a thousand questions any reasonable person in her shoes would ask. She was afraid to know any more. Everything past had been obliterated. Nothing about the future was clear. Had she been honest with herself, Leona would have admitted more suspicion from the beginning.

However, she had handed her fate to fear, as even

the strongest people will when they're overwhelmed by
a great loss. She had chosen the passive course of willful ignorance.

How smart Averill had been, how brilliant, she now
thought. He had convinced her that he was smitten,
that he would take her under any conditions. He knew
she had no option but to take advantage of his feelings
for her, to use him as long as she deemed it necessary.
He let her think that she would one day take her infant
and his best wishes when she left him.

In some respects Leona would come to see herself as a victim of her own narrow attitudes. She had
no idea that Averill understood people and society better than anyone did. Not that first day she spent on
Whitsunday Hill. She knew that he had come from the
bottom rung. Yet she couldn't have imagined that even
then he was using the unique perspective it gave him as
his chief means of climbing toward a tolerable existence. She didn't even suspect that he had learned to
play the affable innocent who lived in eternal awe of his
betters. He was already adept at keeping quiet and making small moves. He had trained himself to put people
at ease by adopting a subordinate and supportive pos-
ture around them. He had crafted a mask of goodwill
and contentment, which reassured all who looked af-
fectionately down on him that he was too simple to experience their superior complexities and tribulations.

People let their guard down. They confided things.
How many times would she watch with resentful regard
as he manipulated far better-educated men, blinding
them with their own arrogance, and gaining whatever
dispensation their positions could offer? He had hidden
his agenda for her behind a thick fog of fumbling adora-
tion. He knew all about her lace-curtain Protestant

strain. He understood its moral murkiness. He knew that she would have to convince herself that she wasn't taking advantage of him. He was counting on the fact that she would blind herself to her basic intentions. It would also prevent her from seeing his own dishonest purposes.

He knew that she was the product of a particular tribe, an insulated little fortress that held itself apart from poor, ignorant people like his. She had been weaned on her innate superiority to trash like Averill Sayres. Strange, he would inadvertently teach her what potent secrets could fester in such people.

Had it not been for his act of inhuman savagery upon the baby, Leona had often mused, she might have called the rest of it a draw and walked quietly away.

People must have their intuition educated out of them. She remembered an almost suffocating sense of boding on that first Sunday morning when she saw the cemetery from the road. It was ancient and it seemed as if the woods from which it had been cleared and sanctified by a now badly rusted iron fence had almost succeeded in reclaiming it. Though, on closer inspection, she could see that some of the graves were still maintained. Several mounds of grass-covered earth indicated it was still in use.

She was glad when it gave way to a thicket of cedars. She was nauseous from the acute sensation of dread. Then the church appeared through the trees and she fixed her mind on its decorous and haunted formality. It was an old plantation house of worship. It was small, probably just one room, and in poor condition. The brick needed pointing and the paint was peeling from the long windows and the wooden shutters beside them. Still, it had an unexpected elegance, a sophistication owing to its careful proportions. Many of its architectural details had obviously come from far away. There wouldn't have been anywhere within five hundred miles to obtain them when it was built in the nineteenth century.

The roof was weathered copper; the stained glass windows were set deep; the eaves overhung elaborate molded trim. Climbing roses arched the paneled wood front door and a pair of eight brick steps curved left and right along a wrought iron railing to the packed clay remnants of a circle driveway. He drove on another hundred yards before he veered hard to the left and they followed the rough, grass-covered driveway seventy feet and stopped where it petered out beside the house.

Half an hour later she found herself being introduced to a church full of smiling country people as Mrs. Averill Sayres. It made more sense than she had begun to think her life ever would. Mrs. Averill Sayres was a disguise, a hiding place from the miserable past. It was a tolerable niche and a part she was more than grateful to play in exchange for the safety it afforded her.

For the first few months Leona lived on gratitude. Averill had spared her the wretched penance of that house in Pascagoula where the months would pass in shame and dread of the unavoidable separation from her child. He had taken her out of a place where every pair of eyes saw her as fallen, a stain on a starched cotton society, a living insult to a decent family. It was good to be where everything she saw wasn't a reminder of something else she had lost.

She tried to express her appreciation to Averill by making a considerable effort to organize and improve the old parsonage, which was precariously close to irretrievable ruin. She also stood beside him in groups of people, using her skills to make him more comfortable. People liked her and that reflected well on him.

Averill worked hard at his calling. He apparently had inherited a church that was near its last gasp. People were already saying that he had turned it around. Leona first thought the place was called Whitsunday after Pentecost Sunday, the day of the Holy Spirit according to the New Testament. She soon found out that there was another explanation. According to local lore, on the morning the church was dedicated in the 1800s, the surrounding woods had filled with white butterflies.

Strange what she chose to believe and why. She was like a child, peering out through the evening haze for signs of the mythical butterflies in the woods. It gave her inexplicable peace. Or was that the new life stirring within her?

Averill was gone most of the time, day and night, calling on shut-ins, looking in on backsliders and making an effort to lure back former members who had drifted away.

Leona loved the simplicity of her days. She could accomplish a great deal with nothing to divert her attention but the peace of the woods. They spent relatively little time alone together. She made his supper; she kept his house; she lent him her support in public. Their conversations were pleasant, if a little more pragmatic than meaningful.

They slept in separate beds, rarely even lying down to sleep at the same time. Averill was usually asleep by the time she went to bed. More times than not, she'd wake up in the morning to find him gone, and two cups of warm coffee left for her on the stove.

One October Saturday he suggested they make a two-hour drive to Grand Junction, Tennessee, where they could make their marriage legal. He said living the lie was bothering him. He also added that a child was always better off wearing its father's last name. She hadn't contemplated the future during recent months. The idea of giving birth occupied too much between her and that.

Averill hadn't done or said anything in all that time to reiterate the deep affections he had expressed the night she left Fredonia with him. She could only assume that they had cooled.

"Averill, I can't let you do this."

"I'd do anything for you, Leona."

"There will be a woman who loves you one day."

"I'll only love one woman the way I love you, Leona."

"I won't be here forever."

"I know a marriage certificate won't change that."

She couldn't have wished for a better solution than the one he'd provided for her. It was working very well. Besides, he was offering her baby a name. In exchange, she could certainly say a few words to a justice of the peace and relieve his shoulders from the burden of living a lie.

What made people believe in something for nothing? What convinced her that there wouldn't be consequences? How did she manage to persuade her better nature that it wouldn't be exploitation if Averill didn't call it that?

Averill Sayres had taught her one very dear lesson. People didn't forget things. Everything Averill did amounted to paying the world back for the indignity of his miserable childhood. People acted indifferent to insults; they smiled and said they had learned values by virtue of having done without. People acquired polish and power and dignified airs. All the same, Averill Sayres had demonstrated it for her: they kept their scorecards. They hid all that past injury and pain way out of sight, where it smoldered like piled leaves or oily rags. They waited. Then they got even.

His spiritual path and compassionate personality were both façade and modus operandi. He was a well-oiled illusion, a brilliant actor playing himself every waking moment. She didn't believe people were born evil. People became the total of their accrued suffering. Averill Sayres had lured her with false humility and disingenuous affection. By letting her think she was using him, he diverted her from his own usurious motives.

What a lie everything was, what a mean-spirited mirage. Yet she had succumbed herself to the ways of the world. She had descended into hell right here on earth. She didn't need another act of this ludicrous comedy. She didn't see the point of learning any more character lessons too late. Did it matter how many pairs of hands shared the collective guilt of her miserable fate? She was here now; she had reached the broken world, the bleak haunt of the jackals from which her dead soul would never escape. There was nothing to do now but wait for them to find him and arrest her.

She caught her reflection in the pier mirror by the front door. She didn't look like a murderer. Then she smiled. It was a lovely smile. It was the same as ever. Yet, looking at her full lips and abundant, even teeth, she began to descry something she had never before seen. It was a removed quality, a coolness. No. No, now she had it. It wasn't merely cool. It was cold—the cold, all-knowing wisdom of the dead.

11

❖

Seeing Audena had upset him. The moment she and that dog she married walked into his church, he remembered why it had been so long since he'd seen her. His sister was a grabby mule. She resented his dental work, his two-year-old Cutlass, his watch, his clothes and Leona's cooking.

Had she but known how much she truly had to resent!

She was his only living immediate family. Well, then, he didn't want any living family. He wasn't about to connect with his dim-eyed, reprobate cousins in Calhoun County for the sake of blood. It was a stupid impulse. He should never have invited her. It was just that he was trying to tie as many loose strings as he could. He and Helen agreed they would never look back. Averill had acted on some leftover, half-wit notion he should see his sister one last time.

Helen didn't want to look back. She had a bad memory here. Her daughter had been murdered on her wedding day last September. Helen didn't have anyone else in town. All her people were dead now. She'd gotten the amicable divorce her husband had promised her—and every penny of their prearranged settlement. Like his marriage, Helen's had been one of convenience. Of course, there was one difference. Helen's ex-husband was a gay man looking for a shield. She was pregnant from a series of amorous escapades. It had never been a real marriage. They had long planned their divorce. Half the time when Averill and Helen were upstairs in bed, Ransom was downstairs entertaining some of his fairy friends.

People could make what they would of all that. It had worked out well for all the involved parties.

Averill had always regretted deceiving Leona. He had no other choice, then or now. There would have been no way to sit her down the night they decided to get together and explain it all to her. He had to have, then and there, a wife whose obvious pregnancy would validate the idea that he had been married for some time and was committed to building his family.

He couldn't very well tell her he'd been fingered in a murder. Nor could he explain that there was compelling evidence against him—which he needed her and the pregnancy to counter.

People were all hypocrites. Everyone lived two lives. There was the person you acted in order to survive in the world. Preacher, teacher, lawyer, Boy Scout leader— you were always some spit-shined perfect version of yourself that the world demanded of you. Then there was the flesh and blood, stepped-on and biting-back you, the one ruled by your inner needs. That was the real one.

Averill, like most poor fools, had been a secret from himself well into adulthood. He had set out to conquer his own flesh armed with the spiritual weapons of his biblical training. He had stumbled on that holy path and discovered his powerlessness over his mortal weaknesses.

He still walked the Christian road, but he held his virtuous postures because he knew that's what the people who fed him expected him to do. He was supposed to believe certain Christian precepts—water into wine, the virgin birth and the resurrection of Jesus Christ—and he did. However, the abstemious nature of Christ, particularly in regard to the temptations of the flesh, was beyond his ability to embrace.

He was ashamed to say it, and he would never say it aloud to anyone, but Averill Sayres had serious doubts about the intimate proclivities of his Lord and Savior as reported. Something was off there; something was missing, something went over the top in the direction of the divine. A young man needed women. There was a wealth of unexplained desires hiding under those biblical robes. Didn't he have charisma? Weren't there flocks of women everywhere he pitched his tent? No. Some tiny little mind had crammed all that chastity in there, probably to keep people feeling bad about wanting to do what came naturally all the time.

When he and Helen were far away, he'd send word to Leona about the baby. No, he couldn't fix everything by telling her the truth. However, she'd at least know the motives and circumstances behind it. He knew that a decent man, one who had the guts to look life in the eye, would never deceive or swindle or seduce the way he had. A better person would never have compromised and slithered his way into this deep hole. He wouldn't have found himself so crazed by terror of his own desperate outcome.

He was a weak man, not a slippery beast of prey—not by intent. He would have been a more respectable man. He had meant to. He had given that his best effort. His failure to repair himself and stand as a man among men would be his everlasting sorrow. Or if he was not just another weak man, if he was evil, if he was a snake, then he couldn't help it. What were his alternatives? Surely she didn't expect him to commit suicide? A man's primary obligation was to live.

Seeing Audena had been a terrible jolt. The time apart had softened his memory of her. He was almost ready to forgive her for certain things. But she was really a mule, a horse-faced woman from hell, standing in the pit of all his past torment, tugging at his billowing, starched white sleeves.

She couldn't even let him alone about his teeth.

"They can chisel down your fangs and smooth your scaly cheeks, but you're the same egg-sucking chicken snake."

She could have helped him. She could have cared. Something rattled. Something quivered deep within. Now a voice like his own spoke from the hissing cedars outside his study window. It reminded him that Audena had been a fat and ugly girl. It painted the lonely image of an upstairs hotel window, a dull lamp flickering with the demon vibrato of an endless freight train. All Audena had to do was be away when things were going on. He was seven. One night a salesman told Mama that aside from his slightly bucked teeth, he was as pretty as a girl. The man had played his fingers in Averill's long, dark curly hair.

What did Audena know? Was she a bastard? Was she conceived in a whorehouse? Was she given to men when she was a child? Had she been forced to endure a decade of the hideous things that men had done to him? Averill slammed his mind shut. That was then, this was here and now. His study had been closed up since yesterday afternoon. The room needed air. He pressed the center section of the double window and opened it like a pair of doors. The cemetery was blurred by mist from the surrounding woods. The old stones were smears of terracotta and gray between patches of yellow-green. He breathed slowly, drawing in the Sunday afternoon.

Now he sensed a distant fluttering. At first he assumed it was a flock of starlings taking shelter in the wild grove of pecan trees about a mile above him in the woods. The notion hadn't taken shape before he understood that it was that memory wrenching itself into his consciousness once again.

There were trains passing, freight trains close below and rattling the windows.

A driving rain pounded the hotel room window around which giant peacock-blue Christmas lights had been strung. It was a white clapboard building in need of paint. There was a dark khaki U.S. Army bus parked in the alley beside the hotel. From the café and bar downstairs Elvis was singing "Love Me Tender." A freight train was passing. He pressed his lips to the window and whispered to the lumbering iron-wheeled serpent rolling away down below.

"Come and take me away, come and take me away."

Behind him at the foot of the bed the soldier with the dark hair was unfastening his pants. On the mattress another soldier was flopping with Mama, whose peroxide-yellow hair glowed blue from the twinkle lights on the little tree they had placed on top of the television set.

He told Audena about the soldiers and their scratchy cheeks and beer and cigarette breath. He told her about their smells and choking on their things and how when they had him on his tummy on the roll-away by the windows it hurt and he was scared they were going to crack him in two. He told Audena. She was twelve. He was seven. She said to shut up or the cops would arrest Mama, and Daddy would break his neck when he came out of Parchman Prison. He told her and told her to tell someone big. She just slapped him and said he'd been turned queer and was a woman and he'd suck the devil in hell through eternity.

He didn't tell her that sometimes if a train was passing while a railroad man was sticking him, sometimes just to hold on to something he repeated to the train in the man's pounding rhythm, *"Come and take me away, come and take me away."*

It was an old country church. It sat in a damp hollow by a graveyard surrounded by dense woods. It was brick. The interior walls sweated the minute you lit the space heaters. Even the best grade of oil-base paint curled off the sand plasters the winter after you applied it. No matter how immaculate he left this room, he always returned to a handful of paint chips lying like the first autumn leaves on the glistening cypress floor. The whole church wanted insulation, and the plaster and lathe would have to be replaced by wallboard. It was hell to keep this way. Though he kept the janitor patching up and painting it every week.

That was all over. That was done. He was going to lay down his robe and his Bible very soon now. He was up to here with trying to figure out God. He was done with it. He didn't need it. He had Helen now. And she had her freedom at last. Maybe it was like her queer ex-husband had observed. Maybe Helen and Averill were attracted by their mutual depravity. Maybe they were a pair of slithering and twining snakes.

All he knew was that when he and she were wrapped up in each other, he didn't hurt. When they were bucking and moaning in the dark he didn't know where he ended and she began. He had Helen and they were going away. What they couldn't give each other between the sheets, her money would buy them.

When they were gone, he could write it all down for Leona about the baby. He could apologize and explain and get that torment off his soul. Once he and Helen were safe and happy in their distant paradise, where Leona would never be able to find or prosecute him.

There was a chill in the air he hadn't noticed at first. He closed and locked the window and sat in the cracked leather chair behind his desk.

Loneliness began to creep throughout his body. He wanted Helen. His need for her was as unstoppable as the late-night Illinois Central grinding past his window. Sitting here without her made him feel as loathsome sad as the diesel wail. It screamed the way his insides had screamed once when two soldiers had him between them. They took turns, switching off between his mouth and his bottom. They were too big, too thick. He screamed because he thought he was going to break in half. But he didn't feel it.

All he felt was the train on the tracks below the window and his heart crying, *"Come and take me away."* He forgot about that for a while as he grew too big to let anyone make him submit to all that anymore. Until

Helen, until they had found themselves irresistibly drawn into her bed, into each other, sharing their excessive stimulation, following pleasure to ecstatic madness. Then he knew that she was his fondest wish come true and that she had come at last to take him away.

Then he heard the door open slowly behind him. It was the last thing he ever heard.

12

Looking back over the months, Soames had to admit that even evil had its pleasant side. She had done a fantastic job on Averill. She'd seduced him with everything from a leather jacket to a new Oldsmobile to an orgy of drug-enhanced pleasures.

He was putty, soft taffy in her fingers. She had been absolutely right about him. He was living in a frenzy of excitation exacerbated by fundamentalist Christian denial. Denial had so overstrained his ability to suppress his human appetites that he had absolutely no control over them. He was also ignorant, greedy and ego-driven. The fool didn't have a clue. He was hers. He had no chance against her persuasive manipulations. She had netted and bagged and twisted him.

She had guessed from the first day he came to see

Henri about the church that Averill was her man. He had that greasy weasel look about him, the shifting eyes and insidious sensuality of the abused. It took one to know one, didn't it? Something familiar smoldered in him, something tightly wound and inevitable seeped through his toothy grins and enervated laughs.

He was always aware of his flesh. He assumed the rest of the world was as well. His clothing was always a little tight here, a little loose there; there was always something shiny or flimsy or opaque about it. He was in a perpetual state of seduction—the way those whose innocence has been stolen always are. He was overwrought with sensing, trapped in his futile pursuit of those who had robbed him. Yet he was ignorant of all that, and worse, mortified by his physical impulses, ashamed and terrified—so distraught with his quivering need that he had turned in desperation to the constraints of hard-shell Puritanism.

If Henri was the dull and sexless lover, thrashing about for a few insensate minutes with his ego, Averill would be that driven animal, that wildly dominant paramour, helpless once aroused to moderate his lust until he and his partner were numb, depleted and bruised.

She was right. From their first time back in September, Averill had been that tender and terrible husband she dreaded and craved. He was insatiable. She was something less than human with him, she was depraved and monstrous and she horrified herself, but she was, from the moment he touched her until he withdrew—sometimes hours later—alive.

Nor was she so devastated by it all to play her part. It was Averill's mind she pleasured with sighs and promises. It was his abuse she molded with her whimpers, his sickness she nurtured with her cries of delight. He came to her against his will. She knew, if he never figured it out, that his lust was a mask for his darker need to violate his own morality, to shame himself with increasing frequency, to drive himself lower and lower into an abyss of self-loathing until he could no longer bear the pain of his disgusting nature, and kill himself.

By now Averill Sayres was deep into the fog and shadows of the thrilling fur-lined trap she had set for him.

"Henri's not coming home for Thanksgiving," she had told him a little over a week ago. They were riding around in the new Cutlass she had given him as an early Christmas present.

"So we'll spend it together." Averill grinned.

"I don't need Henri's money," she lied. "I have my own."

"Money don't matter to me," he said flatly.

"You're a man of God," she concurred, ripping the twenty-six-thousand-dollar price tag off the passenger-side window. Then she told him about her dream. She wanted to live on the Pacific Coast in a modern house set on a tall cliff with every room open toward the ocean. She wanted to spend her whole life with Averill, and—who knew?—maybe, God willing, their children too.

She told him, knowing he was pretending to go along with it, knowing she had no such dream, not for him, though they would have a future, a long golden slide into the lake of fire after he had helped her do what had to be done.

13

SUNDAY, APRIL 23, 2000
5:17 P.M.

She heard a car.

The afternoon had passed like the Dark Ages. She went half-crazy—running to the front porch every time a green persimmon plopped on the roof. She couldn't stop herself. She was out the door at every thud or scrape or fluttering in the trees. Of course, it was guilt—that pernicious dread of getting caught. Though it didn't make sense. Getting caught was the point. She had full intentions of facing justice. She had no plans to flee, attempt to cover her tracks or otherwise circumvent her inevitable trial and conviction.

It was by those means, and only by those means, that Tess would exist—if only in the past tense.

She had checked the kitchen clock at ten-minute intervals. At seventeen minutes past five she was standing in the kitchen and she heard a car engine whine as it climbed the hill. She had hardly heard a soul on the road since Averill had gotten up from the table and walked out the front door at fourteen minutes before two.

He had inhaled two slices of the chocolate cake while she cleared the dining room table. She had set the rest of the poisoned cake on top of the clothes extractor. Yet it wasn't there when he asked for his dessert. It wasn't anywhere. She had to slice the harmless version that was sitting on the kitchen table. Earlier she had watched Winky open the car door for Audena because her hands were full. Leona had given her a dish, a porcelain casserole that had belonged to Averill's mother. It was a cheap glass baking dish and the rim was chipped. Audena had somehow managed to set it on the stove and abscond with the deadly torte instead.

Not dreaming there was a remote chance that anyone but Averill would consume the heavy chocolate pastry, Leona had emptied the carton of Rat Zap into the filling, rendering her dessert lethal enough to wipe out a platoon.

She had watched Averill cross the road and move another hundred yards uphill to his church. She had counted on that. It was his habit to spend Sunday afternoons in his study behind the sanctuary. It was a country church, way up an old clay logging road that wound through the woods another half a mile before it petered out. Odds were very strong that there wouldn't be another soul on that road until Wednesday evening when the choir practiced. She had counted very heavily on all of that.

As soon as Averill was out of earshot, she had ransacked her desk in an effort to locate Audena's phone number. Failing that, she tried calling information. As it happened, she learned that there were two Winky Hodges listed in Calhoun County. Both had answering machines, so both were warned that her chocolate cake would be the last dessert either might ever eat. She didn't waste money on long-distance explanations either.

Now the situation swallowed her last bit of sense. She'd poisoned the stupid bastard. She'd murdered him. Why? She hated this. Now she had lost the point, the reason why it had been so necessary. Now she couldn't quite grasp the triumph of her execution. She was dangerous. She deserved to die. It was all turning against her now. The sky and the woods were laughing at her. She thought of him gagging on his own blood, his flesh on fire, the hopeless torment.

Maybe there was still time. Maybe. She was dizzy. She had to sit down. Maybe she had poisoned herself! Or Averill had caught on to her and switched the dishes. She could hear him laughing. Her flesh crawled. He was in the living room. She made herself go look. No. No, it wasn't Averill. It was the television. Some jungle movie. She needed a drink. She found the bourbon under the back steps. She sat down on the wooden stairs and took several sips straight from the bottle. She sat there for ten minutes. Then she got up. She had to do something. Anything.

One of the McFayes had brought her two pints of raspberries from the farmers market down in Tupelo. She couldn't bear to think of them covered with mold and tossed out by one of the churchwomen. She put a cobbler together and threw it in the oven. While it baked, she dragged a chair over to the chimney behind the stove, climbed up on it and found the bundle of papers tucked in a little hollow at the back. They were letters she had written to Ty during her first six months here and then never mailed. She took them out back into the far end of the garden and burned them. Then she went back inside the house and pulled the cobbler out of the oven and left it on the burners to cool.

She ran a bath, digging out her last bar of lavender soap and holding it under the faucet to dissolve every bit of it. As she luxuriated in the warm, scented water, she made a mental list of the most important things. While the water was running she thought she heard the car. She turned it off and listened. Nope. Just the birds and creaking limbs of a billion hardwoods. She was the only person for miles. She didn't count Averill stone dead on the floor of his study.

When she had dried and dressed herself, she cut a piece of cobbler. She was disappointed. The filling had a bitter metallic aftertaste. Somewhere between the produce farm and her kitchen those berries had spent time in a copper bowl.

Her mother's octagon-shaped English porcelain dinnerware was packed and stored in the attic, all but the teapot, which she kept in the glass cabinet in the living room. It was an old set when her mother bought it at a flea market before Leona was born. She wanted to give it to a cute young couple she'd seen at church. She wrote a note describing all that and stuck it inside of an envelope with their names on it. She left it on the front hall table. She left another envelope in the same place. It contained a note to a neighbor's boy about taking the gray tabby cat that had lived under the house since late winter.

She went out onto the front porch to enjoy the peace of the blue-gray twilight and sat down to wait for that car.

"The prosecutor will paint me as a woman scorned," she thought. "He'll have me an avenging wife."

Well, let him. When he was finished, she'd get to have her say. She'd have a solid forum in which to tell the whole truth at last. No, that wouldn't save her life. The jury wasn't going to give her any out. No plea bargain. There was no dancing around that. Still, the inconceivable truth would be heard and written down as unalterable legal record.

Yes, it would be written down unproven, recorded as testimony, not fact. It would form her rationale for the crime of poisoning her husband. Some would say it was a lie or a delusion or a plea for sympathy. What did that matter? Not one whit—as long as it was said aloud in a public forum and recorded in perpetuity. It would go down as "alleged." Yet someone would hear or read it sooner or later and believe it. It was the truth. Truth wound its way. Yes, it grew as slowly as imported boxwood. But it was inevitable. It got said, told, repeated and accepted at some point. Even her unsubstantiated truth, scribbled by a court reporter who would probably assume she was lying.

"They'll execute me," she said to herself with a shrug, "but I won't die. They'll come into my house. They'll pitch my afghan and the photograph of Mama and Daddy at the New York World's Fair and my high school graduation portrait on the trash. They'll tear my clothes for rags. Yet they won't rid this world of my meaning. Nor will they be able to pervert or misconstrue it."

A life had to matter, even the briefest and least significant. No matter how small, or how quickly it was here and gone, no matter if it had no real effect on the world. No matter if it was tiny enough to hide inside the hollow of a leaf. So she was going to let the world denounce her as a satanic hag all the way to the gas chamber.

She knew she well might avoid execution if she made a big show of remorse and pled temporary insanity. No jury was going to send a young woman to death row if they had any other option. However, she wasn't sorry. She felt no remorse. If what she had done was reprehensible, then she was the reprehensible sort. Yes, she understood that holding on to her fury at Averill had infected her with his depravity. Taking his life was her initiation into his animal kind.

It didn't make her regret what she had done.

If that meant she was insane, then it wasn't temporary. Beyond that she had never lost sight of the consequences she would face. Sorry? Sorry was for cowards. Remorse would imply that there was some part of what Averill did that could be justified. Remorse was letting the world cover his evil with roses. Remorse made her more savage than Averill. It was asking a morally squeamish legal system to turn away from a slain innocent in exchange for sparing Leona's life. As if she was willing to continue living, an amoral worm, caged and useless in a meaningless world.

No. Let them keep their justice. The terrible stone had been lifted off her heart and shoulders. It was all over. She had nothing else to add to this world. She had accomplished her dream. She was Tess's mother. Tess was now created and part of this world. She wanted nothing else from it. She was done.

Leona had never even held her. She couldn't say for sure that her hair was red or brown. She never saw her eyes. Tess hadn't been there long enough to open them. Leona was naked and bleeding in the snow, a dying animal set upon by predators while Tess was born. She lay there unconscious, seeping afterbirth, her forehead black and swollen from the fall. She had to take it on faith about Tess's wavy yellow-red hair like queens of England. She had only seen a round filmy dark wetness. And that was all a flash.

What harm could it have done to let Leona hold her baby a moment before she blacked out there on the icy road? What monstrous cruelty wouldn't let a mother hold her infant? Leona had seen her ghost in the woods once. Seen the wavy yellow-red hair that she took on faith, which had already faded in her imagination, faded with her dying faith in everything.

She had gotten used to thinking about seeing Tess with her bright copper hair in the woods—Tess, her baby, quiet and peering at her from the arms of death. She had gotten too used to it to bother reminding herself that it had been in a dream.

It was no dream that she had been Tess's mother. And now she would speak in a great forum. She would hold her fat, ginger-freckled infant duchess up before a crowd. She would hollow out a niche for Tess and secure her being against people's obliterating indifference.

". . . *hereby sentenced to die*," the judge would say, and she would detest the immutable meaning of his words. But she'd take the opportunity to turn around so that the reporters could hear her. "What does that matter? It's a very small sum to pay for this singing heart and the happiness to say I'm Tess's mother at last and what mother would hesitate to die to ensure that her child will, if not live, then at least exist in people's minds." Not real flesh, no, but the past perfect fact established.

Then she heard Tess cry. She was dreaming. No. She had closed her eyes, but she was still awake on the porch and the sound had come from the church. Not Tess at all, but Averill, distant and muted, calling her name. No. She'd heard no such thing. It was that infernal mewing catbird in the sweet gum tree across the road. How many times had its mournful mewing turned itself into someone calling her name? She had to grab something real, something here and now, like the time: 5:17. And that low sound. It was a car. Five-seventeen and a car was coming.

Five-seventeen and a car was coming and Averill was lying on his study floor up at that church deader than a brick-mason's level. There was no way, no chance that he was still alive. Yet every few minutes the twitter of a sparrow was all it took to convince her the dead could walk. Now the boding whine of that fast-moving car. It was past the house and out of sight by the time she reached the front porch. It seemed to pick up speed as it passed. This was the last house before the road petered out half a mile beyond the church.

Teenagers, probably.

Sooner or later that car had to come back. She'd keep a listen. She was pretty sure it was teenagers, though. That's all it ever was. Getting themselves stuck for life. Would she be at the end of her own lonely road now if she hadn't believed in Tyler Crockett's sweet lies? Sad how there wasn't any magic set of words to explain it to them. How many skinny kids had passed this place on their way into that tender forest of illusions? Sometimes it wasn't even half an hour before they were headed back toward town. How would anyone ever convince those dewy-eyed girls that they had just imprisoned themselves for the rest of their lives?

Oh, it made her shake with frustration. She wanted to shout at them as they passed, "Baby, he don't want you now. He wants to spend the rest of the night telling his buddies all about it. Not that a one of them will remember a word of his bragging when you're starting to show."

Time and event turned over on themselves that afternoon. Leona seemed to be observing, experiencing and reliving every moment. Somehow in all of it she had gone down to the road from the porch to wait for the police and seen the silver Lincoln fly past the house. Soames had gotten the message after all. Minutes before she heard the car—or was it days—Leona had picked up the telephone and confessed everything into Soames's answering machine. No doubt she'd raced over, hoping against hope that she could still save him.

Now Leona heard the church doors screech open. They were heavy and they wouldn't close unless she pulled them shut behind her. So Leona knew by the silence and the diminishing footsteps on the hardwood floor that Soames was hurrying. Then there was a scream. He must have bled through the eyes. They said all of Tilly Crowe's victims did. Next she heard a thud. Or a plop maybe. She must have knocked one of Averill's reference books off the arm of his chair. Now Leona heard her frightened feet on the gravel. Now her car door made that heavenly, heavy gloop sound. Now the whoosh of a fine automobile engine starting. In seconds the Lincoln pulled onto the dirt road and headed toward Leona.

"He's not worth killing, sugar," Soames had so often repeated. "Rare is the man who is."

Leona waved to reassure the poor, startled thing, but Soames didn't slow down. In fact, Soames didn't act like she saw her. Instead, she hit the gas and the Lincoln fishtailed through the silt where the driveway met the road. It came on so fast that Leona had to jump backward to avoid being hit. Before she was back on her feet, the car had sailed down the hill and out of sight.

Two things Leona knew. The first was that Soames had seen her leap back. Of course she'd seen her. The second was that Soames would never deliberately hurt her. Then why hadn't she stopped? That didn't take a whole brain to figure out. Hadn't Leona just confessed to committing murder? Soames was doing the right thing. She had gone to see if by chance she could still help Averill. Then, seeing that it was too late, she had gone to get the law. If she had done otherwise, if she had come straight to Leona first, Soames would be burdened with all kinds of legal ropes and chains that implicated her.

She'd as much as warned Leona not to go off of her nut and do something she'd regret. Leona had all but assured her that she was already way off her nut and she wouldn't have the slightest regret. Soames knew why. Soames knew everything. Soames had landed in the hapless seat of mother confessor, sister, advisor and friend. Leona trusted Soames more than she trusted herself.

The last thing Leona wanted to do was see her friend mired down in all of this.

14

Soames hit the gas when she saw Leona at the end of the driveway—pure instinct. She could have cheerfully mowed down the stupid bitch. She'd screw up a rotten egg, that one. Ignorance really must be bliss. Or maybe the puritanical slut was so bent on her next roll with her redneck lover that she didn't know confectioners' sugar when it stuck to her fingers. The car skidded. She had to slow down. Now, that would solve her problems, running herself into an oak tree at ninety miles an hour.

She had to think. She had no time to think. Her first impulse was to reload her small ivory pistol and head over to Helen Brisbane's house. It was a thousand-percent certainty that Helen would point fingers at Soames. Not that Soames hadn't just pointed one long, straight finger at herself. Now she had to get her head on straight. She had to. Where to first? The sheriff? Leona? Or should she call the county paramedic unit?

No. No, not the last option. He was dead. There was no point in having a big rescue drama up this country road. Go home. Keep shut. Press her luck one more time? The best lies always ran as parallel to the facts as you could get them. She had Leona's confession on her answering machine. She'd admitted poisoning him and why she'd done it. What did Soames have to worry about? How much of the truth could she salvage?

Leona called to say she'd poisoned Averill and wanted Soames to drive her into the sheriff's office. But Averill was still alive when Soames got there. She could sail through a lie detector on that part of it. Then her heart sank because any nut deputy sheriff would ask her why at that point she didn't call for help.

Because Leona said that she already had?

No. Not on her answering machine tape.

She looked at her watch. Leona's call had come thirty-three minutes ago. Her machine always gave the date and the time of each message. Why couldn't she think?

Bingo! She wasn't home when the call came. In fact, she had just gotten it. She was on her way over to the church to see if Averill was all right. Perfect! Would a murderer phone the law to announce she was on her way to shoot someone? No. In thirty seconds she was at the crossroads store, talking into the pay phone.

"Orpheus County Sheriff's Office."

"Blue Hudson, please."

"Speaking."

"Blue, this is Soames Churchill. I'm afraid we have a situation out here. . . ."

*   *   *

Sundays were hell on a divorced man who lived three thousand miles away from his kids. It had been a long one for Blue. He'd spent the whole day alone in the county sheriff's office covering the phones. He didn't see why he should take some poor deputy away from his family to twiddle his thumbs in the smelly courthouse all day long. Besides, it was a kind of penance the way he saw it, an obligation he had. Any man stupid enough to love and lose twice owed himself a strong dose of humility.

Blue was the sheriff. "Interim sheriff," it said on his contract. His predecessor, seventy-four-year-old Warren Meeks, had broken his hip in a fall during last winter's big ice storm. Blue, who was exactly fifty years younger than Sheriff Meeks, was appointed when the board of supervisors deadlocked on their first two choices for the job.

Twenty-four was a little green to wear a silver star. It was only supposed to be temporary. Meeks had been expected to be back at work within six weeks. Instead the poor man had lain in bed for three months growing weaker and weaker until pneumonia set in and he died. In the meantime the young sheriff hadn't disgraced himself. So no one saw the harm in letting him keep the job until a new lawman could be elected in July.

"He's finally driven her to do it, Blue."

What a bitch. Of course, Blue understood Soames. At least to the extent that she meant Leona had done something bad to Averill. However, Leona was still legally married and what was, or had been, between Blue and Leona wasn't meant for publication. Soames was hoping Blue would let her in on it. He didn't know why. Though he knew her well enough not to give her the benefit of any doubt.

"Who's calling?"

"Soames."

"What seems to be the problem?"

Soames made an indignant snorting sound. Blue ignored it. He couldn't stand Soames Churchill. Soames was a waste of fine Southern womanhood, in his estimation. She was one of those gorgeous, leggy redheads who could walk across the courthouse lawn on a dead August afternoon and create more fireworks than a Fourth of July parade. Seeing her from a few yards, a man couldn't possibly deny her anything. Stuck in the same room with her for more than five minutes, however, Blue Hudson would start promising God that he'd become a priest if He'd only make Soames go away.

"Leona Sayres has poisoned her husband, Averill."

It ran all over Soames, playing like that, pretending she didn't know Blue Hudson and Leona Sayres had been acting like two slippery mongrel dogs in heat. Like Blue Hudson didn't know about her and Averill, for that matter. The worst two things a person could say were what they knew and what they meant.

"She what?"

"She called me in a panic, left me a message about half an hour ago. I'm on my way over there now."

"Over where?"

"The church."

"You mean on purpose?"

" 'S what she says."

All he could do was shake and pray to God it wasn't true. Soames was given to wild exaggerations. This had to be one of them. Until six weeks ago, Leona had been all set to walk away from Averill Sayres and marry him. There was no love lost between Leona and Averill, but to the best of his knowledge they had no deep-seated animosity between them either.

Nothing made any sense. Nothing had since Leona

turned cool. He'd never figure it out. One minute they were planning to spend the rest of their lives together; the next she was a piece of stone—unreachable, inscrutable, indifferent to his shocked pleas. Something had happened, something terrible, something that changed everything. One day, she had told him, one day he'd understand that she was powerless. One day he'd realize that she had spared him much greater sorrow than they both felt at their parting.

It was different this time. It wasn't the sharp bleeding agony he'd felt when he and Lucy split up. That was guilt at having failed as a husband and fear of inadequacy and the terror of loneliness and all kinds of things. This wasn't anything like that. There was less self-pity this time. There was no regret or recrimination. This had been more like a constant sick feeling, a nagging sense that Leona was in danger or that she'd had some kind of mental breakdown.

He'd had a lot of ego wrapped up in his hard parting from Lucy. There was none of that with Leona. He couldn't regret much either one of them had done or been to each other. He'd loved her to the best of his ability in every way a man could love a woman. He still did. He'd been worried sick about her. He'd been waiting in a kind of personal hell for something to happen, something to explain it for him.

So this had to be part of that. Leona poisoned Averill? Deliberately. Could that possibly be so?

In the car on the road up Whitsunday Hill, he kept thinking about the kids. Lucy had pulled one last dirty trick, taking off for California with Doctor Kildare and the two younger kids. Their daughter Nancy, she said, wouldn't adjust well to the move so soon after being placed in the Home for Juvenile Incurables. Nancy she left behind, like Blue and the rest of the trash he found all over the house after she moved out.

He was supposed to be spending this month in California. Back in the winter he and Leona had talked about using part of the trip as a honeymoon.

At the crossroads store he veered left, and the road turned to gravel as he began the long climb up the hill. It seemed like some last, impossible mountain. He couldn't shake the godforsaken feeling that the end of everything was waiting two miles above him in the opaque April leaves. It was all so bleak and pointless now. He'd faced up to a million youthful mistakes by now. He'd learned a thousand lessons the hard way. He'd looked at himself from the rest of the world's point of view and tried like hell to change.

Why then was he left with this goddamned nothingness? Why were the woman and the children he loved so far apart and out of his reach? What was the sense of doing your best if the wind had its own ideas? God, he prayed, God, God, God, please tell me this is all some bad joke. Let this be one more of Soames Churchill's dramas. She was an original, he'd give her that. Blue had often thought he'd love to see whatever swamp or hollow she had crawled out of. Henri Churchill's money would never completely erase its impact on her. Then Blue remembered how old Sheriff Meeks had gone to his grave believing Soames had murdered Henri. There was all kinds of speculation when he died in a hunting accident. Blue hadn't been in law enforcement back then. He remembered thinking, like most people, that Henri was just one more dandified idiot who had no business toting a loaded rifle.

Blue was just below the Sayres place. A cloud of dust at the crest of a vine-covered knoll told him a car was coming. He lifted the radio to call for backup.

15

SUNDAY, APRIL 23, 2000
5:46 P.M.

The Lincoln roared into the driveway and came within a hair of hitting the rear bumper of Averill's Cutlass before it jerked to a sudden stop. Soames leapt out of the car and raced to Leona.

"I'm sorry I didn't stop, honey. I just had to think." Tears streamed down her cheeks. She was shaking. "No one with a heart will ever blame you," she said. Then she threw her arms around Leona and squeezed the air out of her. "Blue's coming."

Leona stared at her, incredulous. Blue couldn't possibly come. Blue was on the other side of the country in California visiting his kids. He'd left on Friday night, the fourteenth of April. Wouldn't she know? She had once thought she'd be on the plane with him. She had altered her plans with his in mind. She had deliberately

scheduled this thing so that she would be in jail await-
ing trial before he knew anything about it. She didn't
want him to try to be a hero. This was a culprit he'd
never apprehend. He'd get himself into a lot of trouble,
apt as not lose his job, and then for his trouble he'd get
to watch the state of Mississippi execute her.

"Blue's in Big Sur, California."

"He didn't go."

"Of course he did."

"If you went to town more than once a year, you'd
know Warren Meeks was dead."

"Who?"

"County sheriff for the last sixteen years!"

"Huh?"

"They appointed Blue to finish his term. He didn't go."

It was as if Leona had suddenly found herself sealed
inside a box made of glass six inches thick. She was
screaming, ripping her vocal cords out, but the rest of
the world, which was at that moment Soames Churchill,
couldn't hear her. In fact, Soames sounded miles away
as she repeated her name.

"Leona! Leona!" Soames was shaking her with both
hands on her shoulders.

Gradually Leona started to feel nauseous and Soames's
voice became louder.

"Stop it!"

Soames released her and Leona steadied herself
against a porch post.

"Sit down, Leona. I'll get you a sweater." Soames
practically shoved Leona into a chair on the porch and
then stepped over her as she hurtled herself into the
house. Through the open bedroom window Leona could
hear her opening and closing bureau drawers. She tried
to speak, to explain to Soames that she wasn't shaking

with cold. It was irony or disgust or dread of seeing
Blue's car pull into the driveway.

Then she heard Soames pick up the telephone and
dial a long-distance number. She overheard enough to
get the salient points. Soames was talking to a criminal
lawyer up at Memphis, giving him the gist of the situation and pleading with him to take the case.

"No, Frankie, she can't afford you, but she's my best
friend and I can. . . ."

Strange, but Leona wasn't as touched by Soames's
generosity as she wanted to be. It was almost as if she
was thinking—wait, and see. Soames had a way of in-
undating you with her largesse. Then a day or a week
later you'd see how it all worked out more in Soames's
favor than your own.

"Yes, I know you're expensive. You're the best, aren't
you?"

It was probably just her mood and the bizarre patina
on everything right now, but Leona felt as if the call had
somehow been staged for her benefit. Soames did all
the things people do when they care, but she didn't
seem to feel anything. It was as if she thought the doing
itself would make the reason for it happen.

"Frank Isom is coming to see you in the morning."

"You mean in jail?"

"I'm afraid I do, honey."

"The judge will appoint me a lawyer."

Soames's hollow laugh grated Leona's ears.

She filled Leona in on what to expect. Frank had instructed Soames to tell the law what she'd discovered
up at the church. Period. Soames was to offer no specu-
lations as to the cause of death. Then Soames lost all
her verve and gave Leona another hug. Leona could see
over Soames's shoulder and into the enormous open kid

leather bag that hung by a thin strap almost to her ankles.

It always looked like a portable salon and spa. Nestled
among the sachet and Elizabeth Arden products she noticed the small, ivory-handled pistol that Soames carried everywhere. It was an antique dueling weapon. She
had a pair of them, one of which she had tried count-
less times to give to Leona. It got to be a joke. Leona
would open the refrigerator and there the damned thing
would be. Or she'd recoil at the unexpected cold metal
against her fingers when she reached into her purse.
Soames liked to wear expensive jewelry. "Sugar, they'll
slice my ears and sell them for five grand apiece," she
would say, referring to the diamond studs she never removed. God alone knew what they'd get for her neck
and wrists. She also carried heavy cash. She was forever
pulling a paper Bank of Orpheus envelope out of her
purse and digging through a thick stack of hundreds.
She wasn't exactly hiding her fortune under a bushel.

All well and good for her rich eccentric friend. Leona
didn't have anything to steal. She was more afraid of
guns than she was of thugs and muggers.

Now Soames had that look she wore whenever she
was about to get down to the heart of the matter.

"What?"

"It was that rat poison you bought in Memphis last
month, wasn't it?"

"Yes."

Leona had told Soames what she was thinking about
doing. It had seemed a natural thing to do. It was
Soames who had told Leona that Averill had broken
down and confessed to her that he had killed the baby.

"I meant to keep you out of this, Soames. I should
have thought. . . ."

"I'm going down with your ship, baby."

"You aren't part of this."

"I knew what I was doing."

"You didn't do anything, except try to help me."

"I murdered him, Leona. We both did, I guess."

"Talk sense!"

Soames turned dark red. Even her eyes were cloudy and bloodshot. She looked very old. She turned slowly to touch Leona's chin.

"Sit down."

"It has nothing to do with you."

"I shot him, Leona. I killed him."

16

SUNDAY, APRIL 23, 2000
6:00 P.M.

When Leona heard Soames say that she had shot
Averill, everything she had stored in her head tore apart
like strands of cotton candy—shapes, sounds, thoughts,
past and present. Nothing held any further meaning.
Nothing related or connected. Coincidence ruled. Reality
had turned into the ultimate fantasy.

"Leona, are you listening to me?"

"No."

"I said you miscalculated. The poison wasn't as fast or
lethal as you thought it was." When she went in the
church, Soames went on, she had found Averill rolling on
his study floor in dementia. He was kicking and clutching
his throat and choking with vomit. He thought Soames
was some demon who'd come to take him to hell. He was
soaked with sweat and screaming with pain.

All the while Soames was talking to her, Leona couldn't help marveling at her demeanor. In spite of her ghastly encounter, she seemed as calm as Christmas Eve.

"The bastard deserved every second of his torture."

"He begged me to shoot him, Leona." Her iron façade was finally cracking. Averill had pleaded with her, begged her to end his torture. "So help me God, I did," she finished, breaking down in heaving sobs.

Unreality had triumphed. Soames had shot and killed Averill while he was dying of all the rat poison Leona had fed him. Soames was a heaving mass of hysteria and remorse.

Leona didn't believe a single tear, but she had no concrete reason not to. What made Leona judge and jury over Soames's motives and emotions? It was Leona who had quit feeling. Leona was dispassionate about lives, her own and other people's. Around and around her thoughts ran like the leopard chasing its own tail around a pole in the childhood story. Except that the leopard eventually turned into butter. Personally Leona didn't expect any such golden transformation.

Now Leona did what she had been raised to do. She studied the moment for some opportunity, no matter how small, some measurable good she might accomplish. It had been her father's most repeated advice. Strange that she chose this moment to test it.

"You did no such thing," she said. "I did."

"He was so pitiful. He didn't look or sound human. More like an animal in agony."

"He was dead when you found him. Now that's all."

Why should Soames go to prison for an act of compassion? Leona was the killer. She lifted the weapon out of Soames's purse and walked into the bedroom, where she stuck it into the toe of one of her winter boots.

"Go wash your face, Soames."

They had traded places. Leona was the stronger now. Leona was telling her what to do. There was nothing left to argue, nothing to determine or attempt. She felt grateful for the chance to do this bit of good in the middle of it all. Soames went into the bathroom. Things kept turning inside out; things always had one more layer to peel away. One thing invariably reversed or reverted into another. Nothing ever kept its shape or color or place or outline or meaning. No matter what a thing meant today, it would have an entirely new meaning tomorrow.

Leona almost felt sorry for Soames. She felt as if she had abandoned her. Soames was still part of the normal world. She had to go on bloodying her knees and fighting for her square foot of terra firma. Soames had to keep holding up her lonely existence. She had to fend off an eternal army of lawyers and tax men and bankers whose lives amounted to robbing people like her. Leona had done all her meager business. She was experiencing the unexpected peace reserved for those who surrender everything and seek nothing. She had forked over all her hopes and despairs in exchange for this even emptiness.

She and life had used all their tricks on each other. She and life had failed each other in the end. She hadn't been resourceful or clever enough to figure out its meaning. While life hadn't turned any of its dark clouds inside out to show her any sterling-silver revelations.

In a few minutes Soames was back. So was her self-confidence. She had accepted Leona's decision. It would free her to take charge of Leona's defense.

"Honey, Frank Isom is God's other son. The man never loses a case."

Leona nodded. There was no sense riling Soames any more than she already was. She had no intentions of asking any such man to defend her case. Nor was she inclined to go hoarse trying to make Soames see why she had to lose in court.

"Don't you say one word to Blue Hudson unless Frank tells you to."

What could she say to Blue? He was the last person she wanted to involve in this. How else could she have hurt him by breaking up? She wouldn't have gone through with it if she hadn't felt certain that Blue was in California. She had waited until he was out of town. That way he wouldn't be involved in the investigation or her arrest. She had intended to sign her confession and instruct her lawyer to enter a guilty plea before Blue got back and destroyed himself trying to save her.

It had taken more resolve to tell Blue that it was over than it had to poison Averill. Of course she couldn't tell him the real reason why they couldn't love each other. She couldn't say that it was because she knew that Averill had murdered her baby and she was going to kill him. Blue would have locked her up in the county jail to stop her. Then he would've ruined his career trying to prove what Averill had done. He would have demanded they exhume the infant's remains and conduct a second inquest. They'd already had their inquest and called it a stillbirth. What was going to make them change their minds now? As if Averill wouldn't dissolve into the atmosphere at the first hint of suspicion.

Tess would be forgotten, or worse, remembered as the pathetic and wishful delusion of a grief-crazed

mother. It would ruin Blue and it would rob Leona of
her only means to do anything for her child.

It had been an awful scene between Leona and
Blue. He knew she was lying. He had gotten her within
a hair of breaking down and admitting the truth. He finally left, but not before he said that this was far from
over. Well, it was all over now, Baby Blue. At least he'd
finally know why.

Not why she had to do it. Leona was already beginning to think no one outside of her shoes would understand the forces she had obeyed. Yet Blue would see
that she had protected him and his career by breaking it
off when she did. He'd comprehend the fact that what
she had done wasn't by choice. It was the only thing she
could do to keep her universe from melting into chaos.
If there had been two sane alternatives, she would have
chosen him.

"I mean it, Leona," Soames repeated. "Not one word
to Blue."

What a wonder Leona had created. What detailed
misery and mayhem she had baked into her blue-ribbon
casseroles! She had taken every possible precaution.
For all she knew she'd managed to put Averill's innocent sister and brother-in-law in hell with him. She'd
arranged for her best friend to be the poor soul to find
him, and now Soames was up to her neck in a hopeless
drama to save her. Now Blue, who always did exactly
what he said he would, when and how he said he
would—Blue, who'd had his plane ticket and hotel
reservations for months—was on his way.

Blue, who said she was a sorceress because she'd
broken the curse on him and resurrected him, body and
soul—Blue, who had shot up out of the hopeless dark

and reignited the stars—Blue was on his way to investigate, to interrogate and charge and arrest her. Blue's evidence and testimony would convict and condemn her to death.

She couldn't sit still with all that floating around her. She had to leap out the door and into the yard. She had to swirl around and around and careen with dizziness and terrible laughter. She skinned her knees when she finally fell over. They bled a lot. It was very painful. That made her guffaw even more. Soames was crying and stiff and trying to stay calm and in charge, trying to think, which was a little grandiose with the earth splitting and Averill floating past.

Then something sent Leona into a reeling purple silence. At first it sounded like a baby's cry, but in a moment she realized for the millionth time that was only that damned catbird in the sweet gum tree by the cemetery.

17

It was almost dark. There was all kinds of activity up and down the road now. Two county sheriff's cars and an ambulance had flown past and turned into the churchyard. Leona and Soames could hear all kinds of voices and ruckus. Fifteen minutes later Blue's Jeep stopped in front of the house. The ambulance came back. They could see the body wrapped in blankets and lying on a stretcher in back. The ambulance was all lit up inside like a macabre window display. Blue got out of his car and talked to the driver. The ambulance moved on. They could still hear plenty of activity up at the church. Word was getting around. Several church members rode past during the next ten minutes.

A highway patrolman came up on the porch and

knocked at the screen. He asked Soames to come with him, which she did. Leona figured they didn't want Soames to get hurt if they had to use force during her arrest. Things got quiet. Then Blue's familiar light, steady boot heels clipped up the porch steps. He knocked. He tugged the screen door open. Then he came inside.

Each felt the other must be made of steel at that moment. Neither one of them moved or spoke. They just looked at each other, two metal masks of resolute opposition. Hiding deep inside each of them was the unmitigated will to sacrifice everything to save the other.

"Why aren't you in California?"

"Tell me everything you've done since you got out of church this morning."

"You can't investigate this."

It was dusky, ethereal. Everything was blurred as if seen through gauze; though iridescent too, like frost-covered leaves on a clear night or the glistening fruit she coated with sugar and arranged with waxy leaves and camellias in silver bowls for wedding receptions and rehearsal dinners. Lovely, it was life's unexpected last crumb of chocolate truffle. They sat in total silence.

With nothing to be done about anything, Leona told herself it was better to breathe in this moment, to savor his lime scent, and the unexpected pleasure of Blue's nearness. For all her folly and youth, Leona would take some memories with her out of this world.

She had surrendered certain rights with her decision to visit justice on Averill. One of them was regret for things that might have been. She realized now that she had developed the ability to control certain feelings and to direct them toward whatever made the most appropriate sense. Blue's visit reminded her that she had an enormous potential for loving him. Yet there was no possibility of realizing it. So she experienced the butterfly he stirred in her breast for all the present-tense happiness it gave her.

She became aware that it was cool in the room. She went to shut the door. As she peered out across the porch, she realized that the scene on the road had faded away. Now it felt like any other night.

"Where'd everybody go?"

"I told them to clear the area," he said. "I'm the sheriff. Remember?"

"That must have the whole town awake."

"Let's talk turkey, Leona."

He'd been a highway patrolman before he became sheriff. He had experienced the creeping unreality of highway wrecks, held hands with the dying, pulled mothers away from the dismembered remnants of their children and watched helpless as an explosion engulfed a trapped victim in his screaming hell. He had followed the circuitous and clever trails of killers and child molesters and bank robbers to innocent-looking American dream houses with manicured lawns. He had arrested men in their Sunday suits as they stepped out of church into the sunshine.

There were times when he lay sleepless with knots in his stomach waiting for the hard experiences of the previous day's work to let go of him. Yet he always came back around to the feeling he'd done some piece of good. He'd given a dying kid comfort or locked away some malevolent threat to innocent people. He understood law enforcement. He knew what it meant to protect and to serve.

Until tonight. Now he didn't know the meaning of

anything. It was ignorant to divide the world into good and bad people, not at least based on their records of arrest and convictions. So-called law-abiding people perpetrated all types of violence and robberies against each other and never felt the threat of arrest and prosecution. Instead they died in their sleep at age a hundred and three. There were a thousand kinds of justice. In the end it was the time they did on earth that brought most people to the limits of their immoralities. It was breathing in and out, not prison, that rehabilitated most dishonest souls.

"Tell me everything, Leona."

"I thought you were in California, I . . ."

"Well, I'm not."

"Call someone else to handle this!"

"Tell me everything, Leona."

"Averill murdered my baby, so I killed him."

The particulars, as Leona imparted them, were of little interest to Blue. He was struggling with another irrefutable fact. He should have fought harder to be with her. He should have been more vigilant. Didn't he know she was living in a precarious situation? What was he thinking when he agreed with Leona that they had plenty of time?

He told himself that he was pulling the pieces of his life together after his divorce. His appointment to the office of county sheriff had seemed the most obvious course to follow. He put his focus on getting himself elected the following summer. It was a bitter race. The other two candidates made a mockery of his divorce. He wouldn't risk gossip about him and a married preacher's wife. He took it slow. He got sidetracked with criminology courses at night down at the university.

"It's as much my fault as yours, Leona."

She didn't acknowledge his remark. Though everything about her demeanor told him this was why she had insisted that they were finished. She was keeping him out of it.

"At least I know that you still love me," he said, interrupting her account.

"Do you know why I couldn't let that matter?"

Being with her, hearing her soothing voice, watching the lamplight play off her hair when she moved her head, and knowing her heart hadn't changed cast an uncanny patina of romance over things.

Leona told Blue everything while he dutifully scribbled his notes. The truth was, however, that they had stolen themselves one last night.

A flock of starlings nesting in the thicket across the road made a sudden fluttering storm. She had seen bobcats across the road all winter. One had just seized himself a fowl for dinner. Blue pulled back the shades and stared out into the dark. He did that for a long time while he listened to her breathing.

When he looked into her eyes after he kissed her, his lips were silver-white from the sun and soft like conditioned leather. When they lay down in the velvet shadows, his lips caressed warm circles of flesh where his tongue had moistened her breasts. When they swayed fast and slow, rolling up and down on the bed, she wept with joy. She was seizing gifts of happiness and storing them for the cold, dark season ahead.

When their passion was spent, Blue cradled her in his arms and they giggled and whispered and cried until the sky hung white behind the new green woods.

18

Leona had seen Soames at church. She was an arresting sight, at least six feet tall, a patrician-looking
woman with high ivory cheekbones and sparkling gray-
ish green eyes. She had an eternally haughty expression
dramatized by a magnificent mane of very curly carrot
hair.

She made Leona think of pictures of young Queen
Elizabeth I. She wore the uniform of that strange, faded
breed of old-guard plantation women—the starched
white blouses with pearl buttons, the steam-rolled lace
collar under a sweater when it was cool, always an antique broach, a Victorian diamond dinner ring and boots.

Leona had also seen her on her frequent trips to
the cemetery where her husband was buried. If it was
muddy she came in a pickup truck, letting the tailgate

down so a half a dozen hounds could woof and bay like banshees in the woods while she replaced one enormous faded basket of flowers with a fresh one.

It was hard not to notice her husband Henri's grave. It was situated inside of an old-fashioned family plot with an elaborate iron fence surrounding a dozen graves. A twelve-foot granite obelisk rose from the center. It rested on a three-foot square of matching stone into which the name Churchill had been chiseled and sanded sometime during the middle of the last century. A flat rectangle of bronze served as Henri's headstone.

It was from reading it one day after she heard Soames's pickup truck descend the hill that Leona learned that Henri Churchill had died at age fifty-two on Christmas Day—nine months before Averill brought her here. Soames was cool and friendly. She always nodded when she passed Leona, who went most mornings to sit near Tess's grave. (Though she had taken less and less comfort from the habit as time went by.) Soames had that held-in quality that Leona had observed in British people while traveling in England and Scotland with her mother the summer she turned thirteen. People called it "reserve," but to Leona it was confusing. The signals were always crossed. You couldn't read a person's meaning. You never knew where you stood. Leona let people like that approach her first. Or not. They were a case of good fences, she guessed.

In Soames's case Leona had guessed all wrong. The occasion of their first real conversation was a cloudburst while the two women were at opposite ends of the cemetery. Soames called through the falling torrent.

"Get in, sugar."

The cab smelled of Chanel No. 5. The seat was

made of soft leather. She had Chopin piano music playing. She handed Leona a white embossed hand towel
monogrammed in black.

"I hated to intrude," Soames said. "If it was just rain,
I wouldn't have, but this lightning is so fierce. . . ."

"Not at all. I appreciate it."

Soames backed the truck around, guiding it across
the road and into Leona's driveway.

"The house needs an awful lot of work," Soames observed.

"It's a good house," Leona said.

"Henri, my late husband, always meant to make it a
jewel."

"It's had a lot of work."

It had, of course. Soames had overseen most of it: a
new roof and wiring, a porch floor and basic plumbing.
Averill had mentioned a time or two that Soames wanted
her to call about having some more work done. It was
the last thing Leona wanted to do at the moment.

"Appreciate the ride."

"Young lady?"

Leona was nineteen. Soames looked to be about
thirty. That wasn't old enough to call Leona "young
lady." It irritated her. Still, she appreciated the ride, and
she had nothing to gain from being rude. So she went
along with it.

"Ma'am?"

"You're spending too much time in that cemetery."

That wasn't a subject Leona had any intentions of
discussing with a woman she barely knew. She listened
to the music for about ten seconds, then she gave a little nod and she let the door swing open a few inches.

"Life goes on, angel. It's as unstoppable as a river."

"Just like a river," Leona replied, trying to sound agreeable.

"Nobody has any secrets in these woods, Leona . . ."

"You think I do?"

"Henri had timber down in Calhoun County. I know that ol' reprobate banker London and his liberal ways."

Leona blushed, stunned and embarrassed.

"Sugar, I haven't breathed a word."

"Did Averill tell you?"

Soames frequently left telephone messages, asking Averill to call her about business relating to the church property. She and Averill seemed to have some friendly rapport, at least by the tone of her messages. Soames looked very troubled.

"No, I told you. I've been in the Bank of Fredonia many times."

"You sure?"

"What can you think of me? Why on earth would you ask me if I had discussed such sensitive subjects with your husband?"

She'd hurt Soames's feelings. She didn't want to do that. Still, Soames might be protecting Averill. Leona finally decided to believe her, mostly because it didn't matter anyway.

"I didn't mean anything."

"I thought being childless and losing my husband was unbearable, Leona. But it's just sad, it's just hard, it's just the way it is. . . ."

If she wanted Leona's attention, she had it.

"I don't know how a person endures a loss like yours," she went on.

"The best way I can."

"Why hasn't that charmless holy roller husband of yours brought you to see me?"

"I need something to do, a job. If you know of anything . . ."

"Let me think about it."

The next morning Soames dropped by with a stack of
magazines: *Vogue* and *Architectural Digest* and *Town &
Country* and *The New Yorker.* Leona would have had a
better time reading *People* and *The Enquirer,* which she
used to pore over in her father's drugstore. That afternoon, Soames was back with a heavenly chocolate mint
pie, a "Grasshopper" she called it. "From Dihnstul's
Bakery," she said in a tone that made it sound as if she'd
had it flown in from Paris.

She was rich and young and bored and Leona
couldn't figure out for the life of her why she stayed in
the country or what she saw in their friendship, for that
matter. Soames lived all by herself in a great fortress
fronted by eight twenty-foot Corinthian columns. It sat
on a rise at the end of a quarter-mile driveway, a temple
of things both privileged and past. Leona would have
been terrified to spend one night by herself in that
place.

"Aren't you afraid of ghosts?"

"Without Henri, I am a ghost," she mused.

She had apartments in New York and Paris. She was
on three bank boards and she was CEO, whatever that
was, of Churchill Textiles. Soames was lonely. Her husband Henri's death at fifty-two had been a complete
shock. He had died in a freak accident while hunting
doves on a section of his property last Christmas.

"I'm still in shock," she confided. "He bent down to
pass under a barbed wire fence, his .22 gauge shotgun
discharged a bullet, killing him instantly."

Leona gradually started to read some of the articles
sandwiched between the glossy color photographs in all

those stylish magazines. Like those images of a story-book world, the features detailed a realm of green-and-yellow silk that Leona visited when she walked through the front door of Soames's mansion.

One Sunday Soames drove her to Memphis for a symphony, picking her up in a dark green car Leona took for a Rolls-Royce, but Soames corrected her. It was a Bentley. Leona didn't see the difference, but then finding out wasn't likely to become a priority anytime soon. Leafing through the program, she was astounded to see a full-page ad that read: "The 2000 Sunday Symphony Series is generously underwritten by Mrs. Henri Marks Churchill IV in tribute to her late husband, the noted philanthropist and civic leader."

When Leona pointed it out, Soames shrugged and touched her bottom lip with her finger. It probably had personal significance for Soames and Henri. Though Leona didn't really get the scope of Soames's world until she stopped by her house to return her magazines.

"Oh, no, sweetie, I don't want them."

"These are five- and eight-dollar magazines."

"I don't pay for them."

"How do you manage that?"

Soames gingerly paged through the front section of *Architectural Digest* and showed Leona several advertisements for various rugs, drapes and other high-end furnishings. In the fine print at the bottom of each, the manufacturer's name was identified as "A Wholly Owned Subsidiary of HC Ltd."

"HC?"

"Henri Churchill."

Yet whenever Leona brought up the fact that she needed a job, Soames always put her off, saying she still hadn't come up with any ideas "right" for Leona.

Obviously, she had a rich lady's views on employment. The idea of needing a vocation for the simple basics didn't seem to enter her mind.

"I just need a recommendation for something entry-level."

"I won't help you with a job, Leona. You need a position."

Averill never said much about anything and even less about Leona's activities or companions. Yet he shot from the hip when it came to Soames. "That gal and that house don't go together." When Soames stopped by, which soon became three or four times a day, Averill made himself very scarce. More than once he'd turned into the driveway before he noticed Soames's car and immediately backed out and driven off again.

Averill said Leona was Soames's latest hobby. That wasn't a bad way to put it. She taught Leona how to drive a car and took her for the state license exam. When she found out that Leona could sew, Soames put her to work making draperies and slipcovers for her house. When Leona told Soames she was saving the money she paid her toward buying a car, Soames gave her the '98 Chevrolet Blazer that Henri had ordered a month before he died. She had one of her workmen drive it into town for a cleaning. Then she brought it over after supper.

Leona just stood there trembling. She had no intentions of accepting it.

"Aw, don't be so Methodist about it," Soames joked. "It's just sitting there going to waste."

"I'm so touched, really I am. I just can't. . . ."

"You can't refuse it."

"It's too much."

"You said a few weeks back, you needed a job."

"I do."

"You can do a lot of things, Leona. Figure out which one and sell it."

"I already know," Leona replied, the wheels in her head turning.

"Well, you won't sell them hiding up an old dirt road."

"Let's take a ride." Leona nodded, tears streaming down her cheeks. When Leona gave Soames an impetuous hug, she gave her a tolerant pat on the shoulder.

"I see how it is," Soames said with a tilt of her head toward the next room, where Averill was bound to overhear her. "I'm not putting my nose in," she continued in an ominous tone. "But you better get on with things. . . ."

Leona was thrilled. The Blazer only had nine miles on it, a giant four-by-four with leather seats and a custom sound system. Averill's response was to ask Leona what she thought Soames wanted in return.

"She said it was sitting in the garage gathering dust."

"How hard would it have been to sell it?"

"Averill, why do you have so much to say about it?"

After that, Leona saw the tension between Averill and Soames. For his part Averill said she wouldn't keep her nose out of the church. She was always meddling. She was full of criticism about the way he did everything. Yet she refused to supply him the funds necessary to do things the way she kept demanding. Leona saw the writing on the wall. Averill was making some plans all his own, looking for another church situation. She wouldn't be a part of it.

"Averill, you and I don't have much future."

"You and I don't want one."

"What are we going to do?"

"Keep on a while."

"Averill, we aren't fooling anyone."

"Not forever, just a while."

"How long?"

"I don't know."

"Suppose I have plans?"

Averill looked as if he'd been punched in the stomach.

"Do you?"

She couldn't call them plans. Not yet. She and Blue had agreed to move slowly—and as much as possible, secretly—toward some future together. Each of them had tender scars and bruises to heal. Each had practical situations to resolve. Blue had financial woes in all directions. What he hadn't lost in the settlement, he'd mortgaged or sold to pay his divorce lawyer.

He also had the welfare of three children to consider. He had to figure out the best course for his two boys in California. Lucy didn't seem to think he should try to maintain much of a relationship with them. Of course, Blue didn't see how kids could get too much love. Meanwhile, little Nancy was almost totally dependent on the staff of the institution for any love at all. Nancy was going to be included in whatever future he determined.

He was likely to instigate one type of legal proceeding or another before he had his situation with his kids worked out. That was going to cost money he didn't have. He also was wary of facing down accusations of an affair with a preacher's wife. Time would determine a lot of things for Blue and Leona.

"I just want to get myself situated, Averill."

"Nobody has any secrets in the country, Leona."

"Secrets are all you have, Averill."

"Make a bargain with me."

"I made a bargain with you, Averill, and I want out of it."

"Stay three more months. Make your plans, but don't tell anyone."

"Why would I do that?"

"Seventeen thousand dollars."

He handed her a savings passbook from Union Planters Bank of Memphis. His name was on the account.

"It's from your mama's house."

"You stole my money?"

"No. I was your mother's executor and I'm your husband."

"But, it's mine!"

"Keep your lips buttoned for three months, and it will be."

Averill spelled it out. She had to play like they had a complete marriage. She mustn't tell anyone, no one, that they would soon go their separate ways. That was crucial.

"What if I do?"

"You won't live long enough to spend twenty-two cents." Averill walked out the front door and down the porch steps. Something had been aroused in him. It gave him purpose or maybe focus he had never before displayed. It was hard to pinpoint. There had always been an almost pathetic or slightly unhinged air about Averill. It was as if a hundred strings had been drawn tight and secured near the small of his back.

He had spoken in riddles, but his message for her was straight and clear. She had been advised for her own considerable good to be wary of Soames and feed her no information, even inadvertently. The Blazer had some symbolic meaning for Averill. Was Soames sending him a message? Did they know each other that well? What did she care? If she could believe Averill, and his uncharacteristically straightforward manner almost demanded that she believe him in this instance, she could walk away in three months. Or drive away, thanks to Soames, with enough money to settle into a place and pay for a no-contest divorce.

As for Averill's dramatic warning that she was in peril if she opened her mouth, she had to smirk at that. Averill never could resist a grand exit line.

19

❦

Leona was in a wretched mood. She was on her way home in the Blazer. She'd been around the hill trying to help an ignorant cow plan her daughter's wedding. She didn't like to brand people, especially poor ones. Poor people weren't always ignorant or trashy. Rich ones could turn out to be both. She tried to give a person the benefit of every doubt. All the same, this woman was an ignorant redneck trash cow and her stinky husband would pass for one of the McFayes' bloated Jerseys. The bride was thirteen and swollen to full mast. The groom was twenty and half-reptile. The fact was, three girls from this part of the county had been raped in the last year. The groom had been questioned twice and was still considered a suspect.

Yet the woman went on half a day about a proper

English wedding, which she had pronounced "Englith," because she was missing several upper front teeth. Meanwhile the groom kept touching the bulge in his trousers and grinning at Leona when the others couldn't see him. Well, she could ignore that. This was business, or some febrile precursor of it. She was definitely starting small. Leona had put out the word she was for hire to advise, design and direct weddings. This was her first paying customer—if, that was, she agreed to accept half her payment in the form of poultry and produce and the rest on the E-Z time-payment plan.

She hit a straight stretch where the road crossed a marshy bottomland. It was a low place and the trees were thick overhead. It was almost night here. There was a figure up ahead, a round-looking woman wearing a veil. She was carrying something in her arms. It was a baby. She stepped down into the shallow edge of the swamp as Leona drove past. Leona kept looking for her in the rearview mirror, but she was gone.

She drove on but she couldn't erase the image. It had looked so real and yet it was like a nightmare phantom, some low nursemaid of hell charged with living-dead infants. When she got home, for a change, Averill was sitting there in front of the television. She sat with him and watched two or three mindless series segue into the ten o'clock news. He fixed her a bowl of ice cream along with one for himself. They were almost conversant.

Averill sat up and watched an old movie. Leona crawled into bed. She ran in and out of murky dreams all night long, chasing but never catching that phantom that held her baby in its arms.

20

MONDAY, APRIL 24, 2000
10:34 A.M.

Blue had been in the bedroom making telephone calls for the last forty minutes. The morning was moving on. They had to go. She couldn't imagine how much hell he was going to catch for last night. This was bound to cost him his badge. Every minute he delayed was going to make things harder on him.

She loved the damp smell of the garden on sunny mornings. The sky was deep blue. The wind tossed a scattering of curling white fleece over the new green trees. It was the sort of day she liked to spend with her hands in the dirt. Suddenly she longed to be out there with the warm earth under her knees and the returning sun softening her neck and shoulder muscles.

"Blue!" she hollered back through the house, "let's do this."

If he had any sense, he'd drive off and let someone else bring her into custody. His delay was beginning to have an effect on her resolve, her acceptance of the inevitable and necessary. She kept knocking down thoughts of some possible future with Blue, a way to go on living. That was dangerous. That had to be tossed aside. How could she call herself a mother and entertain the possibility that her pleasure was worth more than her child?

Time was wasting. Time had all been wasted. It was time to go. She went out on the front porch and gazed with strange new affection at the surrounding woods she had regarded her prison for almost two miserable years.

She was caving in. She was losing the transcending peace of telling her story, the immutable conviction that she had taken the only available path that God's hand was in—all that self-obsessed madness was fading away. What had given her the right to take another human life?

What an arrogant delusion it had all been. Now she saw with tragic clarity she had followed the lowest route, the straightest, surest and quickest descending road to hell. She had built silver towers of blind rage, purchased shining palaces of righteous indignation for the exorbitant price of her happiness and Blue's.

There it was, real happiness. Happiness she could hear in the rise and fall of his indecipherable voice on the phone. Happiness she now observed as she eyed his creased leather billfold and the hologram of his key ring with its splayed circle of dull steel and brass. Happiness she could draw in through her nostrils as she found his scent on the back of her hand. Happiness as deep and tender as the lingering, tender echoes he left inside her.

Now she understood as she looked back across a battleground of years from the last precipice of her defeat. The triumph over life for which she had struggled was not to be achieved by the vanity of a holy death. Maybe the thing was too simple, too abundant and available to notice. It had always been everywhere in her life, though never as easy to perceive as it was now framed and illumined by the brilliant corona of her regret. She was overwhelmed with contrition and sadness for the years of loving that would never be. She was flooded with a useless, happy yearning to go on loving Blue. She was riveted to her conviction that the faith and affection she might have showered on him would nurture a lot of good for him. Though her awareness of what she had destroyed radiated beyond that.

She knew the whole truth about life in all its facets. She longed to go on loving Blue, but her heart mourned for life and people in general and the wasted power of all the stored goodwill it contained. She wanted to be in this world, to adore it, to mend and repair and replenish and protect it with all her means. She wanted its troubles and worries and aches and aggravations. She wanted to inhabit the years, to grow weary from beating her fists against their indomitable mystery. Now the irksome burdens she had borne with unceasing lament had shifted and arranged themselves like ballast to steady her for the waving mountains and valleys of life. Now, as she descended the hopeless stone stair of her self-made twilight, she shuddered with unfathomable new ability to beg God for a miracle.

Because her mistake had been no more or less than the summation of all human folly. She had attempted to ascend the throne of God and assert her will above all others.

"Where's the gun?" he asked.

She handed Soames's pistol to him. He looked as if he'd seen a ghost.

"What?"

"Where did you get this?"

"From Soames."

"Cock it and shoot it for me."

They went out into the front yard. It was a fiasco. The gun's chamber was empty. The bullets were an odd size and required special ordering. Besides, Leona had never fired a slingshot, much less a pistol. Not to mention that this one had a special safety latch. Leave it to Soames to be different. Blue looked at her like she was Ma Barker.

"Explain it to me in the car."

As he backed out Leona surveyed the house. The yellow irises beside the front steps had set bud. She'd neglected to put a dry ear of corn in the squirrel feeder. Her bedroom window shades were pulled down to different heights. The flowered cushions on the glider swing were all but faded to solid gray. It grabbed her hard, the sudden notion that she couldn't say whether she loved or hated what she saw.

"Why are you protecting Soames Churchill?"

"Soames Churchill was protecting me," she countered.

When she had explained what happened, Blue seemed to draw himself off somewhere. He didn't say anything. He seemed to be churning it over in his mind, trying to punch a hole in it.

"It's the truth, Blue. Every word."

"I believe you." There was something or someone he didn't believe. Or didn't want to believe.

It was at the very least ludicrous, but Leona couldn't

help the soaring feeling she took just sitting beside him with the clouds skimming the pale green trees overhead. Then she drew air back into her nostrils and giggled out loud. He'd showered in her bathroom that morning and he was wearing Averill's hundred-dollar cologne. Wasn't he a paragon of law and order?

"Mr. Tall Sheriff?"

"Yeah . . ."

"You make one hell of an arrest."

His somber expression reminded her that they were getting close to town, and why. This time the party was really over. So why the hell didn't the sky turn steel gray and a steady rain begin to fall? Why this china blue and white fleece? Why was the sun a splendid yellow sphere this morning, almost like the radiant suns in children's crayon drawings?

What macabre force of nature had surrounded their bleak last act with so much bursting primary color and awakening? As she made out the courthouse clock through the trees and the familiar lead weight pressed her spirit, the April countryside almost seemed a tasteless, insensitive joke.

"Blue, tell me, please, that you're putting someone else in charge."

He was still chewing on Soames and her involvement. Did it buy them anything to hold her accountable for her part in it? It seemed to him that it should. Wasn't she the actual murderer? He meant according to the law, of course, he meant in the technical sense. From a moral perspective Leona was right. It had been an act of compassion. Averill had already been close to death. It was inevitable. Had it not been, then Soames would be guilty of murder.

He knew the answer already, but he made a note

between his ears to ask Arlen about it. Arlen McFaye was the county coroner. Was it a certainty based on his tests that Averill Sayres had swallowed a lethal amount of poison? There was always the chance Arlen would list a bullet and not poison as the cause of death.

His train of thought was making him nauseous. Blue felt like an amoral despot. He didn't like Soames Churchill. He'd never been one-hundred-and-ten percent convinced that her husband's death had been an accident. He had nothing to go on there but a lot of rumor and innuendo about her adulteries and Henri Churchill's intent to divorce her. Blue had actually checked the county clerk's records, but there was nothing on file. Though he had to concede that his negative feelings for Soames were based to a large extent on the fact that she had made him uncomfortable on several occasions by throwing herself at him. It had never seemed real to him. It didn't come across as genuine attraction. He sensed some other agenda there. Maybe he was a thousand miles off. He had never even been tempted to follow her home and find out.

Yet there was nothing in any of that to warrant twisting an act of decency into a crime. Leona was about to run flat into a brick wall. As hard as it was to take, he'd serve no good by destroying another woman, whether or not he liked her. In fact, the only way he could see to help Leona now was to disappear with her.

All he had to do was hang a right at the next intersection, drive a mile and a half downhill through an area that decayed into a semiurban mess of car dealers, car washes, gas stations, drive-in groceries and cheap motels; veer onto the interstate and fly north. Leona would have a cat with a tissue paper tail.

But so what?

It wouldn't kill either one of them. He could cover his ears. He sure as hell didn't have any time to convince her. It was like they taught you in Red Cross lifeguard class. The first thing you have to do in order to rescue a drowning person is knock him out. Otherwise he'll drown you. There wasn't any doubt at the moment that unless one of them pulled a miracle out of their pocket in the next ten minutes, Leona was dead in the water. Or to be more specific, by lethal injection.

He'd do it, that's all. He couldn't live with the alternative. Let her holler all the way to the Canadian border or wherever in hell they'd go. No point discussing it now. He knew her line. She wouldn't run. She knew they'd kill her. It was crazy. She was crazy. He felt responsible for that. He had to make the sane choice for her. He loved her. God Almighty damn, the media would have a ball with them.

SHERIFF FLEES WITH WOMAN SUSPECTED OF CLERGY HUSBAND'S MURDER.

Why did he have to learn the big ones hanging off the cliff by his fingernails? Not even the big ones, just this one. This was the biggest one of them all. How many times had he felt a surging impulse to run to her in the last six months? How many times had his mind and body frozen with the sudden need to see her, to touch her, to tell her he couldn't begin to tell her how senseless and impossible life was without her?

How many times had he gripped his resolve to let the moment pass?

And why?

Had he really thought his promises would keep her head above water forever? Hadn't he known every day of her life was hell? He could hear his father telling him an hour before he died that his sins of omission were what made leaving this world unbearable.

God, he was sorry. It was all fear, wasn't it? He and Leona could have stood beside each other and looked the world in the eye and demanded their right to love each other. Except he'd been afraid, worried about a job he didn't want, cowed by his faithless ex-wife's possible reactions (even though she had already split for California with the kids). Afraid to live, to be, to have or feel his own life!

Now here he was, a poor-ass fool, clutching the steering wheel with cold, sweaty fingers with every desperate thought in his head a prayer. Oh, God, I love her; oh, God, I need her; oh, God, she couldn't take any more of it, please, please help me help her. Oh, God, please save this woman. She's my whole life.

Oh, no, he wouldn't own up to that while he had the luxury of months, even years, to give her the contents of his heart. No, no, that would have made her happy. That would have turned him into a flesh-and-blood human being. Owning the love he felt for her would have made their lives mean something.

If it weren't for his recurring, lunatic hope against hope, he'd hit the floorboard and put an end to this ludicrous torment by veering into the side of the next bridge. Or maybe it wasn't even hope. Maybe now that he had completed his ruin, he finally had the self-control to pass up a chance to play God.

If his heart wasn't bruised and bleeding, if his stupidity hadn't condemned her, he'd have to laugh. It took him back to something his high school football and basketball coaches had told him a thousand times. Blue always figured how to win it after the game had been lost. And his magic formula was always something they had tried to tell him before the game.

He could barely stand to look at her.

"Blue, don't try to save me."

Any response to that on his part was going to render him a useless mess. He couldn't indulge in that, not while she sat there with such quiet grace.

"Things had to go this way, Blue."

"I love you so much."

"It makes all the difference."

"It could have."

"I had to do it. I've known it for a long time."

"I've known how much I love you for a long time."

"A million times I thought about running to you."

"Oh, God, why didn't you?"

"I knew I was eventually going to have to kill him."

"He wasn't worth killing."

"I didn't do it for me."

God, life was a farce. All that reaching and growing, the changes, the losses, the regrets and starting over—where did it get anybody? What for? Where was this climbing path to peace and wisdom all those stupid books talked about? How could she sit there beside him looking so peaceful as he downshifted for soft places in the sand clay road?

Justice, the supreme ruler, man's purported attempt to administer the Will of God, wanted its eye for an eye. Leona, who had never killed before and would never kill again; Leona, who rid society of a worthless man; Leona would stand trial. Judge and jury would purse their Christian lips and shrug and regret that they were morally, legally bound to convict and kill Leona with about as much sensitivity and remorse as the pound displayed when it killed a rabid stray.

All he had to do was hang a right at the next intersection. Yet he kept straight for the courthouse at the stop sign. The road to hell, he knew now, wasn't paved with anything as lofty as good intentions. Its construct was far more intricate than that. It was made of millions of connecting willful ignorances and blind self-indulgences.

"Leona, please, listen to me. . . ."

"I have to do this, Blue."

"Justice is whatever suits those with the most power."

"I agree."

"Then why hand yourself to them?"

She was empty. She had no more words to offer. There was nothing to pull out of her hat that would make him see her purpose. This wasn't something she would debate with anyone. Others might well have better ideas than hers. She was past all that. She had reached the inevitable part, the point of no return. It didn't matter whether this was her insanity, self-indulgence, self-destruction, cruelty or folly. This was her own private cross, her bloody trek up Golgotha. She was seeing it through.

"Answer me, damn it! Why hand yourself to them?"

She wouldn't indulge herself the feelings now. She was too tired, too weak, too vulnerable. Her heart was begging him to overpower her decision, to turn at the intersection up ahead, to take responsibility for her fate. Yet some inscrutable power of intuition had dictated otherwise. Blue was wild with despair. She had to appear calm and resolute. She had to at least convey the steel conviction that he would understand one day. But how? What words could she borrow? Then it came to her with no little irony. She could steal them from Averill.

"Why?" Blue repeated, looking pale and helpless.

"Why did Jesus go to Jerusalem?"

He let the car roll past the stop sign at a snail's pace while he glanced up and down the deserted crossroad. He coasted across the highway, his right foot pressed the clutch and his right hand guided the gearshift into first. Now second, passing the city limits sign, then third. The road widened into a residential avenue lined with two-story houses that sat deep behind ancient wrought iron fences. They stopped at a red light. He looked at her.

"Would the answer make life without you bearable?"

21

❖

MONDAY, APRIL 24, 2000
4:00 P.M.

By four o'clock that Monday afternoon Leona was
about to tear her hair out. Blue still hadn't let anyone
else talk to her. He wasn't willing to face facts. He
was violating his own procedures, wielding authority he
didn't have and listening to no one but himself. Instead
of putting her in a cell that morning, he had locked her
in his office while his staff watched with their jaws
agape. He had been running in and out all day. He was
all over the place. Half listening, interrupting himself,
now on one phone line, forgetting the other was holding. When there was a knock, he opened the door only
as far as the chain lock would allow.

"Blue, they'll be in here with tear gas and machine
guns if you don't take hold of yourself!"

This was nothing like what he had told her to

expect. He was supposed to deliver her into the custody
of a deputy. Then he was supposed to walk upstairs to
see a judge. He needed some kind of papers in order
to remove himself from her case. Meanwhile she'd go
into the interrogation room. When Soames's fancy lawyer showed up, the deputies would question her with
him running interference. Though Leona had her doubts.
Soames was probably grandstanding to keep Leona
from losing control. Surely some big-time Memphis lawyer would know how to force his way in to see his
client.

Instead, Blue was holding her here like personal
property.

She'd been here in his office since their arrival at
eleven this morning. God, she'd never forget that moment. The minute Blue parked in the sheriff's space at
the curb, a pack of lawmen and reporters swarmed.
Word was already out. The deputies pulled Leona out
of the vehicle, handcuffed her and brought her into the
building. There must have been twenty cameras. Half
the crowd was outraged and demanding Blue's resignation. The other half was catcalling and making it all a
dirty joke.

Why the hell hadn't Blue just gone to California last
week as planned?

Blue's men were organized. They had the entrances
to the courthouse secured. The media had to wait outside. Blue lingered behind them to answer questions
and deny that he'd spent last night with his suspect.
As they had driven down Whitsunday Hill that morning, Leona saw that highway patrol cars were stationed
by the crossroads store. At Blue's directive, they'd been
turning curiosity seekers away through the night.

The county board of supervisors was already demanding to see Blue when he arrived. He, of course, ignored them. Instead he took her into his office, locked the door and removed her handcuffs. The only other lawman Leona had seen all day was the confused-looking young deputy who Blue sent across the square for coffee and sandwiches. Around noon she had overheard two deputies in the hall outside of Blue's office during one of his sudden disappearances. Leona and Blue were now "Sheriff Romeo and Juliet" on Memphis talk radio.

"You must think you're God," Leona said after Blue had sent his secretary to inform the board of supervisors he was too busy to fool with them today.

"No, but I think you're innocent in God's eyes."

"Blue, don't prolong this."

There was a knock. Blue opened the door and took a cardboard file box from a young woman who taught Sunday school out at the church.

"Hey, Lu Anne."

"Hey, yourself," she answered in a begrudging tone.

"Aw, now don't be that way," Blue cut in. "Things are rarely what they seem."

"Well, evil can sure look cute and cuddly, if that's what you mean."

"God bless you, darlin'," Blue snapped, closing the door in her face.

"Blue, if that's an indication of what people are saying, then—"

"Sanctimonious slut."

Leona had to admit that she had reached a similar conclusion long before any of this mess. He was taking manila files out of the box and reading them.

"Blue, I'm a confessed murderer. People expect you to uphold the law in this county. . . ."

"Here it is," he muttered, not paying Leona the slightest heed.

They sat there in silence while Blue read a stack of typewritten documents. Leona had no idea what they were or why he was reading them. He was absorbed. The phone rang every two or three minutes. Sometimes it went on for fifteen or twenty rings. It didn't seem to faze him in the least. Then it rang thirty-two times. Leona couldn't stand it anymore.

"County sheriff's office," she said.

"Sheriff Hudson, please."

"The sheriff is unavailable. May I tell him who's calling?"

"Who is this?"

"Leona Sayres."

The man laughed so loud it hurt her ear.

"Oh, that's rich. That's a good one."

22

MONDAY, APRIL 24, 2000
5:55 P.M.

Blue's right hand took the receiver away from Leona.
Then he unplugged the phone.

"You've lost your mind."

He handed her the typed page he'd been reading. It
was from a file that the late sheriff Meeks had made of
his investigation into Henri Churchill's death, an interview with one of Henri Churchill's employees.

"What's the point?"

"There was a lot of speculation that it wasn't an accident."

Leona lost it. If Blue didn't wake up, the county was
going to fire and then prosecute him for obstruction of
justice.

"For God's sake! What difference does it make if
Soames hung him on the courthouse lawn in front of a

thousand witnesses? I measured out that nasty powder and dumped it into Averill's food and watched him eat it for three days in a row." Then, mostly to make Blue calm down a little, she read the damned interview.

Sarah Robbins, now deceased, had been a childless young wife of twenty-seven when she became Henri Churchill's nurse and caregiver. She had come back to work for Henri Churchill as a cook shortly after his first wife died and he began spending more time at the farm. She was seventy-six when the sheriff interviewed her. This was a week after Henri's death. She had already quit her job.

"You don't care for Miss Soames?"

"She has her ways; I have mine."

"Is she nice to you?"

"Real nice."

"You don't think she needs your help right now?"

"I'm old, Sheriff. I'm the one who needs some help."

"Do you think Mister Henri's death was an accident?"

"I never called that boy 'mister' nothing."

"Was it an accident?"

"I didn't see it happen."

"Do you suspect that it wasn't an accident?"

"God help me, I do."

"Why?"

"Because the Churchills been hunting around here since Noah landed."

"Henri knew gun safety."

"Any nut would know what she claimed."

"She?"

"Loaded rifle, safety off, barrel pointed to blow a hole in his head?"

"Who is 'she'?"

"It's not but one lady living here, Sheriff."

According to Sarah, Henri was away on business more than half the time. Soames got bored and lonely. He had taken her all over the world during the early years of their marriage. Now he was drawing in the reins. Her spending had gotten out of control. He clipped her credit cards and to some extent her wings. He sold his big old house in Memphis and rented the apartments in New York and Paris.

"He really put her down on the farm," Sarah had told Sheriff Meeks. Like a lot of rich men's wives, Soames falsely presumed the confidence of her domestic helpers. Aside from Sarah, there was a younger married couple living on the place. The man worked full-time as a groundskeeper. His wife washed and ironed linens and took care of the dozen or so upstairs rooms. Soames made a big deal to Sarah that, in spite of the fact that they were white people, she held the dark woman in higher esteem. (Meeks had that circled in purple. That meant it corroborated something else, probably something about Soames's background.)

Henri had told Sarah that Soames had invented her genteel background in order to seem a good match for him. Sarah was sketchy about the truth, but Henri's investigators had disproved many of her claims. She hadn't attended Smith College. Her grandmother wasn't a Whitney. Her mother had never been an heiress; nor had she lost millions in a fraudulent art deal. Sarah ran on at some length.

Soames, according to Sarah, was dying to have a baby. She wasn't naïve enough to think that would cure Henri's wanderlust. She whined that she had accepted the fact that she had been chosen for a wife by medieval standards. Her bloodlines were more important to her husband than she was. She was his proper public counterpart. Otherwise he was a man like all the rest. He couldn't manage intimacy with a peer. He wanted to do his wallowing with some cloven platinum swine. No, she wanted a baby because she needed love. She deserved love. If Henri was going to imprison her there in his fortress, leaving her behind with the drawbridge raised, then why couldn't he at least avail himself when she was ovulating? Soames wondered if it was deliberate.

Sarah knew it was deliberate. Soames had been very naïve to share secrets with the woman who had raised her husband. They were like mother and son. Henri often called Sarah's house at night when he was away. She knew that he was seeing a woman from Atlanta. He had long since told her that Soames had cuckolded him while he was still blind with grief over his first wife. Soames was a gold-digging sociopath and a piranha in heat, according to Henri.

Sarah also knew how to reach Henri night or day. She was soaking up information from Soames like a deep-sea sponge. Sarah tipped off Henri that Soames had her sources and wiles. She said she had a cache of photographs and receipts. If Henri divorced her, she was prepared to convince the court that he was a philandering wife beater. She'd walk out of the courthouse with millions.

Henri was determined not to let that happen. He told Sarah he'd hire a hit man before he'd spend a dime on a divorce lawyer. Unless, of course, he caught his beloved spouse cheating on him. In that case, he'd get rid of her and she'd be lucky if she got a dime.

"Did she cheat on him?"

"Like a bird dog bitch in heat."

"Who with?"

"With that cheese hot-dog shoutin' preacher up Whitsunday Hill."

"Did Henri catch them?"

"Is water wet?"

"Where were they?"

"Right here in this house on the Savonniere rug in the parlor, two naked potato bug heatherns on Christmas Eve underneath the tree!"

Henri had set a trap. Soames hadn't expected him until the following morning. He had a hidden camera taping them. He waited until they were through. Then, according to what he told Sarah later that night, he strolled into the room and ordered Soames out. She got dressed without a word. She said she would give her address to Sarah, so that she could send her clothes. Henri nodded his assent. Soames wished him a Merry Christmas. Then she drove off with the preacher.

The name (Averill Sayres) was printed in tremulous black ballpoint on the margin.

Leona took a moment to absorb it. Or at least some of it. Soames and Averill had had an affair. So why all her trips to the cemetery to put fresh flower arrangements on Henri's grave once or twice a week? If Henri Churchill hadn't died . . . Then she remembered something. No, it was too obvious. She was mistaken.

"How long after all this was it before Henri Churchill died?"

Blue grinned at her just as if any of it was going to make a difference.

"About twelve hours."

Leona didn't want to get bogged down in what it had all meant in the past. She kept sifting it for some relevance to her current situation. Blue was acting like there was.

"What's it give us, Blue?"

"Us? Nothing."

Her heart went to her shoes. This was infuriating. Blue was spinning nonsense and she was buying into it. She had to knock him back to his senses. She hated him so much in that moment that she could hardly stand to look at him. He kept up his annoying grin. The longer he held on to his toothy Pepsodent smile, the more Leona was convinced of the recent and direct link between humans and apes.

"Blue, what the holy hell has you grinning like an idiot?"

"It gives us nothing, Leona; but it gives Soames a motive."

"For what?"

"For shooting Averill Sayres at close range through the skull."

"What motive?"

"He was both her accomplice and witness."

Blue handed her another page from Sheriff Meeks's interview with Sarah.

Sarah claimed that she had come to the house early on Christmas morning and given Henri his breakfast. He was dressed for hunting. He said he was going out to shoot quail. Sarah washed up. The house was immaculate. Henri was planning to catch an early afternoon plane from Memphis to Atlanta. He would be at his fiancée's house in Atlanta in plenty of time for a six-thirty dinner. He had a four-and-a-half-carat diamond solitaire engagement ring in his pocket, and he showed it to Sarah that morning. Sarah left before eight o'clock and drove fifty miles to spend the day and night with her sister's family in Tupelo.

Soames had called for an ambulance at 11:10 A.M. It

arrived at 11:35. A county highway patrol unit delivered two deputies to the scene five minutes later. The two men later reported that they had walked in on a typical Christmas morning scene. There were open presents to and from Soames and Henri under the tree. She had a ham in the oven. Two plates and the remains of a giant holiday breakfast sat on the kitchen table. The dining room table was laid with all the best things in the house. They were expecting a dozen dinner guests.

Leona handed the page back to Blue.

"Soames didn't have time to kill him, rig up a suicide and do all that stuff inside the house to make it look like she and Henri were celebrating Christmas together."

"Averill helped her."

"I'd put money on it."

"Why wasn't this thing investigated?"

Blue showed her a two-foot stack of documents. The thing was investigated. The coroner's report indicated doubt that the bullet hole was caused by a .22 gauge rifle. It seemed a bit too small. He also indicated some doubt as to whether the weapon had been fired at the close range Soames's story indicated. The damaged area seemed a little too clean. Yet the coroner's conclusion was that Henri Churchill's death was an accidental, self-inflicted bullet wound.

"How?"

Blue shrugged with impatience. He was even more aware of the gathering threat outside of his office door than Leona was. He also knew that the tiny thread of hope he was attempting to ravel could well break off in his hand. The results of his brash attempt to strong-arm the system could very likely mean going to prison.

Yet he understood the tragic nature of justice. Once

Leona was charged with murder, the wheels would begin their inevitable process. The law would take precedence without regard to mitigating factors. People were quick to insist that truth was never absolute. Sometimes the truth was a pair of incompatible facts, neither of which would stand alone. Yet their laws made no such allowances. Right and wrong were pure, absolute, immutable and all-powerful.

Why did people expect so much from the criminal justice system? Most had no idea how it worked nor much interest in finding out, for that matter. They wanted justice, law and order for a ludicrous little bit of their tax dollars. The pay was insulting. The risks and the hours involved were inhuman. Who did they think it attracted?

It attracted two kinds of people. He was an example of one. He wasn't college material. He had three babies and a dead-end job on an assembly line. It was one on a tiny list of opportunities for a man like him to acquire health insurance and some kind of retirement plan. Did people really believe a man wanted to spend his best years hauling in wife beaters and pulling dead kids out of wrecks, ninety-nine percent of whom would have walked away if they'd either buckled their frigging seat belts or left the beer alone?

The other kind of people law enforcement attracted were the ones he called "the nowheres." They were criminals who hid behind the system. They served and protected their own interests. They were bullies who extorted favors from business owners and protected drug dealers for a cut of the profits. If you weren't that kind when you started, the odds were fifty-fifty you'd burn out and cross the line at some point.

There wasn't a law on the books that couldn't be

broken with impunity. All it took was concerted indifference to the lives of others. Blue had a sixth sense about people, an intuition for character. The majority of people he arrested and interrogated were salvageable. They had gotten themselves balled up in situations. A lot of them would eventually serve time. When they lied in an effort to save their own skin, it was obvious. They had an underlying sense of decency that betrayed them.

Not Soames Churchill. Soames was a rare and dangerous beast of prey in the guise of a lost and lonely widow. Soames had an innate lack of interest in others. She could feign kindness and generosity. She could play the awkward, self-deprecating fool. She could play those things so well that people dropped their guard. She could seem anything to anyone when it helped her accomplish her agenda. She could endear or seduce or make love to, even marry, a man and then shoot him in the sunshine on Christmas Day while he begged for his life. She could do that and then walk back inside the house and sit down to an enormous breakfast.

"You mean she bribed the coroner?"

"Or slept with him or paid some goon to scare his wife."

"Maybe he figured he had nothing but guesses and hearsay."

"Or two more stiffs in the cooler and his dinner waiting."

"What about Henri Churchill's lady friend in Atlanta?"

"Sarah claimed she didn't even know her name."

"But she knew how to reach Henri at all times!"

Blue smiled with irony. Did Leona really think Sarah would say anything that would tarnish Henri Churchill?

"Even if it meant Soames got away with his murder?"

"His reputation meant more to Sarah."

"But she could have corroborated Sarah's story."

Leona was too earthy to give much credence to appearances. Other people's opinions were the worst reason for keeping secrets. While it was true that she had taken a fatal turn up Whitsunday Hill for appearances' sake, she had done it in a moment of blindness and pain. She felt at the time she owed it to her mother's memory. Yet even then she had bowed to respectability by the hardest. If she had learned anything from her sojourn in the wilderness, she had learned the tragic price of appearances.

Why weren't children taught to look life in the eye? Why did people wrap their most consequential things in shame and try to hide them from each other? How could Sarah have slept knowing that Henri Churchill's murderer was not only free, but also living like an empress on his estate? If she had known so much about Soames, didn't Sarah at least suspect that Henri had been in danger? Yet she had in effect let him walk into Soames's trap and die. Would she have sacrificed a man's life in order to protect his reputation, a man she loved like a son?

No. Henri's reputation was only the top layer. If thinking and looking and seeing into people and situations were Blue's game, then she had a lesson for the master.

"Look underneath what you're saying, Blue."

"There's nothing underneath what I'm saying."

The subject at hand was Leona's forte.

"You say Sarah loved Henri like a son?"

"She would have died for him."

"There's not a mother on Earth who would voluntarily suppress the identity of her child's murderer."

"Then Sarah was afraid of Soames."

Blue looked away and back and away again. He was thinking. He was trying something on for size. A person might just as well be a rock when Blue was like that.

"Leona?"

He looked at her as if there were smoke coming out both of her ears.

"What are you gawking at?"

Blue answered her with a strange smirk.

"Why are you looking at me like that?"

"You said no mother would hide the identity of her child's murderer."

"Who'd know better than me?"

"But you kept your child's murder a secret."

"For obvious reasons."

"The minute Soames told you what Averill had done, did you decide to kill him?"

"Not that very second, no . . ."

Could he possibly mean what she was thinking? Had Soames used the old trick of persuading her to do it with bad arguments against it? The idea made Leona blush with shame. Was she really so willing to live at any price, even pointing fingers at innocent people? Yet Blue seemed to think there was some merit in it.

"Leona, how exactly did you deduce that Averill murdered your baby?"

"Soames."

"Soames deduced it?"

"No, he told Soames."

"Why?"

That stopped her. She hadn't really questioned it at the time. Blue looked as if he was about to go into a trance. His features were frozen, his eyes glued to her. She had to think. She had to remember it in detail.

Blue could worry the horns off a billy goat picking at it. Though something was slithering down in her sub-conscious. Something that made her afraid she was about to find out she'd been a fool one more time.

It was a Wednesday night in late March. She knew it was a Wednesday because Averill had gone to make an appearance at choir practice. Soames had turned up at the door acting glum. She had something on her conscience, she said. Something was going to drive her insane if she didn't tell Leona the truth. Of course Soames made a one-act play out of spitting it out. She had to dramatize her mixed emotions, her fears for what it might do to Leona, to their friendship, what Leona might do—all of that.

Then she told her. She said Averill had turned up at her door one night the week before, weaving drunk. He was a mess, she said, puking on the kitchen floor and—

" 'Kitchen floor'?" Blue interrupted.

"Yeah, 's what she said, 'kitchen floor.' "

"Go on."

"I'm trying to. . . ."

Then Soames finally said it. Averill was drunk and bawling and guilt-ridden and upset because he had gone completely insane the night the baby was born and strangled it. He couldn't live with it anymore, but he didn't have the guts to blow his brains out or turn himself in.

"Soames!" Blue hissed, "Soames's word is all you had to go on!"

"I have reason to think she was making it up!"

"Finish your story, Leona."

What else was there? Soames had gotten her mes-sage out. A minute or two later she left.

"A minute or two later?"

"She had to be somewhere."

"Where?"

"I don't know."

Like she had cared where Soames had to be that night. It was strange, though. When Soames told her that Averill had confessed to murdering Tess, Leona had felt a surge of some kind, as if she were being lifted to a different plane. Everything since then had taken place here on that surreal level.

She hadn't screamed or lost her temper or tried not to believe it. She had somehow in that moment separated all the unimportant things, like Blue, like the rest of her life, like the fact that killing was always wrong, from the thing that she knew in a moment she was going to do.

"It's called shock, Leona."

"I'm beginning to see that, Blue."

Though she couldn't see it much since she was still experiencing it. She had no capacity there and then for considering the possibility that Averill might not have done it. In order to even consider that, she would have to figure a way out of her own body first. Or go permanently berserk. Instead there had been this lead calm that she shook off for a few minutes, but never longer than that.

What was it? Something was happening. She was falling. She was sitting still. It was as if someone had turned up the lights and the volume of the world around her. Emotions as well. She was feeling everything and too much of it at once. It was roaring, excruciating, and then everything was fury as she leapt at Blue and punched and kicked and pounded and somehow his voice was saying as if through a roaring waterfall that she was all right. She was feeling. She was coming out of it.

Though it was another five minutes before she understood that he was Blue and not Soames telling her what Averill had done. She was frowning at them both in this spewing rage.

Then it was quiet and she was opening her eyes. His shirt was torn, his nose was bloody. His face was scratched.

"You fainted, thank God." He grinned.

Did he understand that she had broken some wall inside of herself that had protected her from what she had just felt?

"Blue," she said, throwing her arms around him, "Blue, I'm so afraid. Blue, help me."

He held her for a few minutes. Then he kissed her.

"Welcome home, Leona."

It was like that, almost as if she had been in space. She was back on planet Earth. What was the point, though, if all she had done was come home to die?

Leona was letting Blue know that she understood him a little. If he was going to do her any good, then he had to connect her situation to something wider, some chain of events and people he had been investigating for a long time.

If it was a useless effort, then at least it was more rational than she had first thought it was. Her ideas had led her into the bottom rung of hell. What did she have to lose by following his? Beyond that she was simply awed by Blue's unbridled willingness to risk any consequence if it kept a shred of hope alive. It was as inconceivable as it was undeniable. Even if it failed to help her fend off the outside world, it gave her an immense feeling of worth deep inside. It was as if she had somehow developed the power to experience two congruent realities. There was this terrible tumult of dark facts and pain. Then next to it was a vein of astounding happiness. Blue had proven his deep and unselfish affection for her. If it was only another route to her execution, well, so what? It flooded her diminishing existence with unexpected meaning.

He was tapping the number pad on his telephone. She watched him roll his desk chair to the wall behind him and then lay one foot over the other on his blotter. Colored with all that she felt for him, he looked magnificent to her.

"Blue?"

She could hear the telephone on the other end of the line ringing.

"Yeah?"

His mind was off where an exhausted male voice had just said hello. "Thank you." His hand was up, telling her not to disturb him. "Arlen?" The county coroner apparently had anticipated Blue's questions because Leona could hear a steady, if indecipherable, stream of words. Blue's face went blank. It lost all its former tension. Yet it didn't change as much as it seemed to pale and diminish.

It was bad. They had been whistling to each other in the dark all day. Arlen was bringing Blue back to earth and it was obvious to Leona that it was a hard landing. Why else would he sit there with the receiver still in his hand, not moving, not saying anything? All of Leona's golden transcendence from moments before had evaporated like rubbing alcohol in the searing August sun.

"What?" She hadn't meant to sound so whiny, so desperate and unable to swallow her inevitable, just deserts. Blue cleared his throat. Then he pressed the Redial button on his handset.

"Arlen? One quick question." Blue took a long, slow

sip of close, damp air. "Is this a joke?" Blue hit a button on the desk unit and the coroner's easy listening radio station sent "The Tennessee Waltz" through the speaker. He had regained his color.

"Okay, one more time. What killed Averill Sayres?"

"A bullet."

"What about poison?"

"What about it?"

"Who did the toxicology testing?"

"Memphis."

"How much did you tell me they found?"

"Zip."

"None?"

"Zero."

"Did they find anything unusual in his stomach?"

"They say he'd ate about a pound of baking soda."

"Then why is everybody hollering for Leona Sayres's neck?"

" 'Cause she's too damned pretty to be a preacher's wife."

"Arlen?"

"Ap."

"Turn up the music there, will ya?" Blue said as he hung up the phone.

The look on Leona's face was almost worth the whole stinking ordeal.

"Baking soda?"

"Somebody pulled a switch."

"Soames?"

"Why would Soames put you up to it and then switch the poison to baking soda?"

"It doesn't make sense."

"Averill figured you out."

"But Soames . . ."

"She was expecting to find a corpse."

"Why'd she shoot him?"

"You know what they say about a woman scorned."

"Especially by a man who can finger her for murder."

She was shaking. Her head was throbbing. Something terrible had passed behind her back. This was forbidden territory. Or she was insane. Whatever it meant, she was sure the punishment would be eternal and unbearable.

"You bribed him, didn't you?"

"With what? I'm six bucks overdrawn."

"But . . ."

"My guess is the Reverend Mister Sleaze had the last laugh."

Averill figured it out? Averill switched baking soda for poison and let her think she was doing him in.

"How'd he know I had it?"

"Where'd you get it?"

Leona felt a rippling in her veins from head to toe. It was either God or a stroke.

"And the angel of the Lord found her by a spring in the wilderness." The line was from a story about an unmarried, pregnant woman who had fled in shame. Leona had many times over the last year and a half thought of herself that way. She was Hagar in the wilderness. Now here he was, her delivering angel, two days past due for a shave, unreal, yet real. Everything around her seemed to shine, and a giant burning circle in her chest began to shrink. There was an orchestra playing "The Tennessee Waltz" in her head, and Blue was floating toward her. She seemed weightless as he took her in his arms and they waltzed like a pair of helium-filled refugees from hell around and around his office.

23

❧

An hour later Blue had his third conversation of the day with Arlen McFaye.

"Who else knows about this, Arlen?"

"Zilch."

"You and me and the gatepost?"

"Ap."

"Can we keep it that way?"

"All my reports are public record."

"Twenty-four hours?"

"No can do, sir."

"Not even for a case of Jack Black?"

"I'll need a chaser."

"You need ice too?"

"Ice, I got, this is the morgue, remember?"

Blue had no sooner hung up the telephone than he

jerked open the door into the hall and a din of confused
voices fell off like a choir obeying the director's cue.

"I need Jenkins, Smith and Lefferts in my office.
Now."

The three deputies appeared and the rest of Blue's
staff squeezed into the hall to witness whatever was
about to happen.

"Lock her up."

"Do we interrogate her?"

"Or should we go ahead and book her?"

"Hell, no," Blue growled. "She's been interrogated
and we're not booking her as a suspect. I want you to
charge her with murder." An agreeable buzz in the corridor and the sudden calm on the faces of the three
deputies signaled general relief and a return to nor-
malcy.

Leona observed all this as they cuffed her wrists behind her back. People had an inveterate need to cling
to what they saw as the status quo. All the violations of
his duty, all the threats to his position, the rumblings
about possible charges of obstructing justice, every bit
of it had vanished. The crack in their universe had been
repaired. The invading extraterrestrials had rocketed
home to their galaxy. The tried and true had conquered
all. They had no intentions of learning any more than
that. The strange events of the day had been one of
those ephemeral aberrations of life. They had their
good ol' boy Blue back on the job. They had a compre-
hensible murder, the madness of one more evil woman
scorned. She would never have believed it if she hadn't
experienced it. Their hostile attitude toward her had
vanished. She hadn't twisted Blue Hudson's mind after
all. No, he'd only put a big toe over the line by taking
some advantage of her last night. Well, he was, after all,

a healthy young man and a lonely one. She had her own
lascivious needs in light of her husband's neglect. Blue
was a finely cut young fellow. How much could she
have minded? Now it was already a mile downstream
and about to disappear over the cataracts. They were
grateful to Leona for turning out to be no more inexplicable than any normal young Jezebel who took it all too
far.

They were afraid, terrified to know anything they
didn't already know or at least believe to be true. Yet so
little of what the average person did or said was true.
The way to get on with people was to figure which lies
they wanted you to tell them. The way to succeed was
to figure out how much of what you saw or felt was acceptable. With so much self-deception and willful ignorance, it was no wonder nothing ever turned out to be
what it had seemed at first. It wasn't death they feared.
It was life, meaning themselves and each other. No
wonder so much evil went unnoticed until it created
enough pain to spark some riot or war.

Yet she knew she had only seen this fearful herd-
ing instinct because she had been removed from their
society just then, cast down and branded something
other than they. It was a perspective that clarified a
great deal.

She and Blue had decided that her arrest and incar-
ceration would accomplish several important things.
She would be safer in a jail cell than anywhere else. If
Soames Churchill was looking, then she would continue to assume that Leona was willing to plead guilty.
It also took a great deal of pressure off of Blue, allowing him to maneuver about and retain his power as
sheriff. Soames had shot and killed Averill for reasons

all her own. Yet she had insisted it was no less than a compassionate, last-resort act of mercy. She had invented a ghastly scenario and let Leona think the poison had worked unbearable torment on him. Of course, there hadn't been any poison. Yet, as Blue observed, the least possible aspect of Soames's account was her claim of empathy toward another human being. No. Soames wanted Averill dead and she hadn't trusted Leona to accomplish the job.

Soames had wanted Averill dead. She had given Leona several strong motives for killing him. Then she showed up one afternoon with a two-pound sack of tasteless, odorless and super-powerful rat poison. Not because she was concerned about Leona's suspected vermin under the house.

Leona and Blue were trying to figure out Leona's value to Averill and Soames. What was it Averill had wanted from her in the first place? Why had he gone to such lengths to help her out? He had come back to Fredonia shortly after Henri Churchill's murder. To that time he and Soames had carried on their affair. Odds were high that Averill had participated in Henri's killing. Why? Had he and Soames planned to be together?

It was easy enough to imagine Averill smitten by Soames. Her vampish airs would have titillated him. Her potential millions would have also aroused great passion. Wouldn't it have been easier to lay low for a while? Did he think arriving with a wife and a baby on the way would lessen suspicion? Blue countered that Averill wasn't so worried that he didn't come back here to live. Was that Soames's doing?

"Maybe."

"I know what she wanted."

"No, before Averill brought you here."

"What did I have that either one of them wanted?"

"A baby."

Blue winced and shrugged. It was tender territory, to say the least. She'd had a thousand years' worth of hell in one day. Yet there wasn't time to sidestep and soft-paw his way to it. Soames Churchill was taking on evil in his mind. She was becoming a sorceress, an accomplished dissembler and the first one-hundred-percent carved-granite criminal mind he had encountered in his law enforcement career. She had murdered at least two men so far.

"Then why was she so nice to me after all that?"

"Manipulation."

"Like the wedding business?"

"She got you into that?"

"She hounded me into it."

"Why?"

"I don't know. I don't have a clue."

"Did she steer any business your way?"

"Rhea Anne Brisbane's wedding."

Blue leaned forward with rapt attention. He was listening, but he was also praying Leona would tell him what he was desperate to hear. "Take your time," he said, knowing how little either of them had.

Leona had helped Soames plan a huge party in her garden. It was in honor of a young couple who had become engaged. The event was life and death to Soames. It shocked Leona to see that Soames didn't know how to achieve the effects she wanted. She was lost. Using more common sense than experience, Leona went to town and had a great time spending Soames's money to create an arresting Arabian Nights theme in a billowing tent of parachute material. It had an exotic, royal and romantic ambiance that captivated all the guests. Several had asked Soames for Leona's number.

Leona was hired to decorate churches for several weddings that summer. By fall she was becoming an enterprise. Leona didn't think twice when a young bride-to-be from Orpheus named Rhea Anne Brisbane knocked on her door. Rhea Anne told her that Soames Churchill had insisted she hire Leona to decorate for her wedding.

"That hateful snit," Soames later whined, "that lying, hateful snit."

"What do you mean?" Leona asked.

"I never sent her to see you. I wouldn't get you involved with that pack of trash."

Leona didn't see the big deal. They might be trash, but they had ready money. She was thrilled to have the income. Soames was burdened with the constant need to be upset with someone. This was going to be a giant production and real cash cow for Leona. It would also spread Leona's reputation. It might even put her on enough solid financial ground to leave Averill.

Besides, in the high-handed, old-fashioned sense of the word, the Brisbanes were nothing like trash. Far from it. This was tall cotton all the way. Rhea Anne's marriage was dubbed "the merger," as two of the old guard families were involved. How many times had Soames told Leona to showcase her talents for the crimped-cucumber-sandwich crowd. Suddenly the Brisbanes were "nouveau trash" and Soames denied that she had ever sent Rhea Anne to see her.

All the same, Soames volunteered to help Leona get the wedding greenery to town in her truck. She had promised to be there by seven-thirty that Saturday morning. She finally showed up around ten o'clock. She looked half-awake and she acted totally hungover. Leona had given up on her and called one of the Spakes when Soames finally pulled into her driveway.

"It's a wedding, not emergency surgery," Soames said when she saw the irritation on Leona's face. Leona was organized. She had used the time to finish the ivy ropes. She had other garlands coiled in tubs of cold water. The wild roses were soaking in the creek in potato sacks. Nearby there were giant ferns growing in clay pots in the shade at the edge of the water. The honeysuckle and the privet and the lacework gypsophila and the white silver-throated lilies were standing in buckets on the back of the truck. All she had to do was clip the peonies along the cemetery. They had to be cut last or they'd open too soon.

Leona had a gift for classical embellishments, an inexplicable comprehension of looping swags of fruits and floating silks and wreaths of ordinary leaves that took on Greco-Roman majesty. She could take an armload of the most despicable common briar and dry brush and Johnson grass and turn an old slop pot into a fountain of ancient splendor.

The Episcopal sanctuary was too dreary, too dark with its mahogany ceiling and trim blackened by decades of oil heat. The stucco walls were pink, the carpet and most of the stained windows were deep crimson. Back in the twenties some diehard Victorian had been determined to elevate the modest church with abundant splashes of imperial Anglican blue blood of the Lamb. Rhea Anne had some taste. She asked that it be airy and NeoClassical.

"Then I'm afraid you better call an architect," Leona

had advised her when she took a look at the place. Leona had expected some argument. For all its Gothic darkness and smothering red, the old building had lightness, a delicacy that had obviously been ignored for the last seventy years. However, Rhea Anne looked overwhelmed. She wasn't much more than twenty, but she had the resignation of a much older woman in her eyes.

"What do you think, Mrs. Sayres?"

Leona thought Rhea Anne was a very weary-looking young bride. Something about this event had been omitted from the articles on the society pages about pre-wedding parties. Whatever it was, Leona had the feeling she was supposed to make it disappear with magic swags and loops of greenery and cascading summer flowers. That she could do. Rhea Anne listened to Leona's suggestions with an air of general relief and a vague attention to details.

"That's fine," she said.

"It's not the most economical way to go," Leona said, by way of bringing up the eternally unpleasant subject of money. She quoted an outrageously high price. She was testing Rhea Anne. If she agreed to it, then she was talking out of turn. There had to be parents waiting in the wings, people whose money she was spending.

"That's fine," she said. Then she lifted her checkbook out of her bag and used the flat surface of the altar rail to steady her hand as she gave Leona the specified amount.

"You think we can make it respectable for that amount?"

"Don't you want to discuss this with Mama and Daddy first?"

Rhea Anne replaced the gold cap of her fountain pen and dropped it into her shoulder bag.

"I'm sorry if I insulted you," Leona said.

"I'm not insulted. It's just that I don't have the week it would take to answer your question."

"I see." Leona smiled, though she didn't have a clue. "Soames Churchill told me I could count on you."

"Soames Churchill told you the truth."

24

FRIDAY, SEPTEMBER 17, 1999
4:46 P.M.

Timon Baird, the sixty-two-year-old Episcopal rector, had just stepped out of the Bank of Orpheus into the muggy September afternoon. It was Friday. Rhea Anne Brisbane's wedding was scheduled for the next evening. It was a social do. All kinds of people would be dropping into the rectory all day. They'd expect hors d'oeuvres and wine and liquor. He needed help. As if in answer to his silent prayer, he spotted Darthula.

"Good afternoon, Mother Darthula."

"Evening, Father Baird."

"You're veiled in blue today."

"Dark, dark blue, Father."

"What's it mean?"

"What do my white veil mean, Father?"

"White means the angels are watching."

"It do. And when I got my red veil on?"

"Red warns us the devil is here about."

"Ain't I told you it do?"

"Indeed. So, what's blue?"

"This here veil on my head is dark blue, Rev. . . . You look like you standin' up straighter, Holy Paws."

"Once more before I'm stooped," the priest replied. She reminded him of a dark blue veil on a tree stump. There were as many stories around town about Darthula as there were people to tell them.

"I was sorry to hear your mama passed, Father."

Darthula had prepared many fine meals for the old bat's dinner parties. Queenie had ruled over her table like God ruled the world.

"Timon tells me the most interesting things about your sanctified church, Tallulah."

"It's Darthula, Mother. . . ."

"I think we have wonderful race relations here in Orpheus, don't you, Tallulah?"

"Yessie, Shining Star of Love, and you the mother wonderfulest of all relations."

Timon asked her to polish the church pews for the wedding.

"I think you glad Old Squirrelzrina gone to the worms, Father."

"You look tired, Darthula. Can I give you a ride home?"

"Not that you ain't sorry about your blessed mama."

"She's in a better world, Darthula."

Father Timon backed the Buick out of its parking space in front of the bank. He already knew the general meanings of the veils. "What does your dark blue give us to understand?"

What the hell had happened to Buicks? Darthula

wondered as the car lurched forward. She'd had her ass kicked less setting in back of Lonnie John Spakes's pickup truck.

"Say what?"

"Dark blue, dark . . ."

"Dark mean the area is still clean of Mephistopheles, but a tall indication he's coming and he ain't far."

Father Timon hadn't been "called" to the priesthood. The truth was more that his mother, who was now gone to her reward, had driven him into his robes. He was deeply ashamed to admit it, but he equated faith with ignorance. Darthula's comforted him for some reason. It was real. He drove past Whitsunday Pentecost Church and circled with the road as it turned around in a clearing. Then he stopped the car and Darthula got out.

"Darthula, can you work for us tomorrow?"

"You and no other, Father."

"I'll pick you up at seven-thirty."

She nodded. Then she disappeared into the thick bramble. As she did, a handful of white butterflies rose behind her.

25

❦

Soames waited by the back of the truck while Leona maneuvered the soft bank of the creek. "Overdoing it a little, aren't we?" Soames said when Leona had crammed the last two sword ferns into the truck bed.

Leona shrugged. "Better to have too much." She had a long day ahead of her in that church. She was determined to give Rhea Anne her money's worth. She knew exactly where she'd use every garland and loop of flowers and leaves. Soames was getting on her nerves. Why had she volunteered to help Leona if she was going to be so critical and oddly resentful?

"Don't delude yourself into thinking the Brisbanes are going to appreciate your efforts," Soames moaned as she dumped her purse on the seat beside Leona and put the truck in reverse. Leona didn't say anything. She had already deposited the Brisbanes' appreciation in the Bank of Orpheus.

Soames chattered like a starling with a toothache as they headed down the hill under the sparkling trees. Leona half listened, counting dogwoods, drawing pictures of raw countryside still wet from last night's rain. The wind in the trees always reminded her of some outerspace cathedral choir. They roiled around the big curve out of the woods, and farmland dropped down a mile on her right, then rose into a long wooded hill. She could see the familiar courthouse clock tower just above the trees.

It always made her glad to see that clock poking its rounded slate roof and white face just above the high horizon. She always felt grateful for the sight. To her it meant she had survived the darkness of the wooded hills behind her and that another world, one better lit and familiar and sensible, hadn't disappeared with all the things she had lost. It was still there and waiting for her. This wedding was her biggest step toward it to date.

"That odious bitch!" Soames had stopped at the light at the southwest corner of Court Square. It was just after eleven. There weren't any other cars in either lane. She didn't see anyone on the sidewalk.

"Who are you talking about, Soames?"

She hissed with irritation as if Leona were the dumbest person alive for not knowing. Soames could be like that. If it was on her mind, it was the most important thing in the world.

"Excuse me for breathing your air, ma'am."

"Whoever taught you it was good sense to play dumb all the time?"

"I'm not playing dumb, Soames. I am dumb!"

They went on in silence, bristling, the pair of them. Soames pulled into the alley behind the church and got out to help Leona unload the truck bed.

"Don't bother," Leona hissed.

"Oh, for God's sake, Leona," Soames moaned, picking up a fern. "You can't haul all this by yourself."

"Please put that down!"

"Fine," she minced, letting the giant green plant drop to the asphalt. She got back into her truck. After Leona had finished unloading the bed, Soames scratched off up the alley.

Weird, the very idea of a wedding upset some women.

Two hours later Soames walked into the sanctuary wearing a good as new smile and carrying a boxed lunch. She had one of her housekeepers with her. That was her way of rolling up her sleeves and digging in.

"I'm sorry for this morning."

"Don't mention it."

"Sweetie . . ." Soames began in a mournful tone. Then she stood and motioned for Leona to follow her through a door beside the altar that eventually led them up a set of stairs and into the church parlor.

"I thought you knew, Leona."

Soames was having a little drama. Leona never knew where the facts began and the fantasy would lead. She was baiting Leona to ask a lot of questions. Leona had hours of work ahead of her.

"Soames, I have work to do."

"Of course you don't know."

"What?" Leona stood up and laid a hand on the doorknob. Soames could drag one of her scenes out for a week. She didn't have the time. Time seemed to be all Soames had.

"Averill is having an affair with Helen Brisbane."

Funny how the reality of a situation hit you first. When Soames told Leona that Averill was sleeping with the bride's mother, Leona's first thought was that now she was really dying to meet her. Clearly Soames was hoping that Leona would at least explode as if a torpedo had just hit her.

"I'm sorry," Soames whispered. "I thought you had a right to know." Soames knew the lay of the land between Leona and Averill. She knew Leona was getting her enterprise off the ground. Leona couldn't have cared less if Averill was sleeping with the bride or her mother. Why did Soames? Soames followed Leona back downstairs into the sanctuary. She kept cramming the thing into Leona's ears. She thought it was the height of deception. That guttersnipe Rhea Anne had known about it all along. This was all designed to humiliate Leona. Soames stayed to help her decorate the church, taking every opportunity to object on Leona's behalf.

Did she not see that Helen and Averill would soon be making a move? She had no doubt Averill would make his move sooner rather than later. However, Leona was preoccupied with her own moves at the moment. So she tried to ignore Soames until, mercifully, she left to have her hair done for the wedding around four o'clock. Soames had succeeded. Leona was riled. Leona was angry. Though not with Averill—with Soames for trying to push her buttons.

Rhea Anne and Helen showed up around five-thirty. Like most legendary seductresses, Helen was a little disappointing in the flesh. She was a small, quiet woman with dyed black hair. She wore a little too much rouge. She was charming, though. She seemed genuinely moved by the decorations. She was very complimentary. In fact, both she and Rhea Anne hugged Leona with tears in their eyes.

Not that Leona was inclined to let anything tarnish the little glow of goodwill she felt toward the Brisbanes when she stopped to consider the fact that their check had immediately cleared upon deposit.

The last person Leona saw in the church was Ransom Brisbane. He crept into the sanctuary and stood at the back while she was gathering her things. Despite his considerable height and broad shoulders, there was a balloonlike quality to Ransom. He seemed always to be straining his neck or poking his heavy frame glasses back up the bridge of his nose with his index finger. That and a host of rumors about him and the Episcopal rector was all Leona could claim she knew about him.

"Mother fuck," he moaned, dropping his jaw with exaggeration, "Mother of God . . ." He moved slowly toward her, taking in the canopy of ferns and wildflowers over the aisle. He had a fancy crystal and gold glass in his right hand, part of a large set she had seen on Father Timon's dining room buffet.

"Exquisite," he spat. Leona smelled vodka. "Helen and I will always be in your debt." He spoke with casual intimacy, as if this were the continuation of a previous conversation. People did that a lot in Orpheus. She supposed it was because they knew so much about each other, it didn't seem relevant whether or not they had actually ever met. In Ransom's case the familiarity seemed closer than that, almost a violation. He was drunk.

Leona was tired. She wanted to take some pictures for her customer book and get out of the church before the guests began to arrive. Ransom was talking ninety to nothing about weddings and fashion designers and swirling his arms like snakes as he conjured up all kinds of images that he found a great deal more exciting than Leona did at the moment.

Did the self-important shit not see she was busy and exhausted and not the least bit interested? Did he think she had some obligation to put up with him? Was she supposed to believe he didn't know about her husband and his wife? Or did it make the moron feel high-class to stand here talking on with her and making a show of not knowing a thing?

"Where did you study design, Leona?"

"I'm afraid I never did," she replied, turning to pick up a metal basket filled with leaves and flower petals.

"Idiot savant?" he asked with a goofy grin that identified the true idiot to Leona's satisfaction. Then he lunged with one arm toward the metal basket in her hands, grabbing it in what was meant as a chivalrous gesture, but which landed him facedown on the floor while the glass in his hand flew across the sanctuary, smashing into a thousand pieces against the baptismal font. There were twigs and leaves and pine needles everywhere.

"Mary Mother of God!" he shouted as he got back to his feet. "Timon's goddamned Medici cocktail glass! Look here!" He pointed to a rise in the edge of the oriental runner at least five feet away from where he'd stumbled. "Haven't you ever heard of tacking down a carpet runner?"

Leona dared not open her mouth. The smallest amount of oxygen would ignite the coals of rage and God alone knew where things would end. She just stood there shaking with gritted teeth while Ransom fled down the aisle.

Because of Ransom's drunken melee, it was five minutes before seven o'clock when Leona walked out of the sanctuary. She was exhausted. She took the route along the side of the church that was away from the parish house lawn. She was avoiding the first wave of wedding folks. She had called one of the Spakes for a ride home. The boy was waiting in his shabby pickup truck in the alley where she and Soames had unloaded the plants that morning. Across the alley were parking places behind the stores along the east end of the square. Most were abandoned at this hour on a Saturday. Just before they reached the street, she spotted Soames's Lincoln in a narrow bay behind a shoe store. Soames had parked there to avoid the wedding traffic along the street.

It was eight-fifteen when Soames pulled into her driveway and got out of her car. She had just come from the church. She was shaking and crying. Rhea Anne had finished dressing for the ceremony upstairs in the church parlor. The church was packed to overflowing. A madrigal was playing. At seven twenty-five the wedding party lined up on the church steps. Ransom Brisbane stumbled upstairs to collect his daughter and lead her down the aisle. He found her asleep on the parlor sofa. He called to her, but she didn't hear him.

Moving closer, he saw the pistol on the floor and the tiny trickle of blood from the hole at the middle of her forehead.

26

MONDAY, APRIL 24, 2000

10:45 P.M.

Leona had been so deep into her account that it
took her a minute to reacclimate to her surroundings.
She had been a long way off. Now Blue looked over his
desk at Leona as if he had just seen the Rapture. Then
he opened his desk drawer and took out a small ivory
pistol. It was identical to the one Leona had seen in
Soames's purse yesterday afternoon.

"Where did that come from?"

"It's Rhea Anne Brisbane's suicide weapon."

It was a pair of antique dueling pistols. Soames had
tried to give her one of them at least a dozen times—for
self-protection! She had even put it in Leona's purse.
Did Leona remember the last time? Now she did. It was
on the afternoon before that doomed wedding. She had
gone into her bag for her scissors and there it sat. She

hadn't even bothered to protest. Instead she had just slipped it quietly back into Soames's purse.

"You messed her up big time," Blue grinned.

Leona shuddered. Soames had tried to frame her. Thanks to Leona's aversion to firearms and her stupidity, she had failed.

"You ready to get yourself arrested?" Blue asked.

"Yeah, but I'm too dumb to pull off a murder," Leona answered. It was chilly in her cell. The odor was revolting. All around her voices echoed. The cot felt like concrete. None of it made any difference to Leona. She put her head down and slept like the dead.

27

From the dining room window Timon could see the old ladies starting to swarm. They had experience with overflow wedding crowds. If they waited until seven-thirty, parking would be a consideration. They could well wind up walking several blocks, not a daunting prospect while it was still daylight, but maneuvering the uneven sidewalks in the dark after the ceremony could be disastrous. They could all name hapless contemporaries who had fallen and broken their hips on an unseen tree root or listing section of concrete. Some recovered, many after long hospital stays and improper healings that required surgical intervention and painful months on canes and walkers. Others had taken arthritis into the breaks and died bedridden from pneumonia within a few months.

Seven-fifteen was too early if getting a seat was the only motivation. There would still be plenty of seats inside the sanctuary at seven-thirty, but this seasoned crowd had known the pitfalls of every church in Orpheus for decades. They knew the most accessible seating, the places with the best views and the ones from which you had the best chance to be viewed, the clunkers in the Presbyterian church that dipped when you leaned forward to take your hymnal off the rack, the Episcopal creakers that squawked during a prayer, the unfortunate pew in the Methodist church above a furnace vent that would scorch your ankles.

Besides, they moved more slowly and they didn't like to be huddled up along a stair rail with a young deputation on their heels. They liked to climb straight-backed, to enjoy the floating sensation as they headed into the sanctuary. They enjoyed being situated and ready to watch the next generation lumber in around seven thirty-five. Though it never failed to startle them how the years had begun to show on the next generation.

Watching them cluster at the church steps, Timon acknowledged that he had accomplished one thing in his life. He had become an expert on old ladies. He would very soon be one himself. Five minutes later the curtain was rising on the spectacle. Darthula was covering platters of leftover hors d'oeuvres with clear plastic. He couldn't count the people who had stopped in all day. They had their ostensible reasons. People never said, "Hi, we're here for the free food and drink."

It was seven-forty. The bridesmaids and groomsmen were sitting in two gray vans across the street from the church steps, where they would line up behind the bride at two minutes until eight. The groom was standing in the alley behind the house, smoking and talking with his uncles. From their laughter he assumed there was a bottle of liquor moving around their narrow circle. Timon wouldn't be part of the wedding procession since he was going to lead the closing benediction from the back of the church. It took a bishop to perform a Brisbane marriage ceremony. He was planning to hold down the church foyer during the ceremony, directing latecomers to the parish house and keeping general watch.

It was almost dark by seven-fifty. The candles flickered behind the stained glass windows in the sanctuary. A trickle of late-arriving guests was being routed into the parish house, where a pair of remote stereo speakers would allow them to hear the ceremony. It was an odd egocentricity of the town. People paid good money for black tie and formal wear and then sat on aluminum chairs at the same folding tables where they sometimes sold rummage, other times played bingo and on Shrove Tuesdays ate pancakes and sausages. It seemed atrocious enough to Timon that airlines oversold flights. Sending engraved invitations marked "black tie only" under the same auspices was extraordinary bad taste. Not here in Orpheus. No one ever complained about it. In fact, there was a regular handful who seemed to prefer it. For obvious reasons the parish house was labeled "the smoker." It always made Timon think of some blitz-era MP's dinner guests waiting out an air raid between courses in a London shelter.

Ransom Brisbane thumped his cigarette into the grass and trotted toward the parish house. He'd take the back stairs up to the second floor and bring Rhea Anne down and across the lawn to enter the church. As he went in, he stopped to hold the door for Soames Churchill. She was wearing a crimson feathered hat. She had a gangly air about her, as if she needed ballast. Maybe she was drunk. Soames moved toward the front of the church, displacing half the wedding party on her way up the steps. Ransom disappeared into the parish house.

Timon had to get over there and take his prominent position at the rear. Darthula came back into the room. She had switched her white veil for the red one.

"Close, is he?"

"Close as you," she replied.

Moving toward the front door of the rectory, Timon passed a gallery of framed photographs that told his unremarkable pictorial history. How he longed for the millionth time for the courage to take what remained of his life and live it. It was one thing to lose your faith in God. There were thousands of theologians and religious scholars whose religious experiences were intellectual rather than spiritual. Timon would settle for faith in life.

How he wished he believed in something as much as Darthula did. How he would give anything to wake up just one day and possess the immutable sense of purpose she did. All he wanted to do before he died was feel himself become God's mortal instrument for good or change or truth, but something. At the door he remembered the little book of prayers he always gave to the bride and groom. He went back to get it.

The rectory was air-conditioned. The dining room windows were closed and the drapes were drawn when Timon took the prayer book off the marble sideboard. It was only the rare sound from outside that penetrated the cool stillness. So it jabbed him between his shoulder blades, the piercing tenor wail from the second-floor window of the parish house.

Meanwhile, fifteen feet away where she was cleaning the kitchen, Darthula's hand reached into a canvas bag and took out a wrinkled red veil.

28

WEDNESDAY, DECEMBER 24, 1997
11:00 P.M.

Averill had rented a small guest house in Orpheus. The parsonage needed more work than his time and budget would accommodate—at least in the beginning. Once Averill had built up a congregation, it was hoped that the funds would materialize. Of course, Averill grew less and less interested in the future of the little church and its ministerial manse as time went by. He was more comfortable in town. There were two or three decent restaurants close by. He could walk up the block to the dry cleaners or the bank or post office. There were people on the street and in the cafés he came to know as speaking acquaintances.

Who was there to see out on Whitsunday Hill except Soames Churchill? Things had gone from a little wild to insane between Averill and Soames. As the situation between Soames and Henri deteriorated, Soames visited her affections on Averill with increasing frequency. She said that it was just her need for physical release. Averill could match her in intensity and appetite. It was all just harmless fun. At first he didn't really connect the little "gifts" she always had waiting—a portable CD player, a dozen hand-sewn broadcloth shirts with Averill's monogram on the cuffs. And cash—she sometimes tucked a pair of hundred-dollar bills in his palm before he left.

When the mechanic told him it was going to cost him a thousand dollars to get his truck in decent shape, he actually caught himself calculating how many times he'd have to bed Soames to raise the cash. Though even better, or much worse, than that—he couldn't honestly decide which—Soames paid the garage and told them that "Mr. Henri" had instructed her to keep his minister in dependable transportation.

As if those weren't enough incentives for a lusty young profligate, Soames always had lavish meals or Averill could sit in Henri's sauna and then let Henri's automatic shiatsu massage chair pound and knead him into a waterlogged noodle. Every time Averill got ready to explain to Soames that he had to stop the affair, she silenced his carefully rehearsed parting speech with a suit or a new pair of Church's English shoes.

It was ironic. Soames's gifts actually decreased Averill's sense of obligation to her. They were more like payments than presents. She knew she could buy his attentions and she lost no pride in doing so. That spared Averill the need to explain the shallow nature of his passion. It alleviated any guilt he might otherwise carry because of his growing attachment to a woman in town.

Averill had drifted into a quiet affair with his landlady,

Helen Brisbane. She and her husband, Ransom, lived in a sprawling white Victorian mansion across the street, which the locals called "The Wedding Cake." They had, by any standards, a very civilized marriage. She was a sweet, sweet, pretty woman with a quiet, impeccable air.

She was the soul of discretion, appearing like a surprise bundle of softness between his lightly starched sheets, dissolving into the darkness like a dream before deeper sleep. She was wild and tender, all silk and fire, and what she drew out of him was something finer than he had ever believed himself to be.

He didn't know when he had started to love her, or where it would lead. He only knew that she made him want to be healed. Like Soames, she had a husband. Unlike Soames and Henri, Helen and Ransom Brisbane had understood the purposes and parameters of their marriage. For reasons Averill didn't quite grasp, or need to, Helen and Ransom would remain for all public appearances husband and wife until their daughter Rhea Anne was married.

Averill assumed that the issue was respectability. However, he would later discover that respectability was a by-product of a far more pragmatic agenda.

All this had evolved in secret during his first year in town. However, it wasn't until he found himself listening to Soames's hollow arias about their future in a glass house overlooking the Pacific Ocean that Averill began to realize how strong his attachment to Helen had become. Soames was too strident, too capricious and self-absorbed. There was a disingenuous quality about every grand thing she said and did. It was all the worst or the best with her; it was all deafening roar or stone silence, all frenzied, excessive ecstasy or "excruciation," her favorite word. Or maybe it was just that no matter how hard he worked to please her, she was eternally dissatisfied, somehow ungenerous in spite of her lavish gifts and, in the end, perpetually unwilling to surrender control in any situation.

It had to end. He had to find a graceful exit, and not just from Soames, but the church as well. He had a vague and gathering sense of a real life with a real woman who he was beginning to hope would be Helen Brisbane. When the day came that she was free, he wanted to be wholly available to pursue her.

By now he had also begun to perceive the undercurrent of panic that fueled Soames's excesses. She was in more trouble than she had ever revealed to him, though he almost thought it was something inside of her. Whatever it was, and whatever raveling messes her languishing marriage would create, Averill was determined to avoid them.

All of which was heavy on his mind the morning of Christmas Eve when he walked out the front door in time to see a wrecker towing his Cutlass away.

"Averill, Henri's lost his mind!" Soames was on the telephone, sounding a little insane herself. "He's dumping me for his little screw-around bitch!" she sobbed, as if he and she hadn't made love almost every day for the last year.

"What went with my car?"

"He cut off my money! They're repossessing it!"

"Why didn't you tell me?"

"Don't yell at me!"

"What the hell is going on?"

"You don't love me."

"Sure I do."

As if the imperious witch had ever loved anyone.

"You've been using me."

That was the truth, of course. In a lot of ways this was a godsend. Except for the car. He figured he'd earned it. That made him a kind of a whore, he guessed. But he had recently come to the conclusion that certain moral ideas were a luxury of the privileged. He'd save his remorse for better days. He wasn't about to let go, not yet.

"Of course I love you."

"You know that pistol we bought me?"

"Yes . . ."

She had gotten increasingly worried, almost paranoid about Henri. She was afraid to be alone in the country without protection. They had purchased her a .45 pistol last week in Memphis. He had tried to show her how to use it, but she freaked. Or acted like it. Lately it seemed everything she did was acting like something.

"I'm going to use it on myself." Then she hung up. He dug around and found his truck keys. The truck was sitting on the alley where it had been since Soames Churchill had decided he could drive a Cutlass. Well then, the Lord Soames giveth and the Lord Henri taketh away, he mused. It took him half an hour to start the truck.

Soames was berserk with anguish and shrieking in terror every time the house creaked. Henri and she had battled through the night. He had ordered her off the place and then left. He had taken Averill's car and padlocked the church. He was going to have Averill up on all sorts of charges which a well-connected hypocrite like Henri Churchill could make stick. It took Averill half a quart of Seagram's Crown Royal to get her to sleep for an hour. He had to cut his losses and run. But where? And how? He didn't have fifteen cents to his name.

"Angel of God!"

Soames was awake, feeling "miraculously better." "Famished," as she always said. No trace of the former terror. This was Soames on top of the world, Soames, the eternal optimist. Or Soames the nutcase, he wasn't so sure anymore. "He can't hurt us, baby," she purred. "I've got stacks of evidence to use against him. He'll send us on a honeymoon that will last the rest of our lives." Averill knew she was seducing him. He knew it was all bravura. Was it habit, ego or lack of a better idea? He didn't know. There they were, tugging at each other's clothes on the parlor floor. This was going to get him killed someday. He couldn't help it. Soames just had a way to get him all "famished" too.

29

❦

When he left the courthouse, Blue paid a call on Arlen McFaye. He lived down a sharp hill of squat, shingled bungalows. Arlen's wasn't big enough to turn around in. He lived there with a wife and four kids and his mother. There couldn't be more than two bedrooms. Yet there was no sign of anyone else when Arlen let Blue into the living room. The place was immaculate. Every surface glistened. Everything that could be stowed had a niche. At the side of the room, a neatly taped plastic tarp revealed the skeletal outline of a room in progress. If Arlen was a McFaye, he was the trying kind. He'd been in the army. He was only four or five years older than Blue, but he was already bald.

"I can't believe what I'm hearing about you, Hudson."

"Then don't."

"What do you want?"

"Did you autopsy Rhea Anne Brisbane?"

The question caught him off guard. He had to catch hold of it.

"No. Nobody asked for an autopsy."

"You didn't examine her and fill out the death certificate?"

"No one suspected foul play."

"Did Sheriff Meeks ever discuss the possibility that it was a murder?"

"Of course not."

The two men were silent for a moment.

"A little over a year ago. During the big January snow, you examined a stillbirth?"

"I have no recollection."

"A stillborn infant girl born to the Reverend and Mrs. Averill Sayres."

Something behind Arlen's eyes had just added. It made him uneasy.

"It was born dead."

"Why?"

"Who knows?"

"It just happens, huh?"

"All the time."

"What kind of tests do you run?"

"None in this case."

"Why not?"

"Am I suspected here?"

"Hell, no."

"Then I done you enough favors for one day."

Blue explained. He hadn't meant to insinuate that Arlen wasn't doing a fine job. There was a killer loose. His odds of getting that person locked up before someone else died were getting slimmer by the minute. He had a real situation on his back. There was an element of the birthing of that child that related to something else. He'd been presented some strong hints of possible foul play. Did anything on record indicate even the remotest possibility?

Now Arlen looked very uncomfortable. He crossed the room, switched on his computer and dug into his files. He pulled up the record. The official cause of death was asphyxia during the third trimester.

"What's that mean?"

"It means we had to give it our best guess."

"How extensive was your exam?"

"Off the record?"

Blue held his breath.

"If this bites me—"

"You have my word."

"A man of God comes to me grief-stricken over his wife's stillbirth. He tells me the baby came a week ago while they were snow- and icebound. His poor wife went psycho with grief. She held on to it for two days. It was starting to smell. Phone lines were down. He had to knock her unconscious. Then he went across the road in the ice and snow and dug a grave with a pickax. He can show me where. Now, I can put this tormented couple through the hell of a useless exhumation. Or fill out two forms and sign them. Which would you do?"

"You never even examined it?"

"What would you do?"

"What you did, Arlen." Blue leaned over Arlen's

shoulder. He fingered the keys and the screen glowed yellow. He hit one more and the information vanished.

"Why the hell did you do that?"

"Now kill the backup copy."

"Why?"

"To save both of our asses."

30

❦

TUESDAY, APRIL 25, 2000
12:13 A.M.

There wasn't much moon and the ground was wet. All around him it felt like eyes peered at him from the woods. Sometimes when he let the pick fall into the soft clay, his eye held the image of the dark parsonage across the road through the iron cemetery fence. Over and over as he worked, he saw Averill sitting on the porch wearing one of his straw hats and watching his progress. Sometimes a deer cracked the brush or a screech owl let loose with a paralyzing cry and he almost expected the dead all around him to rise.

Sometimes he caught an indecipherable murmur near the path that split the woods as it climbed the hill. Then he knew Soames was on to him. He pitched one shovelful after another onto the pile that slowly rose as he sank in the slowly deepening hole. Every time his head followed his arm upward to release a load of earth, he expected Soames to be standing on top of it, taking aim with her delicate ivory pistol.

When the woods were blurred with the blue-gray mist of approaching morning, Blue felt the shovel scrape against something wooden. Redoubling his efforts, he had the top protruding a few inches out of the moist earth in about five minutes. Using his pickax, he pried it gently open. It was wrapped in infant's blankets and bound with wire. He lifted the mummified relic over his head and let it roll slowly off his hands and onto the ground. The wire was coated with plastic and it was hell to break.

It was almost full daylight by the time he could unwrap the blankets, which soon began to look almost new after he had loosened several layers. Then the last blanket was opened.

Nothing. Not a trace or remnant of any kind.

No, hell, no. Of course not. He'd known as much, and so had Leona, but it was too obvious for either one of them to see it. Leona hadn't relied on her fragmented memory of the night the baby was born. That wasn't what convinced her Averill had murdered the baby. It was the set pieces all around her. The grave. The empty crib. The autopsy. Other people's accounts of what happened. Those things fit together as they had been designed to complete the picture. Averill had actively worked to create that picture. It was a very convincing composite portrait of a stillbirth.

A stillbirth. Not a murder. It was Soames who had altered their original design. Leona had told him as much—without realizing what it meant. Soames had come to Leona, and "confessed" her "past" affair with Averill. Then she had convinced Leona that Averill had murdered the baby.

Blue stood up. Behind the woods the horizon was red. He turned toward the road. The parsonage windows gave back the angry sky. It was still dark there. Glancing off his shoulder as he slipped the car into drive, Blue caught one last image of Averill peering off the porch at the gaping hole and the new mound of dirt in the cemetery.

Let them bury the bastard in it.

31

She kept Blue waiting an hour in the double parlor while she bathed and dressed. She had laid this scenario out in her mind, even practiced a few French phrases to give her performance a smooth finish. She kept him waiting an hour because she had expected him all day yesterday and into last night. When the housekeeper woke her at 6:30 A.M. to say Sheriff Hudson had called, she was furious. She fumbled with her makeup. Then she drank a Bloody Mary to settle her nerves. Then she couldn't decide which housecoat was the most becoming. Blue had waited for an hour when she finally waltzed into the parlor.

"Why, Mister Blue Hudson, sir! What are you doing on my love seat looking like Caravaggio's 'Cupid' at this ungodly hour?"

She had swept through a gigantic arched doorway with marble column supports that separated the front parlor from the back one behind his head. Sneak attack, of course.

"What have you been doing for the last hour?"

She stood at the far end of the room, a wary lioness waiting for her cornered prey to make his inevitable, fatal move. The early sun flooded the gilt-and-velvet parlor with lurid yellow. The intense light revealed dry, pallid flesh under a veneer of makeup. She had rubbed a white substance into tiny dark folds of flesh under her eyes. She was an aging carnivore, embittered by years of stalking lesser warm-blooded creatures through sleepless, solitary darkness.

"Why have you hauled me out of bed at this ungodly hour?"

"I need your help."

She despised getting out of bed before ten o'clock in the morning, but Soames had an intuition that this was going to be worth it. Was he investigating a murder or trying to cover it up? No one had really bothered to question her about the murder, despite the fact that she had been the one who called Blue's office to report it. She had heard plenty of lurid tales about his inappropriate conduct with Leona in the last day or so.

"Leona needs my help."

"Leona isn't worth helping," Blue said.

"You bastard! She was in love with you!"

"You think she's so damned good?"

"I won't help you send her to death row."

"Then you'll help Leona send you to death row."

Blue had to admit that in spite of all the circumstances, he was beginning to enjoy his visit. Soames was always acting. Didn't it figure then that she would fall for his performance?

"Send *me* to death row?"

"She says you shot Averill Sayres."

Soames had plenty of color now. She pasted on an incredulous mask.

"I'll let you see yourself out."

"Look, we know she's lying."

She regained her aloof expression.

"Me? She turned on me like that?"

Blue wasn't about to waste a cue like that.

"I know all about how Leona turns on those who care the most."

That worked. He had reassured her.

"Don't you want something to drink?"

When he was finally back at the wheel of the Jeep, he went all jittery. He had given her quite a performance, pretending that he had recently come to the reluctant conclusion that Leona had not only murdered Averill but Rhea Anne Brisbane as well.

"What?"

This time there was unmistakable triumph in her incredulity. Blue ran through the various incriminating facts surrounding that case as it related to Leona. He was hoping Soames would indicate some kind of satisfaction that he was basically saying that her setup had succeeded.

"She was not only the last person alone in that church with Rhea Anne, but the only person in the county who had any motive for killing her."

Yet Soames seemed to weigh what he told her about the gun.

"The clinker is the gun. We know Leona used the

same one to kill both Rhea Anne and Averill. But we can't find it."

"I'm afraid I don't see what any of this has to do with me."

"I was just hoping she might have said something."

"About the murder weapon?" Soames asked with disdain. "You must think I'm an accomplice!"

This was going to be his exit line. He had to say it just right.

"Not about the weapon, Soames. About me."

"You?"

"Yeah. Like whether or not she ever really loved me."

Moving down the long driveway toward the road, Blue kept checking the rearview mirror, half expecting Soames to step out from behind a giant Corinthian column and fire a pistol at the back of his head. Well, if she did, he mused, the county would have all the evidence it needed to free Leona and convict Soames.

Of course the real question was, now that he had set the trap, was she going to take the bait?

32

❦

There had been nothing to do but wait until dark in the woods. He had pulled the truck into a dry creek bed and under a sandstone ridge. Folding his fleece-lined jacket into a wad behind his head, he stretched out across the seat. He kept fading in and out. After midnight Blue drove without headlights as close as he felt it was safe, then he crept through the woods about a mile before he came out in the cemetery across the road from the parsonage. The house was dark. The Oldsmobile and the truck sat where they had been last night. All the same, he kept his head low and moved from tree to tree, making a wide arc that took him to the porch.

Once inside the dark house, he searched in the shadows, feeling around in drawers and at the backs of shelves. The little pearl-handled pistol was wrapped in a piece of velvet and tucked into the toe of Averill's galoshes at the bottom of the bedroom closet. He examined it for a moment, removed a bullet, and then wrapped the pistol and put it back.

Nothing to do now but wait. He sat in the silent house, crouched in a dark corner of the living room, and watched the moonlit face of an old Seth-Thomas shift from nine to midnight to three A.M. The longer he waited, the longer his list of unanswered questions grew. He had miscalculated something. Then around four A.M. he heard footsteps on the driveway. The door had been unlocked when he got there. He had locked it so she would have to jimmy a window. He wanted her to think her secret was locked tight.

Either she wasn't much of a thief or she was drunk. It took her fifteen minutes to get a living room window open. She went straight to the bedroom. He followed her, standing in the door as she knelt at the closet. She didn't start or even scream when he flipped on the overhead light. She just sat back on her haunches and threw her hands in the air, one of which held the weapon she had carried for protection.

"Drop it," he said.

"I'm sick to death of it," she said. Then her right hand aimed the gun inside her mouth and as she fell forward, his face was splattered with blood and brains.

33

❦

Soames had no intentions of spending any more time in this hot sheet motel. She had woken up around six-thirty and dressed, leaving Averill in Birdland while she took care of business. Now it was after eight and the worthless bastard could start earning his keep.

"Lover . . ."

He opened his eyes, moaned and shut them again, turning away from her.

Where the hell did the shiftless piece of Holy Roller trash get the idea he had the right to sleep until noon? She pulled back the sheet and he drew his long torso into a ball. He reminded her of a hairless lizard in bikini briefs.

"Get your bony ass up!"

He stared at her, incredulous.

"What are you looking at?"

" 'S wrong, baby?"

"I have a little Christmas present for you."

He sat forward, grinning like a juvenile.

"It's not here. It's out at the house." She threw him his shirt and trousers. He tried to shake off the rest of his sleep and confusion. Henri had thrown her out for good. She couldn't go back to the house. He shouldn't be here or anyplace close to here with Soames.

"You can't go to the house right now."

"Baby, I can go to that house anytime I like for as long as I like."

"Henri . . ."

"Henri had a little accident this morning."

Averill felt ice water running down his back.

"What kind of accident?"

"Hunting," she said with a bored expression, swooping his socks off of the floor.

"How is he?"

"To my way of thinking? Henri has never been better."

"Dead?"

"Death doesn't close for Christmas, Father Feelgood."

"How'd it happen?" he asked, carefully avoiding any direct reference to the strange name she had just called him. She was souped, high on something or out of her mind. She had an ominous air, a boding irony about her that scared him.

"I shot him."

She'd flipped. She had a gun in her purse and she was going to use it on him. He dove for the door, jerked it open and ran into the afternoon drizzle without belt or shoes. By the time he was halfway across the parking lot toward the café, Soames was outside the room, bent double, laughing. She had left her purse in the room and her hands were empty.

"Horny little worm."

He followed her back inside the room.

"You think I'd shoot you in the broad daylight in a motel room?"

"Yes, you're acting that crazy."

"Well, I'm not even half that crazy, idiot."

They had to get out to the house and make things look like a big Christmas dinner had been planned. She wanted him to help open a mess of presents so it looked like Henri and she had exchanged gifts that morning. She wanted breakfast leftovers with hers and Henri's fingerprints on them. Then they would have to drag the body out into the fields and arrange it with the pistol she'd used so it looked like a self-inflicted wound.

He was certain now that she wasn't armed. However, her assurances about her sanity hadn't convinced him one iota. What made her think he'd have any part of murder? He was clean and he was going to stay that way.

"You go on, I'll visit my sister and her husband."

"You'd abandon me?"

"This is murder you're talking."

"Premeditated murder." She nodded.

"Then you know I can't get involved."

Soames gave him a dazzling smile. Then she laughed. There wasn't a trace of cruelty or sarcasm in it. She was genuinely amused. "I don't know how to tell you this, Reverend. But you're an idiot."

She took obvious relish in explaining it all for him. He'd been the adulterous paramour of a murdered man's wife. Without thinking, he had cosigned papers last month that made them joint owners of a home in Laguna Niguel, California. Henri had not only taken his car away from him yesterday, but he had thrown Averill and his wife into the street. He had taken Averill's church away from him and his lawyers were planning to name him in a series of lawsuits. Henri's body was already stiff and cold, and nearby the gun used to murder him was lying in plain sight. Averill had purchased that gun a week ago. Averill's fingerprints were all over it, as well as Henri's bedroom, bed and widow. Averill had checked into this establishment last night with the deceased's wife and both had been seen here today by the staff.

"I didn't kill anybody," Averill stammered.

"Not as long as you do exactly what I tell you to do."

"I've got the truth on my side."

"I've got the evidence on mine, stud. . . ." She grabbed his groin area with her fist and squeezed his testicles lightly. "Merry Christmas, lover."

Later, when everything had been done as Soames commanded at the house, she called town for an ambulance. "An accident. My husband, Henri, was climbing a fence with a loaded pistol—a Christmas gift—it went off and I think . . . I think he's . . . Hurry!"

Averill waited in the silence after she hung up the phone while she busied herself opening a stack of Christmas cards.

"Oh, the Heathertons!" she cried as if it was the merriest Christmas ever. "Look at the girls!?! Aren't they gorgeous?" She handed him a photocard of a family of four in green plaid.

"What do you want me to do now?"

"Do?"

"I can't be here when the cops arrive."

"Who called the cops?"

"There's been a murder here!"

"There's been an accident."

"I can't stay here."

"No, lover, you can't."

"What about the house in California?"

"You don't really think I bought a house in California?" She chuckled with delight.

"You said . . ."

"I lied."

"Why?"

"To make you my accomplice."

"To murder?"

"To my life."

"What do you want from me?"

"Your mind, body and soul."

"You really are a witch."

"No, I'm not that special; but I am a good liar."

"Then why do I get the feeling you're telling me the truth?"

"We're rich, lover boy. When the smoke clears we're going to sail around the world on the QE 2."

She could think that if she wanted to. He was out of there. He'd go on foot if need be. "I'm leaving."

"Your car's in the garage."

"What?"

"I had it towed."

"You said . . ."

"I told you, I lied!"

"To trap me."

"Yes."

"Why?"

"Because I love you."

"You don't even trust me."

"That's different."

"Well, I'm leaving you."

"No, Averill, you're leaving—but you'll never leave me."

Over and over as the Cutlass rolled down the highway, he heard the sound of her voice telling him that he would never leave her.

34

❦

Eight months after Averill left Soames to explain Henri Churchill's body, he moved down the front steps of the Clay house in Fredonia and slipped up the block in the twilight past the neat bungalows and squared hedges of the saved. In his pocket was a yellowed envelope containing seventeen thousand dollars, Viola Clay's life savings. She had ferociously held on to it through the bad years, believing she would spend the money on Leona's wedding one day.

By his own reckoning Viola couldn't survive more than a day or two. It had taken all her strength to lift the envelope and give it to him.

"Leona's in a familial condition and I ask your help in getting her away." He said that he would. He meant what he said. He'd been to visit as part of his duty as a part-time assistant to the Church of Christ minister. Since Viola was Methodist to the bone, the minister considered his obligation to her as secondary. Averill had gone to visit her twice a week in his stead.

"I assure you we'll find her a respectable option," Averill said.

He felt sorry for the girl. The whole town was spinning on the fact that the Crockett boy had ruined her. She was a pretty thing, full of spunk and warmth. Now all he had to do was find a way to keep his promise and Viola's money as well. Was he supposed to turn a girl's whole life around for free? As long as he left Leona in good stead at the end of the day, he was sure Viola would consider it a bargain.

He turned the corner and moved toward the boarding house where he'd taken a room. Soames was sitting in a raveling wicker chair on the porch. He'd spoken with her on the telephone twice since last Christmas, but this was the first time he'd seen her in person.

"What are you doing here?" he asked, with undecorated dismay.

"Who are you doing without me?"

The answer was Helen Brisbane, but he and Helen had taken extraordinary pains to meet in secret. He was sure Soames didn't have a clue.

"What are you doing here?" he asked her again, almost angry.

"I have news from heaven."

Henri Churchill's death had been investigated every way the old sheriff knew how to do it. The coroner had finally closed the inquest, and Henri Churchill's death was forevermore an accident.

"Congratulations."

"I'm lonely. I miss you."

"That's your bid'ness."

"I shouldn't have tried to involve you."

"It turned out all right."

"I was Henri's prisoner, Averill. It made me crazy."

"Done is done."

"We're not done!"

"I am," he said, feeling the power of a dying woman's seventeen thousand dollars in his pocket.

"I'll give you anything you want, Averill."

"I don't believe you, Soames."

"I'll deed you that church and the parsonage and pay you a good salary."

"Why?"

"I'm not too proud to buy your love, Averill."

"Suppose it doesn't work out that way?"

"Give me a chance at least."

"I'll call you," he said, feeling more than a little triumphant as he waltzed past her into the boarding house and let the screen door close in her addled face.

It was a trap. He knew it was a trap. He told Helen it was. She saw his point, but she was in love with him. She wanted him near. Her daughter Rhea Anne was engaged to be married next September. After that, they could go their own way. In the meantime, Soames's offer would keep him close to her. She was miserable without him. She was afraid of losing him.

Averill knew that Helen loved him. Or needed him in that desperate way some women called love. There was no question he wanted the things her money could buy. Yet he sensed that he was able to earn it in some ways. He pleased her in bed, as he had never felt he could please any other woman. He didn't find her as alluring as Soames. However, he didn't feel what went on between him and Helen was dark and wrong in ways he couldn't understand. Helen was easy. She had made a lot of compromises long before she met Averill. He seemed to possess enough of what it took to keep her content.

They meant a lot to each other. They weren't holding out for anything like perfection. They would work it all out just fine.

Leona was a complication. He had a promise to keep. Even his easy morals wouldn't let him feel right about keeping her money and leaving the poor girl out in the cold. Still, he had to play it all Soames's way.

He didn't tell Soames his plan until the day he and Leona had left the town of Fredonia in his truck. They had stopped near Grenada to buy gas. He called her from a pay phone while Leona went inside to use the rest room.

"Soames?"

"Yes," she said with a voice full of sleep.

"I'm going to accept your offer, but . . ."

"That's wonderful, darling."

"I said, but . . ."

As if one small Mississippi town was an island to itself—as if Soames didn't know, hadn't spoken with any number of connections in the Fredonia area. As if Viola hadn't told half the world that she had given the nice young man her money to see about Leona's future.

"But what, angel?"

"I'm bringing a wife with me."

That was to create a boundary, a wall of decency over which Soames would find it more difficult to climb—and behind which Averill could hide with Helen Brisbane as long as it was necessary. Of course he didn't say any of that. He said that they could use Leona as a decoy. Soames acted thrilled.

"Since when did a wedding band overpower destiny, Averill?"

What an idiot he'd been. What a fool! God, she loved it. Did he really think she hadn't watched his every move during the last six months in Fredonia? No, of course not. No more than it would have occurred to him that Soames could use his so-called wife as a means of communicating with him whenever he decided to play hide-and-seek. There was no legal limit preventing further investigation of Henri's murder. Yes, the coroner had been forced from lack of evidence to rule it accidental. That didn't mean a judge and jury had legally declared it. She still had everything she needed to pin it on Averill if she decided to. In fact, she had long ago decided to. The only question was, when?

At the time of their romantic reunion on the porch of his boarding house, Soames still had good use for Averill Sayres, more than ever, in fact. Of course, she knew all about Leona. She had hired an investigator who had spent a week in Fredonia going from house to house pretending he was a Bible salesman. The man knew his trade. Under the pretext that he always gave a leather-bound copy of the Holy Word to every clergyman in town, he invited Averill to his hotel room, spiked his Sprites with pure grain alcohol and got all the information direct from the jackass's mouth.

Averill's self-serving rescue of the desperate girl not only was fine with Soames; it sounded like a godsend to her. It would provide her what she wanted more than anything else. This was no white trash mess-up. Leona

came from respectable people. Tyler's family had plenty
of distinguished ancestors. This was going to be a child
of good old Southern stock.

"I hope this Clay girl appreciates your generosity,
Averill."

Averill was playing right into her cold, ivory hands.
Leona Clay would go into labor next winter, but she
would never know what happened. As far as she had to
know, the baby would be a stillbirth—"decently buried"
while they kept her under heavy sedation for a day or
two. Averill would go along with Soames's plan. She'd
see to that.

As soon as Averill and Leona were settled, Soames
called and demanded to see him. When he didn't show
up at her house as promised, she called him again. He
broke his second promise as well. She sat in the parking
lot next to the church and waited several hours the next
afternoon. When Averill finally pulled up, he saw her
and quickly drove away. Finally, Soames hid her car and
cut through the woods. Then she jimmied his office
window open, climbed in and hid in a closet. She was
about to leap out and surprise him when she heard him
speak into the telephone receiver. In three minutes
Soames knew the whole story of Averill and Helen
Brisbane. Soames stayed in the closet until she heard
Averill's truck start.

The next time Soames broke into Averill's office and
waited for him, she was holding a dear little white pistol
and she had it cocked and pointed when he opened the
door.

"What do you want, Soames?"

He was trying not to look scared, but she could see him trembling.

"You."

"We both know better than that."

"If I can't have you, then no one can. . . ."

"You'll have to kill Leona, too; she's waiting in the truck."

"Love me like you used to. . . ."

"Put that gun down and go!"

"Two bullets, Averill. One for you, one for me."

"Stop it!"

"Make love to me!"

"I can't!"

She fired over his head, though close enough to make it seem like a genuine miss. The bullet passed through the open French door and lodged in a tree, with a soft ping.

"One bullet now, Averill. One for you."

She took aim.

"Don't! Please . . ."

"Tell me you love me."

"I love you."

"Make love to me."

"Later."

"In my silk and velvet bed?"

"Yes."

"I'll kill you if you stand me up again."

That night in the breathing shadows, Soames showed him his sickness. She understood his inescapable, base nature. It wasn't mind, body or soul that turned into passion between them.

"Do you know what makes me want you, Averill?"

"No."

"You hurt me the right way."

"You're crazy."

"Do you know that you're broken?"

"In some ways."

"In identical ways, you and I . . ."

"Then we need other people to fix us."

"We're irreparable, Averill. We're damaged goods."

"I don't want to be."

"Do you know why you came here tonight?"

"You threatened to kill me."

"That excited you."

"It scared me!"

"Pain and terror are all you and I can feel, Averill."

She was frightening him. He understood her. The conversation and its morbid tinges were having the intended effect. He could feel new desire boiling in every pore. It sickened him. That drove his lust into frenzy. She called him a mule and dog and she shrieked with pain and begged him for more and he couldn't stop, not with the heavy aphrodisiac scent of death filling the dark.

Later she bathed him, caressing his spent flesh with warm oils and teasing and whispering her desire. He would bring her the baby, the bastard his wife carried; she would explain how to do it. When he told her she was out of her mind, she agreed. He would do it all the same, she told him. He would give her this happiness in exchange for his own. Or the state would execute him for the crime of breaking into her house on Christmas Eve 1997, tying her and raping her repeatedly, then murdering her husband. What did he want to see? Semen stains or fingerprints? Though she had so much more evidence.

So he agreed. He gave in. He tried to convince himself

that somehow it would mean a fresh start for Leona as well. He also worked hard to avoid Soames and resist her invitations, but he seemed weaker than ever. He rehearsed how the event would take place with Soames: the signal, the meeting places and the drug that would keep Leona unconscious for several days. He agreed. He resigned himself to the ugly scenario. Though in the end, he had shocked himself with the drastic act that became his death sentence. Instead of bringing the infant as promised, Averill had turned and run into the woods.

"Soames?" He had awakened her about two A.M. with his phone call. "You aren't going to believe this. . . ."

He told her the infant was a stillbirth. She said all the things he would expect her to say if she believed him. Then she told him that in spite of her desperate edges and threats, she held no enmity for him. She was grateful for his efforts. Acts of God were beyond his control. She had only meant to love Averill. She had finally realized that she loved him enough to want his happiness. She convinced him that he was free of her demands, threats and influences.

She knew that he had believed her. The best way to deceive a person was to tell him exactly what you knew he most wanted to hear. She also knew that Averill was lying. Leona had seen the doctor in Orpheus the day before. How difficult was it for Soames to call his office, pretend she was throwing a last-minute baby shower for the preacher and his wife and extract the information that Leona was at full term of a normal pregnancy.

Averill had murdered that baby. What else could it

be? What Soames Churchill claimed became her property. Averill had murdered her baby. Whether it was from insanity or anxiety or for vengeance against Soames for blackmailing him, she didn't care.

He had done it, and after Helen Brisbane's daughter was married in September, he and Helen were going to dissolve into the blue. Unless of course some unforeseen calamity prevented it. Unless the groom got cold feet or the bride's went so cold that rigor mortis set in. That tragic turn had cost Helen a daughter, but it had cheated Averill of something he held equally dear. The terms of Helen's legal arrangement with Ransom stated that their child had to be married before she would legally pass "Go" and collect her million dollars. How long would Averill's eternal love for his overripe pear last after he realized her purse would always be empty?

When Soames Churchill sent a wedding gift, she sent one that lasted forever.

35

❖

The sky was already pink and silver through the little window above her cot. The night had dropped down chilly and the cotton blanket they had given her was worthless. She was asleep and awake. As she sat up, she thought for an instant she saw Blue sitting on the empty cot across the cell from hers.

"Hey." He grinned.

"Hey, yourself," she said.

"It's all over. Soames is dead."

Then his arms were around her. She realized at once that this was that waking dream called life. She couldn't fathom it. How had he set her free? The whole scenario was impossible. Life twisted around so fast. Everything shifted. Everything changed or shed its outer layer and turned out to be something else.

He had left the cell door open. People were gathering around. There was shouting and explaining, and one by one, the voices died away. Somehow she was sitting beside Blue in his truck, driving home.

"You saved me," she said, thinking out loud. He was more pensive than she would have expected. He shifted his eyes toward her and then back to the double beam on the narrow road.

"You saved me first," he countered. It almost angered her. She had spoken a fact straight out. He was being ridiculously modest. It was self-deprecation to the point of falsehood. She owed him her life. He couldn't make anything like such a claim.

"I tried to kill Averill."

"That's attempted murder."

"I'm bound to face charges."

"No evidence."

"I signed a confession."

"Gee, you know what? I completely lost it."

"That's police corruption."

"Yes, it is."

They were coming through that brief, boding bottom land she had hated since the night months earlier when she had imagined the stooped figure running for cover with a baby in her arms. She had never told him about it. It seemed to her now that she never would. She would leave this place. She would abandon as much of it as she could and live with the memory of the rest. She still thought she might be more use to herself and the world in a city.

Leave him? She owed him everything. She was suddenly aware that she had no power over her feelings for him. It frightened her a little. She had no means to protect herself from this immutable, imperishable bond with him.

Neither one of them could sleep. They lay side by side in the blue dark, listening to the faint hissing of the wind in the trees. It was only now that the impact of the last two days let its brutal, transforming jolt echo and shatter a thousand familiar shapes and perceptions.

"Blue?"

"Yes?"

"Do you feel old?"

"A thousand at least."

"Why did Averill want me?"

"I think you know."

"The baby."

"Soames wanted a baby."

"Averill and Soames? I don't get it."

He had to tell her. They had driven past the cemetery in the dark. She was going to see that mound of dirt across the road when she went outside in the morning. He had to tell her. Yet it was condemning her to an endless, raveling agony. The notion of her infant strangled and buried was devastating. It was loss and grief and everlasting sorrow to carry. But there was finality. There was a changeless, cold marble fact to be resisted and then very slowly taken in and accepted.

What did an empty grave mean? Had Averill simply hidden the real burial site from fear? Was he afraid of an exhumation? Had he murdered it after all? Had he cracked its skull or left some other signature of his killing? Or did he have another purpose? Had he been thwarted somehow in an attempt to present Soames with a child? Had she promised him money? Or was she blackmailing him, using her ability to prove his involvement in Henri Churchill's death?

There were endless questions, enough to torture Leona for the rest of her life.

"Leona?"

"Yes?"

"There's no body buried in Tess's grave."

"I know."

"You know?"

"He wouldn't risk it."

"You mean you figured it out."

"Everything except why he did it."

"To punish you."

"For what?"

"For your sins."

She had been very calm, very controlled and logical. She had taken the view that it could only mean Averill hid his savagery with it in a secret, unmarked grave. That would shift like the wind. It would crumble every time she heard about some couple that had an adopted daughter. The inescapable hope would haunt her forever.

They passed a night of brooding silences interrupted by troubled fits of unfinished conversation.

"Blue, do you think Tess is dead?"

"Yes."

"How do you know that?"

"I don't know it, I . . ."

What could he say? He had a theory. Soames Churchill figured into it. But his theories weren't hypotheses. His wasn't an x-equals-y way of thinking. His theories were plain gut instinct, what in a woman would be construed as "intuition." The way he saw it, Soames

Churchill had Averill Sayres by the ying-yang with a downhill pull when he brought Leona home. Sayres was scared to death. He didn't just show up with a wife who was expecting a baby. It was all to some hidden purpose.

"Did Soames ever say she wanted a baby?"

"I don't remember."

"Did she act any certain way around you while you were expecting?"

"I didn't know her then."

"You must have seen her everywhere."

"No."

"At church?"

"Maybe, but I don't think so."

"Wasn't she in the choir?"

"No. That was after the baby."

That had some significance. Soames went where she had something to gain. Period. Otherwise she wouldn't have bothered. So Leona had nothing Soames wanted directly from her until after she'd lost the baby.

"What'd she want from you, Leona?"

"What did I have?"

"Sayres."

"No, Helen Brisbane had Averill."

"He was a scared rabbit, Leona."

"What's that got to do with it?"

"He had the world screwed on backward."

"Blue, I know Averill was insane. . . ."

"He worshipped his own worst fears."

"I know he was paranoid! I know scared little rabbits do stupid things!" She was pounding his chest with both fists, furious.

"Why are you doing this, Leona?"

"Why the hell did you have to play tall sheriff!?!"

"I saved your life!"

"You made it worse!"

Her words stung. She could see that. He could see that she felt guilty for saying them. Yet neither one of them could deny their meaning. The loss, when Leona had believed that she had simply given birth to a stillborn child, was almost unbearable. Yet she had somehow come through it, at least the immediate, searing pain of it. Then she discovered that it was no ordinary wound. It was infected by perversion and cruelty. It hadn't healed at all. It had only been festering. Its poison had slowly worked on her until she had tried to relieve her tortured mind by taking her own demented justice.

Now, after all of it, there was this terrible hope, this raw belief that had the power to turn everything else meaningless again. He had given her baby away. Or sold it to one of those illegal adoption rings you heard about. Why else would that grave have turned out to be empty? No. No, he had simply made double sure there was no hard proof of what he'd done. Maybe he figured Leona would put it all together in time.

It made no sense. Who could he have given a newborn infant to in an ice storm way up a dirt road? Someone had helped him. Someone knew. Soames? Why would Soames help Averill kidnap or kill her baby?

"Blue, he must have given her to Soames."

"Why?"

"I don't know!"

"Then where is she?"

"Maybe Soames gave her to someone else."

"Why?"

"I don't know yet. I'm thinking. . . ."

"Leona, you'll never know. You'll have to wonder for the rest of your life."

"If I don't find out what happened to Tess, I won't have a life!"

"*We*, Leona, *we* won't have a life."

He looked even sadder than he had on that day he first came to see Averill. She flooded with shame. He had appeared out of the gray woods, and slowly the world had turned green with possibilities. He had made her believe in life all over again. How had he done that? He hadn't given her back the things she had lost. He hadn't explained life to her any better than she could interpret it for him. If his power had been love, then why did they both feel doomed now?

Could she just go on for the rest of her life without ever knowing? Had Averill murdered her infant and buried her in the inscrutable black swamp? Could Tess be alive? Could she be walking now somewhere in the vast world beyond the circling treetops? Were people like trees? Would time surround and protect Leona with a tough outer layer while her insides turned to wood? Was that what people meant by putting one foot in front of the other one and plodding on?

Their eyes met as eyes do when two people in conversation have drifted into wordless scrutiny. Why did his eyes always seem to see something that hers didn't? There was something indomitable there. It had drawn her to him. Now it made her sad because she had begun to think that Blue simply believed in some eventual good that she couldn't.

He hated her sadness. It scared him. It took her deep inside of herself, way beyond some impenetrable wall. It left him floundering in solitude. It showed him how small he was next to her overwhelming loss. It forced him to admit that at times her despair was greater than her ability to overcome it.

"What is it, Blue?"

"What you want is a miracle."

"I know."

"No, you don't."

What could he tell her that she didn't already know? What passionate beliefs could he foist on her that weren't tinged with his needs and desires? What pure and immutable good thing could he produce that might change the raveling future and prevent her inevitable descent into hell?

"You want me to be your miracle."

"That's ridiculous."

"It's the condition you put on your affections."

"I don't know how to live with these feelings."

"I don't doubt that."

"Then why don't you understand?"

"No matter how much pain you bear, you can still love me."

"I do love you."

"Well, I can't make all your sorrows disappear."

No, he couldn't. She had never consciously felt that he should. Yet she had communicated that by resenting his faith in things. She had begun to feel there wouldn't be room in her heart for all the obligatory emotions she owed Tess and her overwhelming affection for Blue. She felt disloyal, so she was pulling away from Blue, as if she had no right to hope for any good.

"How many times are you planning to break my heart, Leona?"

He was right. No matter how much justification she had for the way she felt about things, she was in no way entitled to let those feelings cause Blue any more pain. There was no doubt about that. After all, she could still love him. She could comfort him. She could reward and reinforce all the good in him. Doing that was her path through this towering forest of overwhelming sorrow. It was life. It was what people meant by faith, by putting one foot in front of the other one—without answers, without clues, without reasons—because that was all any living thing could do.

"If I have to live without the answers, then I'll live without the answers."

"Are you sure, Leona?"

"I'll lose you if I don't."

"You realize there may never be any answers?"

"Yes."

"You accept that?"

"I have to."

"Then I promise you, as long as I live, I'll keep looking for them."

36

Leona stood eyeing the white enameled perfection of the porch floor. Its narrow planks had been laid an eighth of an inch apart to allow air in and moisture out. It was a seemingly endless wraparound portico with a swirling Victorian railing that curved outward here and there to accommodate sitting areas furnished with white wicker sofas and chairs cushioned in narrow black-and-white stripes. A maid had just greeted her at the door and shown her to a conversation area that overlooked a rose garden divided into an intricate geometric pattern of low, dense boxwood hedge.

"Lovely, isn't it?"

Her hair was gray, no doubt rinsed with silver. It lent strange glamour and dignity. Her clothes were different as well. Something harsh in her appearance was softened. There was nothing lurid or lascivious about her ivory linen dress. She didn't seem at all worldly or wanton here. It occurred to Leona for the first time that she must be at least fifteen years older than Averill.

"That's African boxwood. . . ."

Helen paused as Leona's eyes met hers directly for the first time.

"People always ask how we grow such dense, low hedge."

"Are you a gardener?"

"Lately I've taken an interest."

Helen offered her a seat. Their conversation ran the gamut of all the polite topics two women seeking to establish their mutual civility could cover. After a while the maid brought an elaborately prepared tea, which she served from a cart on ivory plates trimmed in black and gold and monogrammed with a "B" at the center. Leona was strangely ravenous. Helen identified the various pastries for her, as well as kiwi fruit, which Leona had neither seen nor imagined. Finally, when the maid had cleared their places and rolled the cart away, Helen's mask of respectful affection became somewhat more intense.

"I believe you have some questions for me."

"Well . . ."

Leona wasn't prepared for the ordinary facts confronting her. Helen was a lonely, middle-aged woman whose best years had been spent living with a man who never touched her. It was the price she had paid for her daughter's well-being. She had probably married Ransom with the same desperate feelings that guided or misguided Leona toward Averill. People gossiped about her agreement with Ransom. They said she had done it for a million dollars. Who would slice twenty years off her life for a million or even ten million dollars? No, it was all over Helen's face. She had paid a terrible price all her own. In the end she, like Leona, had lost her child by the very means she had chosen to protect her.

"I did love him, Leona," Helen offered by way of accommodating Leona's obvious discomfort. "It was created more by limited circumstances than Cupid, but I think Averill and I had a fair chance at a good life."

"You don't have to explain."

"I thought in time I might help Averill find himself."

"Don't say anything good about Averill Sayres to me."

"I'm not defending the wrongs he did. . . ."

"You knew?"

Helen's warmth disappeared. She glared at Leona with controlled contempt. In a moment, she stood. "So good to see you," she said in that dismissive tone of false kindness people in Orpheus used when they wanted you to leave.

Leona didn't get this at all. She had obviously insulted Helen, but how? Helen's sudden aversion to her question was an answer. She must have known what Averill had done. Had she known he was planning to kill the baby? And did she know why? Now it occurred to Leona that Helen might be afraid of her culpability. In the eyes of the law she might be an accomplice.

"Helen, I don't mean you any harm."

"It's a little late for that."

Now Helen was the accuser. Or trying to put her off by acting like one.

"All I want is the truth."

"Then you'll have to tell some truth first, Leona."

"Why wouldn't I?"

"You attempted one murder. It's not so difficult for me to believe you were an accomplice to another."

"What?"

"You got yourself hired to decorate the church."

"I got myself . . . ?"

"Hired! And who else was there when Soames did it?"

Had the border between real and unreal disappeared forever? She had come here to beg Helen Brisbane for any shred of information she might have about Tess. Now she was accused of helping Soames Churchill commit murder.

"Helen, you can't think I knew—"

"I think Soames made excellent use of you."

"If she did, it was all—"

"Easy! You made it all so damned easy for her!"

Helen was crying now, overwhelmed by sorrow. She looked so lost and helpless and vulnerable that Leona couldn't hold on to her own moral indignation. Helen's loss was too genuine. How could Leona stop the flood of empathy? People were connected by deeper forces than blood: frailty, mortality, incomprehensible loneliness and loss. How could she shield herself from that mutual, all-encompassing grief? Thank God, life would pass in a wink. Thank God, this terrible vulnerability they shared wouldn't last forever. They seemed to be drawn into a vortex of dying things, of losing and aging and shrinking into inevitable nothing.

It was strange, the two women, embracing, feeling their unsuspected union of common haplessness. What would either gain by accusing the other? Then, slowly, the mundane, material, temporal, here and now, living and breathing world reclaimed them. They somehow managed to regather their wits, wash their faces and settle down in the comfortable yellow silk parlor because the afternoon sun was weak by now and it was cool outside.

"Leona, you didn't know . . ."

"Helen, I don't really suspect . . ."

All the same, Leona saw it all much clearer now. She had been Soames's conduit to Averill and her unwitting means of tracking his every move. She had also provided Soames access and a credible explanation for her presence in the church; she had indeed facilitated Rhea Anne's murder. All of these things she wasted no time sharing with Helen, along with the fact that she regretted them very much.

"Leona, I have a favor to ask of you. . . ."

Would Leona provide testimony to help prove that Soames murdered Rhea Anne? Of course she would. She'd tell everything she knew.

"It might get embarrassing, Leona."

"We'll sit together in the courtroom."

Then Leona asked Helen why she hadn't gone to the authorities with her suspicions.

"Soames would have countered by accusing Averill of Henri Churchill's murder." There was more in Helen's eyes. She was assessing Leona, waiting to see if she knew or at least suspected the rest.

"What is it, Helen?"

"We were also afraid for you."

"For me?"

"She had a brilliant case against you."

"Why wasn't I a suspect?"

"Your connection wasn't obvious."

All Soames had to do was point it out. However, no one had accused her of anything, so she kept it in the arsenal of damning evidence, true and false, that she maintained.

It was getting dark. Leona and Helen had drained each other. It was time to leave. Yet Leona hadn't asked her about the baby. Had she and Averill ever discussed it? Did she know the truth? Would it serve any good to ask her about it? Or would it just hurt someone who had already been badly wounded?

"Helen, do you know anything about Averill I should know?"

Helen darkened. Leona had kept the question general on purpose. Her instincts told her there wasn't much point in asking it.

"Yes, I do, Leona."

"Please tell me."

"I know how he felt. . . ."

"About what?"

"Every day, his existence, how it feels to struggle every waking moment . . ."

"With himself?"

"With the damage that only you see and no one can fix."

"You mean his background?"

Helen let a small sigh escape. She seemed to be studying Leona, evaluating her honesty.

"I mean, Leona, that there are two kinds of people in the world: the ones who lose their innocence as young adults and the ones who are robbed of it as children."

Helen could make all the moist-eyed pleas for sympathy she wanted. Leona would never feel sorry for Averill Sayres. She had to let it be. They were crossing the porch now.

* * *

"I read where it's supposed to be a warm, dry summer," Helen remarked, looking at the dark leaves tinged with the dying amber sun. They eyed each other one last time. Maybe it was because the twilight lent Helen an aura of lost beauty. Maybe it was inevitable. Before she realized it, Leona found herself asking the question.

"It was the baby—that's why he married me?"

"Yes."

"He knew all along what he was going to do."

"Averill married you to help you and himself."

"But the baby . . ."

"Soames wanted the baby. She blackmailed him into stealing it."

Now the two women, each with missing pieces of the same puzzle, sat on the porch, oblivious to the dropping chill and the damp mist, and made a shared picture of their individual fragments.

They came all the way to that January night. Averill was supposed to drug Leona as soon as the infant came, and keep her sedated while Soames made off with it.

"Then why did he kill my baby?"

Helen turned ashen.

"Averill did everything in his power to protect your baby."

"By strangling it?"

"Who told you that?"

The terrible implication of her unspoken answer was all the information Helen needed.

"Soames Churchill. You tried to murder Averill based on information you got from Soames Churchill. . . ."

Leona felt a freight train roaring in her chest. She

had an image in her head that she couldn't keep of Averill grabbing her baby. Then everything was blood, snow and ice.

Helen's hands were on her shoulders. She was driving her words into Leona's head. This was the truth as she had heard it from Averill. There was no reason to doubt it.

Averill had never planned to conspire with Soames. Helen had gone to Memphis with Averill the week before the baby was born. They had drawn Leona's money out of an account in Union Planters Bank. If things had gone as expected, Leona and her infant would have been safely settled into a life of their own within a week of its birth. The stillbirth and the phony grave were ploys meant to fool Soames. Averill had arranged a safe, temporary situation for the newborn infant. He would take it there right after it was born. Leona would be sedated and allowed to rest and recover as necessary. As soon as she was able, he would take her to collect the infant and explain everything.

Everything went wrong.

The snow and ice made the roads impassable. He couldn't wait. Soames was checking for signs of Leona's imminent delivery every few hours by then. He had to get the infant to safety that night. He was trying to shrink the distance to town by cutting downhill through the woods. It was dark. He was panicked. He was worried about the baby in his arms. Something happened. He tripped and fell. He hit his head and blacked out.

"So that's how she died?"

"That's as much as Averill ever told me."

"So she's buried there in the woods?"

"He went into shock. He didn't know."

"Lie to me, Helen! Please, lie to me! Tell me he said he buried her."

"I can't imagine he would have just left her there."

"Not even in shock?"

"Not even in shock, honey."

37

Father Timon switched out the porch light and moved through the downstairs rooms turning out lamps and sconces and overhead lights. Then he fixed himself a plate of leftovers, which he heated in the microwave and carried with relish upstairs to his bedroom, where he planned to stuff himself like a Poland China pig while he watched the evening rerun of *Law & Order*.

God had other plans.

Darthula showed up at the back door. She was carrying an enormous bundle of rags, which he insisted that she leave on the porch.

"Heard about the murder?"

"Of course."

She was standing in the doorway. She had replaced her soiled garments with a purple velvet robe. Her red veil remained over her face. She looked like she was going to a costume party as his late mother. He didn't laugh at that because he didn't have the energy to explain.

"He was the devil hisself, Reverend Mister Averill."

"Really?"

"Know who done it?"

"Who?"

"Miz Evil Thang."

Father Timon didn't follow.

"Miss Soame' Churchill."

"Why?"

"Crazy."

"Has she been arrested?"

"No, nor will she ever be."

"She fled?"

"Shot him dead and herself next."

"Chased him all the way to hell, did she?"

"You pretty funny."

"She went crazy thinking he kill the baby."

"I didn't know Mrs. Churchill had a baby."

"She ain't."

"Whose baby did he kill?"

"Nobody baby killed."

"I don't understand."

Darthula turned around and grabbed the bundle of rags. He thought she was leaving, but she turned toward him, lifting a blanket and revealing the sleeping visage and gossamer curls of the most beautiful baby he had ever seen.

"Where did you get that baby?"

"Found her in the snow."

"When?"

"Last January."

"Where?"

"Where the devil laid her down."

"Why didn't you tell somebody?"

" 'Fraid the devil would find out and snatch her."

"We have to talk to the sheriff."

"You have to give me something to eat first."

38

SATURDAY, APRIL 29, 2000
10:00 A.M.

It was the first hot, sticky day of the year. Averill's sister Audena and her husband, Winky, led the parade from the church to the cemetery where his fervid flock laid their slain angel to rest. Leona and Blue watched from the front porch. It was all very sad, yet there was an undeniable circuslike edge to it. They had to smile at the silhouette of Leelinda Spakes's silicone breasts as she pranced through the mud in her formfitting choir robe and spiked heels. She couldn't have seen them from this distance, but Leelinda looked over at them and turned to step out of the line of mourners and cross the road.

"Hey there, Leelinda."

She just stood there, beaming her disapproval at them through her false eyelashes.

"Need something, sugar?" Blue asked.

"A harlot may be hired for a loaf of bread . . ." she said, quoting scripture, "but an adulteress stalks a man's very life." Then she drew in a long breath that made her already enormous breasts seem to inflate and lift as if she were about to float away. She was all unmitigated satisfaction as she turned slowly toward the cemetery.

"Leelinda?" Blue called in a subdued tone.

"Yes?" she inquired with a haughty glare.

"If you crash in water, can those things be used for flotation?"

Blue had no sooner fired off his remark than a sudden streak of lightning and an immediate peal of thunder aborted the ceremony at the grave, and mourners raced for the parking lot beside the church while Blue and Leona dove inside the house. The air was copper. Then a sea-green wall of water fell like a tidal wave out of the sky. Suddenly Leona was exhausted. Her fragile hilarity gave way to a weary sense of gloom. She went into the bedroom and tried to sleep.

There was something he wasn't telling her. Blue had been acting strange since last night. Father Timon, the Episcopal priest, had called him. He'd gone into the bedroom and whispered into the receiver for half an hour. After that he was downright silly.

"What was that all about?"

"Nothing."

It was late afternoon by the time Leona woke from her nap. The rain had stopped and the sky was pewter blue above the trees outside the bedroom window. Blue was in the front yard arguing with someone. It was Audena and Winky. Their voices grew louder. She peered through the dusty screen over the bedroom window. Winky and Audena were barreling down the driveway toward the road. Blue swirled around toward the house. He was doubled over, laughing.

"What?"

"I caught Winky trying to hot-wire Averill's Cutlass."

"What'd you tell him?"

"I told him I was sheriff and he was under arrest for car theft."

She showered and changed and then went out on the front porch, where Blue was watching the shadows spread over the green hills. Her nap had given her some ballast. The world didn't seem as frayed and tattered.

"You have something on your mind."

"Yeah," he nodded. "There are some things better shown than told."

"Then show me."

"Twenty minutes."

"Is it bad?"

"No."

"Please tell me."

"It's not bad," he countered. Then he went in and took a shower.

"Ready?"

"I'll get my purse."

"You don't need it."

He let her walk down the porch steps in front of him. She moved to get into his car.

"We're walking."

He took her hand. They crossed the road and stepped over the low iron fence at the front of the cemetery. He went straight to the flower-covered mound, but he didn't stop there. Instead they moved up the path into the woods for about a hundred yards. In another three or four minutes, however, Blue turned down a side trail toward the swamp.

"There's snakes down there."

"I hope you understand why I did it this way," he said, making less sense as the black surface of the swamp came into view. To this point she was on familiar ground. Now Blue was guiding her to the left, where another path she had never noticed descended the hillside. In another minute Leona had to admit that she was completely turned around. Blue had taken them down into a gorge she had never seen. In another minute, she saw the shack. So this was where Darthula lived. It wasn't through the swamp, as she had led people to believe.

"Darthula?" Leona called, so they wouldn't startle her.

"She's not home."

"What's going on, Blue?"

"I'll give you the details later."

Then he sat her down on the rocky hillside and took both of her hands. There was something he was having a hard time telling her. She might just brace for a shock, a good shock, but a shock nonetheless. She took her cue from him. She waited for him to tell her whatever it was. She was sure he was doing it the best possible way.

"Leona, I have wonderful news."

In a heartbeat, he could see her beginning to hope against hope and dread that she might be wrong at the same time.

"She's alive. Tess is alive and she's here." He was trembling and crying. He was going to pieces.

She was by some inexplicable quirk of human nature as calm as the moss-covered rocks. "Where is she, Blue?"

"There in that crib on the porch."

Leona floated through the surreal purple and gold haze. Yet it wasn't surreal or dreamlike. She could smell the pines and hear the birds. The past two years were the dream. She had somehow fled her own being and moved off, leaving the rest of herself behind in that nightmare just past. This wasn't to be confused with that dim place. This was where she had somehow overtaken and stepped into her own lost being once more.

Now she was moving up the porch steps. No, nothing fantastic here. An old crib. She crept toward it and peered down at the sum of it all. Tess sat cross-legged, sucking her thumb. She was a cherub, a peach, a perfect, freckled angel with swirls of curly silver-white baby hair and ice blue eyes that danced when she looked up at Leona. Yet she was no dream or angel. She was altogether tangible, here and now.

"Hey," Leona said in a soft, hoarse voice. Then, leaning toward the curious baby, she wrapped her hand around a wooden side rail and let her fingers flutter slowly. In another minute Tess touched her knuckle and Blue saw Leona's color deepen, but she didn't move or make a sound.

"Hey," Leona repeated, smiling at Tess.

"Hey," Tess shouted, clapping both of her hands.

"Come?" Leona asked after Tess had shown her an earless stuffed cotton bunny.

"Yeah!" Tess shouted, jumping up and down.

Then she lifted the dancing baby with both arms, resisting the urge to hug, for fear of frightening her. Sitting her up under one arm, Leona swung Tess around so she could see Blue, who was trying to stem his tears with his handkerchief.

"Hush, baby," Leona commanded.

When it was full dark and Tess had fallen asleep on the bed, Leona went out to the front porch, where Blue sat looking at the stars.

"Whatcha know?" he asked.

"Less by the minute," she said.

Across the road the moon had plated the flowers on Averill's grave silver blue. A breeze stirred the tops of the pines. It was clear, but she could smell more rain coming from the opposite side of the hill. She drank the soft scent. Far up the hill an owl hooted. They sat in the quiet splendor, leaving each other to the dreams and battles and reflections that lie within. Slowly the cloud continent appeared over the trees, and after a while they could feel the first scattered drops of rain.

"Coming in?" she asked Blue, who seemed to be asleep with his eyes open. He stirred himself fully awake and stood next to her, watching the jade green tops of trees bristle in the gathering wind.

"I love these old woods," he said.

She was falling asleep. The shivering limbs of the trees seemed to echo the breathing in the darkness on either side of her. Husband and child, partner and promise, breathing in and out, their chests lifting and falling with the floating pines. Was it a pattern or an accident?

Did it matter if she understood that it was lovely?

It was life, and she could feel her own breathing with theirs; life, and now a muted drumming on the roof. There, in the little house under the sighing trees, she pressed her shoulders into the pillow and imagined the Earth curving all the way around from the head of her bed through town and the ocean and Asia and back to the foot of the bed. For now she understood that she was at this place on that curve for this time.

Happiness was a here-and-now, breathing thing.

It was enough, all this warm breathing and creaking and holding on to the curve of the Earth. It was magnificent, the slight swell of moonlit curtains, the comfortable squeak of tired bedsprings, the far-off wail of a wild dog. She was tired. Sleep was tugging at her. Tomorrow with all its cloying improbabilities and toil was lurking in the darkness, waiting like a snare in the tall grass near the empty grave across the road. Tomorrow and dying, and bending time could wait.

She slept. She woke. Blue got up in the night to close the window. He kissed her, and soon he was breathing in deep sleep again. The storm had passed. The room was silver. This, she thought, drawing the moment into her breast, probing it with her eyes, this sensing moment of bliss is mine. Then her eyes caressed the sleeping baby. She touched Blue's shoulder. She let her cheek graze his upper arm.

It was earthbound enchantment. She peered through the thin veil of curtains over the window into the moonlit woods. Closer in the yard there was a catbird in the sweet gum tree. Then something flashed and disappeared. She waited. It was gone. Then something else fluttered. She slipped quietly out of bed so as not to disrupt their perfect breathing. She slipped into her robe and went out onto the front porch.

It was cool now. She watched in the stillness. There, across the road out of the feathered mist, rising here and there from the blackness between the silver tombstones, as lovely and ephemeral as all living things, a hundred or else a thousand flickering white butterflies rose and drifted like holy snow among the trees.

ABOUT THE AUTHOR

DAVID HILL divides his time between Los Angeles, where he writes for the stage and screen, and Mississippi. His first novel, *Sacred Dust*, won the Commonwealth Club of California First Work of Fiction Award.